TOEHOLD

A Novel

Stephen H. Foreman

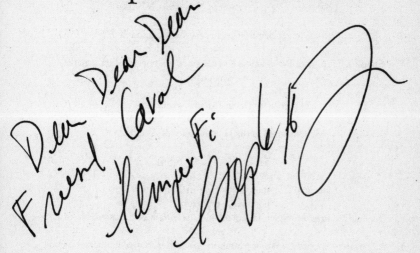

Dear Dear Dear
Friend Carol
Semper Fi
Stephen F

Simon & Schuster Paperbacks
New York London Toronto Sydney

SIMON & SCHUSTER PAPERBACKS
A Division of Simon & Schuster, Inc.
1230 Avenue of the Americas
New York, NY 10020

First Simon & Schuster trade paperback edition 2007

SIMON & SCHUSTER PAPERBACKS and colophon are registered trademarks
of Simon & Schuster, Inc.

Designed by Davina Mock-Maniscalco

Manufactured in the United States of America

1   3   5   7   9   10   8   6   4   2

Library of Congress Cataloging-in-Publication Data
Foreman, Stephen H.
Toehold : a novel / Stephen H. Foreman.—1st Simon & Schuster pbk. ed.
p. cm.
1. Taxidermists—Fiction. 2. Women hunters—Fiction. 3. Single mothers—Fiction.
4. Alaska—Fiction. I. Title.
PS3556.O7227T64 2007   813'.54—dc22
2007018327
ISBN-13: 978-1-4165-4331-2 (pbk)
ISBN-10:   1-4165-4331-7 (pbk)

To Jamie Donnelly

Who kept the faith

And kept the faith

And kept the faith

And kept it.

TOEHOLD

S omething new had been set loose across the land. The locals called it break-up. True, the river remained three feet thick with ice, in some places four, but in other spots the ice had definitely begun to move. The underwater currents now flowed swiftly, responding to the warmth of a Spring sun that appeared, finally, in the northern sky after months of arctic night.

Only a week ago the temperature had been fifty below, but Toehold, Alaska, knew that break-up was only days away. If you lived in Toehold and didn't have a calendar tacked to the wall of your cabin you wouldn't be able to tell the difference between the last long week of a grinding Winter and the first sneak peek of Spring. Most of the folks accepted the Winter months with grace and pride—if you didn't want the weather, what the hell were you doing here?—but people got grumpy when the sun didn't appear as expected. When it finally did come out even the geezers had smiles on their faces. Suddenly the snow glittered like a mirror ball on prom night. It made you want to dance. Arctic Spring also brought an end to the uncommon silence of that deeply frozen other world that called itself a river. Spring brought the screams, groans, and great cracking shots of ice as glomerations the size of industrial-strength refrigerators fractured, heaved up out of the river, and ground against each other with a sound like locomotives slamming on the brakes.

Each year the forest service hired people to walk the rivers and report back on the progress of the break-up. It was a cold and lonely way to spend the time, but there was an upside: it paid real cash money in a place where a wolverine's hide was considered a good week's work. This year the job went to Mary Ellen Madden, called Mel, and she didn't even have to apply for it. Old Fritz McFadden, a sourdough who had prospected, hunted, trapped, and connived for the better part of seventy years in the country, had monitored the river for the past ten, but Fritz had a boil on his ass the size of a jawbreaker and was also incommoded by a major dose of influenza. He couldn't walk three steps without the world starting to swirl, and the prospect of bouncing around on a snowmobile with a fester that size was inconceivable. So, when Mel stopped by to see if he needed anything, Fritz said he'd cut her a deal. He knew she could use the money. That was no big secret. Everybody in town knew she could use the money.

This was the deal: "You walk the river for me," Fritz said. "Tell me how it is, I'll radio the report to Fairbanks, and you can have the money."

"All of it?" she wanted to know.

"Half," he said.

"I do the work, you get the money?" she said.

"You do the work, we get the money," he answered. "Most people would jump at this opportunity, but I thought of you first."

"You're a first-rate human being," she said.

"Don't piss me off, or I will give it to someone else," Fritz said, emphasizing the word will as if he were a drill sergeant.

He was right. She did need the money, always needed the money. Mel and money were not normally on a first-name basis, which is how she found herself out on the ice in a blizzard that caught her completely off guard. It followed three days of above-freezing temperatures, baby-blanket-blue skies, and cloud cover like an eiderdown comforter. Icicles were dripping like Jack Frost's nose. The river ice was groaning nonstop.

Time to check it out, Mel thought. *Strap on the snowshoes.* This was a good day to be alive. Her parka was unzipped. She didn't need the heavy hood around her face. Lovely. Lovely. A flock of white-cheeked geese veered down below the clouds and followed the river loudly looking for open water. She climbed a rise overlooking the river to take in a great length of it before she went down and walked the shore. To look out over this country from on high was a gift. You could see forever. The limits of self-consciousness dissolved, and you were swept into the infinitude of it all. Each breath taken from the wind given back to the wind. Once you got down into it you would be lost in its vastness: eternity in each step taken.

Mel caught movement from the far shore of the river, a half mile or more away. A caribou was running through the deep drifts along the bank. It was remarkable how a four-hundred-pound animal could move so easily through such deep snow. George Nanachuk, patriarch of an Indian family that had hunted this area for centuries, explained one evening while she watched him skin one that the caribou has a wide hoof that acts like a suction cup to give him purchase on ice and snow and steep rocky terrain. A painting of a man on a cross didn't do it for her, but a hoof like a suction cup did.

About a hundred yards behind the big deer Mel spotted two more shapes—no, three: wolves. They were loping along on a steady trajectory with the caribou, but instead of closing the distance they merely maintained it. They never got any closer, but they didn't fall back much, either. Mel knew that a caribou could outrun a wolf. In fact, it seemed to Mel that the wolves were tiring, losing interest. The one in the lead stopped running altogether and lay down in the snow, breathing hard. The other two did the same. The caribou continued on for a few yards, then it, too, stopped and looked back. The wolves remained where they were. When the caribou seemed reassured that they were no longer in pursuit it began moving again, hooked a left, and headed for the tree line, only now at a slower pace. At that moment, when it seemed at last to be safe, when it seemed that in another second it would be into the trees and lost from view, four more wolves burst from the forest directly in front of it and cut it off. It was an ambush, and the three wolves behind closed the distance to the caribou until there was no escape at all. They had outwitted the faster animal, and now they would take it down and devour it. Dodging sharp hooves and slashing antlers, the wolves circled the caribou, darting in and out, each time tearing away another hunk of flesh. They packed the snow and turned it red. One wolf, a black one, managed to lock onto the caribou's nose, its powerful jaws splintering those of the deer. Now free of the antlers, the black wolf hung on and used its leverage to yank the caribou off balance. The caribou's forelegs buckled, but it stayed up. Blood poured from the desperate animal's savaged flanks, but it kicked and slashed till its sinews hung in strands and its bones showed through the skin left on its legs. Finally, when those legs could no longer bear any weight, it collapsed into the snow, and the wolves swarmed over it like maggots. So much for the kindness of strangers.

So intent was Mel on watching this spectacle that her radar failed to sense a shift in the weather. She had forgotten what Esther Nanachuk, George's wife, had told her about how to tell weather in the mountains. "Just wait five minutes," the old woman said. "It'll change."

And so it had. The breeze became a wind; the skies darkened; a late-season blizzard caught Mel out in the open with so much whirling snow she could no longer tell one direction from another. She knew that if she could get to the base of the hill, she would find some shelter from the driving wind. But when she got down there she was shivering so much she mentally prepared to die. When, when would she ever get old enough to know better? Now she knew the answer: never. The only thought that gave her comfort was that she knew, from listening to people talk, that the death was quick and not unpleasant, a speedy deep freeze. Zap, you're ice and you're gone. But how the hell did they know, sitting comfortably inside next to the warm stove drinking homemade from a jar? You could believe anything. Mel began to shiver uncontrollably. Hypothermia was setting in. Her body shivered, trying like hell to warm itself up, but no way. It had to be seriously below zero now, and the temperature was dropping steadily.

When she first came into the country she figured what the hell was the difference between twenty below, forty below, seventy below? Cold was cold, right? Bundle up. But two weeks into her first Winter taught her a lesson: choose twenty over forty, forty over seventy. The differences were real. At twenty, saliva froze in the corners of your mouth. At forty, frostbite took seconds. At seventy, moose piss froze before it hit the ground.

Before she realized what she was doing, Mel dropped to her hands and knees and began digging in the snow like a dog. At the edge of her consciousness she heard Esther Nanachuk's voice telling a story about how her grandmother got caught in a blizzard in the old days. The old woman scooped out all the snow she could, then got into the hole and let the falling snow cover her up. She said it was so quiet and peaceful and warm that she fell asleep. She did not know how many days later it was that the snow stopped (she learned it had been three days), and she crawled out hungry but alive. There was a feast of thanksgiving when she showed up back in the village, though first she had to convince them she was not a ghost. She did this by puncturing the flesh of her thumb with a needle made of bone and holding her hand up high so everyone could see the blood form like a small, red pearl.

Mel lay on her side, her knees drawn up, her arms around her, like one of those Peruvian mummies she had seen in the *Geographic*. *This could be worse,* she thought, as her eyes shuttered down. Warmth wrapped itself around her like an expensive coat. Not so bad. *If I die,* she thought, *will I die happy? Now's the time for answers, right? Let's start with a simple question: "Will I die happy?"* She would, she thought, except for a few really annoying details:

"Did I leave the Mr. Coffee on?"

"Will anybody miss me?"

"Will whoever gets my truck know enough to pump the gas pedal real hard three times before turning on the ignition?"

"Would they scoop me up after the thaw or leave me for the birds?"

There was another thought, too, but that one she pushed back. That one Mel preferred to keep hidden. She hoped the moment of death held some kind of, well, some kind of what? Glow, maybe? Johnny Mathis singing, "It's wonderful, wonderful," from these great speakers she could never afford but always wanted for her truck? The sensation of golden French vanilla ice cream on the tongue? But all she felt was curious, and after a while, she wasn't even that anymore. What she knew was that the wind howled like spirits come to get her. Then the wind went silent, and she didn't hear or know anything at all.

At some point in the darkness, her eyes opened, not because Mel willed them to; they just did. She could claim no spectral visitations, no dreams, no answers. Her only vision was a lot of white, a surround of white, in fact, but really kind of cozy. Not one howl to be heard. Mel wondered if this was heaven. *If I'm frozen stiff,* she thought, *what am I doing thinking?* which she was. *And, if I'm thinking, maybe I can wiggle my toes*—which she did—*and make a fist*—which she also did—*spit that annoying strand of loose hair out of my mouth* ... And then it was like a geyser punching skyward from the center of the Earth. She blew out from underneath that snow having no idea how long she'd been there but dead certain that she was alive. Trial by ice and snow: she had been tested; she had won.

Mel felt light as a leaf. She wondered, would the wind carry her away? But her feet, when she stamped them, told her she was on solid ground, and that was really what she wanted.

The day was quiet and lovely, and she could see clearly in all directions. She didn't feel like a ghost because she was ferociously hungry and had to pee. Then again, how would she know, having, to her knowledge, never been a ghost before? She was pretty sure, though, as she stretched herself out and the blood flowed back into each of her limbs, and she could still hear the river trying to disgorge itself of ice.

She wiped herself free of as much snow as she could and walked to the river, where she could see that the ice had pulled free of the bank, exposing a ribbon of water. It was happening. The river was in extreme break-up. A few more days of decent weather and the water would run free again. She watched as two plates of ice ground against each other until one slipped up and over with the sound of an ax blade being sharpened on a grind-stone. It remained a solid slab almost perpendicular to the other. Behind it, one which she hadn't noticed 'til this one moved, was another, oddly oval in shape, and moving slowly but steadily forward as if it had legs. Mel figured it to be noon or close to it. The glare from the sun on the snow was now so bright that she pulled a pair of sunglasses from her parka pocket to protect against snow blindness. Only once had Mel made the mistake of not using the sunglasses. The remorseless light had hammered her eyes, and she'd spent the next seven days feeling as if a file were being rasped across her eyeballs. She put on the glasses and watched the unusual slab of ice move toward the bank maybe twenty yards down from her.

This wasn't right. Ice didn't move like that. Maybe it did where dead people went, but she thought she had already answered that question. The oval slab rose up out of the river at a steady pace, totally encased in large plates of ice. It was like a colossus from ancient Egypt rising ponderously but implacably from its throne to its feet. It seemed to be walking. It *was* walking! This colossus covered with ice. The sun made this apparition shine so brightly that, even with her sunglasses, Mel had to keep looking away, and every time she looked back, the thing was closer to shore. It was alive! She saw what had to be legs encased in ice, big as trash cans, and in that instant she knew: a massive grizzly bear looking even more fearsome than it no doubt was. It must have spent the blizzard out on the ice of the river, only a few feet away from her, and now it had awakened at the same time she had, this sleeping giant, covered every inch with slabs and plates of ice. If it saw Mel it took no notice. She watched spellbound as this astonishing creature followed the river until it disappeared into a patch of frozen willows along the bank.

Toehold made absolutely no pretense whatsoever at being anything it wasn't. It was what it was, which was exactly what it wanted to be: a bush village about as far away from everywhere else as its residents could get without getting wet. A few clicks more and they'd be in the Arctic Ocean. Toehold had never seen better days, which was just as everyone liked it. It didn't want to glory in its past, even if there had been anything to glory about. Anyway, its past was its present. As for its future? Well, Summer followed Spring, Fall followed Summer, and Winter eclipsed them all. The goal of the average citizen was to live through each one and start all over. It was not a place for those who shirked, and it was not a place for those in despair.

A raw and naked force brought people here, a force that could not be ignored, one that demanded your participation in a hundred thousand ways. The place itself buoyed your spirits if you just went with it. You did not come here to rule over anything. You came because you felt it was a grace note from God that this wild and good country let you be a part of it, not just another harried citizen crossing off his list of chores on a crowded city street. Anybody who came into this country had to be prepared to work hard, and, if they stayed, they did. All anybody asked was to do it on their own terms. Nature dictated what you needed to do, and that was all right, as long as it wasn't a dyspeptic foreman on your ass for eight plus overtime.

No one knew with any certainty how long the village had been there. George Nanachuk, the Athapaskan head man, knew from his grandfather who knew from his own that it had always been a traditional campsite for hunting caribou during the great Spring migrations, though he doubted it was called Toehold then. For eons, thousands and thousands of these majestic animals moved through their range south to north, their graceful antlers curving back along their bodies like the bent bows of ancient archers. George thought the first permanent structures must have been smokehouses to cure the meat. Esther Nanachuk remembered sitting between her grandmother's outstretched legs in a circle of other old women with their own granddaughters sitting the same way as they chewed the tough hides with their teeth to make them softer and ready for tanning.

Fritz McFadden might not have been the first white man to set foot in Toehold, though he was the first one who stayed. He moved here from Montana at the age of twenty to run a trapline. Montana, wild as it was when Fritz was a kid, wasn't wild enough for him. He was born and raised in the Bitterroot Valley. It was a good life, real tough, but there was always food on the table and a blanket over you when you went to sleep. But his father remembered a time when there were no fences at all, so he inculcated his son with the belief that living in the valley was like living in a big corral. Fritz's father was the one who got him into breaking horses for the army during the Great War, and he could remember crossing a frozen Jenny Lake in the Tetons in a horse-drawn sled to visit relatives, the only white family settled there at that time. His dad died from the pneumonia picked up on that crossing and was buried in ground that later became a scenic route. In fact, Fritz heard that every last inch of the place was roads and resorts now. He had absolutely no desire to see it again. Ah, but Alaska! That was another matter. The population of the entire state was less than in Helena, Montana's capital. More to the point, the bounty of fur-bearing animals was much greater in Alaska, a fact that set Fritz dreaming.

Fritz didn't recollect that Toehold had any name at all when he first arrived. At some point somebody must have christened it, and the name stuck. But nobody, including Fritz and the Nanachuks, knew who or when. The number of residents who now called Toehold home was about two hundred. All of them had a story, some ridiculous, some bordering on the Homeric. But everyone has a reason for winding up in Alaska. Fritz's will suffice for the time being.

To comprehend the logic of Fritz McFadden's migration to Toehold, you first need to know something about chickens. Then you've got to know something about mink, and, finally, you've got to know something about Montana water rights. Water rights were a valuable commodity in a range so dry. If you were registered in the water rights department of the local courthouse as numbers one, two, or three, the chances of your running out of water during a dry spell were, in the words of Fritz's mother's second husband, a shithead named Johnny Foss, as good as finding balls on a heifer, so everybody else had to covet what they had and worry about not having enough. But the biggest worry was ornery bastards like Johnny Foss, low man on the hydro totem pole and a son-of-a-bitch as evil-tempered as a man could get

without having a red-hot poker shoved up his ass. He stole all
the water he could by sneaking upstream and diverting it across
his land, which, by the way, abutted McRossin's place, probably
the most successful chicken ranch west of the Continental Divide
and owner of first rights on the water coming down from Ward
Mountain, 12,440 feet of which were practically in his backyard.
Johnny referred to them disdainfully as the McCluckens.

One September, a time of normally low levels of water, the
drainage crossing McRossin's place was lower than usual. The
culprit was, as it turned out, not the time of year but Johnny Foss,
who got his hind parts handed to him by Mr. McRossin's ranch
hands at the old man's request. McRossin himself made sure he
was there to give his thieving neighbor a final kick in the ass. By
this time, Fritz's mother had died, so she wasn't privy to her husband's humiliation, but humiliated he was, and vowed revenge.

Now the thing about minks that you've got to appreciate is
that they are damn near the meanest animals on Earth and will
kill just for the pleasure of killing. And the thing about chickens
is you don't want them anywhere near a mink. Even one mink
can and will literally destroy a barn full of chickens, which is what
the McRossins had, and the mink will kill them all without even
eating a single one, leaving little tiny holes in their necks like a
vampire.

Johnny Foss's demented idea was a work of evil genius. On
the border of the two properties, only a few yards away from
McRossin's barn, Johnny Foss built a barn of his own, and popu-
lated it with cages full of minks. His idea was to start a mink
farm, and since mink breed quickly, Foss soon had hundreds of
them, a legal fact of life that caused Mr. McRossin a truckload of
aggravation and insomnia but about which he could do nothing.
Johnny Foss hoped to shorten the old man's life. It would be the
perfect crime. Except for the fact that his plan came back and bit
him in his own ass.

One dark night, one of the minks got loose—nobody knew

how—invaded McRossin's barn, and killed every last chicken in it. The needlelike bite marks on the chickens' necks could have been made by no other animal. It was a disaster for McRossin, and shortly after that, Johnny Foss disappeared. He was found floating down the Bitterroot River with a bruise on his head that appeared to have been made by a collision between his skull and a shovel. The coroner, a good friend of old man McRossin, ruled it suicide. After the incident with the chickens, there wasn't any place Fritz could go in the valley where people didn't look at him cross-eyed, a guilt-by-association thing. So Fritz sold the place he had inherited, went to Alaska, and started his trapline.

Toehold dug out of Winter and sloshed into Spring. The residents celebrated by sobering up. Life in the bush was defined by the seasons, and the seasons, particularly Winter, were defined by the consumption of alcohol, legal as well as homebrew. You had your solemn drunks, your sorry drunks, drunks who liked to party and drunks who drank alone, mean drunks, happy drunks, dumb drunks who thought their bonehead ideas were gifts to civilization, and crying drunks. Those were the ones you wished stayed home. There were drunks who drank beer first thing with their Cheerios and put a little Christian Brothers in their coffee. There were even a couple of drunks who never seemed to eat anything solid at all, namely Floyd and Lloyd, twin brothers nearly ninety years old who nobody could recall putting so much as a piece of dry bread in their mouths without washing it down with whiskey. One snowy night somebody noticed there were no lights burning in their cabin and no smoke coming from the chimney, so a search party went out looking for them. The way Buddy Barconi told it was that they found Floyd and Lloyd's truck nose-down on an embankment. A strong winch was needed to get it out, but Floyd said not to worry about them 'til the morning when it was light. The heater wasn't working but they had a couple of jars of Fritz's applejack brew to get them through the night, so they didn't have anything to worry about. They'd already seen that evening's episode of *The Rifleman* anyhow.

For folks who claimed to drink only at night, the arctic night was a godsend. A nightcap lasted for seven or eight months, so nobody had to violate their principles. If you did your work properly in the Spring, Summer, and Fall, if you harvested and canned and smoked what you needed, there really wasn't much else to do in the Winter except to every once in a while put some fresh meat in. One popular activity was to drink beer in Sweet-ass Sue's bar, the Pingo Palace, the only establishment of that nature in town. The drink of choice was, of course, beer, because it was all most folks could afford, and the beer of choice was Olympia (as in "Gimme a Oly"), a brew indigenous to the state, Alaskans being as chauvinistic as anyone else, probably more so.

The only citizen in town who wouldn't touch an Oly if you stuffed it in his Christmas stocking was old Fritz McFadden. "I ain't never paid tax one to the 'gummint,' and I ain't about to begin," he declared. Yet that didn't keep the man away from his daily portion of homebrew. Fritz made the best damn bush lightning between here and Point Barrow, and the man was rightly proud of it. He kept a still in back of his cabin which always seemed to be cooking something, from potato skins mostly, as Fritz was a demon for boiled potatoes and harvested a whole year's worth every Fall. People said when Fritz died nobody was going to have to embalm him because he'd pretty well embalmed himself already.

Mary Ellen Madden could drink with the best of them, but

what she preferred was homegrown weed. (To tell the truth, what she really preferred was chocolate liqueur, but she didn't keep it around because if anybody found out, everybody in Toehold would think she was a sissy.) She kept a plant the size of a small tree out back of her place, but nobody gave a shit either about that or about Fritz's still. It was just folks making stuff for personal consumption, and damn it, that was their God-given right. There was no police force, anyway, no 7-Elevens to stick up, no grocery carts to steal, no juvenile delinquents, no real crime to speak of, just a bunch of nuisance stuff like pissing out your front door or sleeping with somebody else's spouse. The feeling was that if you were that dumb and willing to die, it was your business. Mostly it amounted to nothing, anyway, because if you were making it with somebody's wife, he was probably making it with yours, so eventually it all evened out of its own accord.

Sweet-ass Sue always kept a few bottles of the good stuff around. Most of the time it was under lock and key, but she did break it out on special occasions, the most special of which was when hunters arrived from out of state. Hunting season was in the Fall, and a few of the locals made some cash as guides. That's when Sue got out the Johnny and the Jack because the out-of-state hunters brought the cash to pay. Of course, they'd stand their guides to a few, and probably the guides' wives would show up as well. So Sweet-ass cleaned up, and the locals got a taste of what they were missing when the out-of-state hunters weren't around.

As Winter shifted to Spring, diets shifted from caribou and moose, with maybe a little bear and a few ptarmigan mixed in, to fresh fish. Until she arrived in Alaska, Mel had never eaten so much meat in her entire life. She was by no means a vegetarian. She could always be talked into a steak, rare, I want it to moo, thank you, but in the Alaskan bush the craving for rich, fatty meat came on her an irresistible five times a day. She couldn't get enough of it. Nobody could. That was what the cold did to you. Up here, a vegan was a freak of nature, surely a creature of unsound mind, and probably unpatriotic. Mel really wasn't crazy about fish, but with the sun back and the snow gone, she couldn't stand another mouthful of moose, either.

It was good to be outside again without putting on thirty pounds of clothing and boots like tractor tires. In the old days, all of the Indians would take up Spring and Summer residence in traditional fish camps along the river, each family on its own time-honored piece of real estate. Many families still did, but not as many. The nets strung across the river hauled in a feast of arctic char, grayling with their large dorsal fins, silvery white fish, and the ferocious pike, able and inclined to eat all the other fish plus an assortment of birds and small mammals if they happened to find themselves in hostile waters. Traplines were abandoned as life shifted to the river. Animal hides wouldn't be thick and rich again until the cold set in once more.

All in all, Mel managed to make it through another Winter with her skin intact. Making it through a Winter was a matter of great pride up here. No matter how good you were with hook and bullet, you'd always be considered an outsider unless you wintered here. Love it or leave it.

What surprised Mel most about the warm weather was how much she continued to think about the ice bear. In her waking hours, it was always in the corners of her consciousness. He entered her dreams at night where she leapt upon his back and rode him high above the Earth. It was cold, yes, freezing as the icy tail of a comet, but she punched her fingers through the ice on his ruff and hung on as he bucked the wind and soared. She thought it might explode under her. Never had she experienced such a thing as this.

One late Spring day, when the young grass was that lovely shade of bright golden green, Mel was out on the river just looking things over. Her mind was blessedly still, nothing roiling up from the bottom of her brainpan as it often did to disturb her peace. It reminded her of Beat poet Gregory Corso's statement, "True power meant standing on the street corner waiting for nobody." At this moment, that was just how she felt, too. Isolated as she was, she didn't feel as if she were missing out on anything at all. Well, maybe there was one thing. No maybe about it, there was. One. One that, when she couldn't turn off the thought of it, bored into her brain like a beetle after it crawled through her ear. But that was it. The news? Hell, wasn't it just like a soap opera? Tune in the TV three weeks later and nothing had changed. The latest movies? Not a chance. She liked the old ones better anyway, the black-and-whites: *Winchester 73, How Green Was My Valley, The Maltese Falcon, The Grapes of Wrath*. Did anybody really give a shit about a fake meteor crashing into the Earth, and what if they did? She didn't want to hear about it. But even those old black-and-whites, if she never saw them again it really wouldn't be such a big deal. But if she never again saw the rosy dawn sun break over a glacier and paint it pink, it would be.

Mel did, however, like to read poetry. She had a few battered anthologies she'd picked up in used bookstores and carted around wherever she went. She wasn't sure she understood it all, or even much of it, but it felt nice. "I grow old, I grow old, I wear the bottoms of my trousers rolled," like those bent old men lining up waiting for the soup kitchen to open, bent old men on a broken street where weeds grew up through the cracks in the sidewalk. That line broke her heart. "Do not go gentle into that good night" was another one. Don't worry. She wasn't about to. But poetry wasn't about the now; it was about the forever. And so was Alaska.

As for music, she liked country stuff, bluegrass in particular. She could do without all the redneck bullshit that went along with country, but she loved a song to tell a story. Those stories were eternal: hurt, pain, hope, jealousy. "I gotta get me a job," "She's thinkin' single; I'm drinkin' double." Shania Twain singing, "That don't impress me much" about some bozo with a big car. Alison Krauss singing from the quiet fullness of her heart about a room filled with so much good love there was no need for words. Wasn't that what everybody wanted? Mel didn't need to be near any fast lane to know it.

She had just rounded a bend in the river when she saw him again. Not at first, though. Mel had negotiated some modest white water in a dented canoe that Old Fritz had given her in exchange for lancing his boil (a truly odious job considering where and what it was) when her attention was taken by an enormous grayling that vaulted from the water toward the midday sun in an extravagant defiance of gravity. The fish hung in the air above the river, flipped its tail, and shivered in the light. Droplets of water flew from its body, each drop catching the sun, then the water parted and exploded with the colors of the rainbow as the big fish plunged back into it.

Then the great bear was suddenly there, crossing the river about ten yards downstream. Most of the ice was gone and his coat was golden, but it had to be the same one. No two grizzlies that size could exist in the same range. One of them would either leave or die. Bits and slivers of ice remained in his fur and flashed in the light. His thick, golden coat glowed in the sun. Muscles flowed under his hide. She could only imagine the strength of such a beast, though she knew that this bear could crush the skull of a full-grown moose with a single swipe of a paw ten inches wide.

Mel had to rouse herself. There was no time to sit and stare because the current was taking her directly toward the bear. She back-paddled quickly, but the splashing caused the bear to look her way. He stopped, stood on his hind legs, and faced her, all ten feet of him. He couldn't get her scent because the wind was in her face.

Just stay still, she thought. *Please, just stay where you are and go away.*

She managed to back up about twenty feet, but he splashed down and moved toward her. Panic began to rise in her like the temperature on a thermometer when you hold a match to the mercury. He wasn't moving quickly. He showed no signs of anger. Still he came closer with each step. Just curious?

"Oh, God, what do I do?" she said aloud. He heard her and stopped. This time his jaws popped, a sure sign of agitation. Mel jacked a round into the chamber of her thirty-aught-six and snicked off the safety, though it flashed through her mind that this might not be enough gun for a beast this size.

The canoe began to drift downstream toward him. The cross-hairs were on his head, but she knew that a grizzly skull was so hard and so concave that it was possible for a bullet to carom off. Whatever advantage the rifle gave her began to slip away in her mind. She wanted to turn and run, but he would chase her down and that would be the death of her. She was afraid to put down the rifle and continue back-paddling. She was afraid not to. He stopped and stood to his full height again. Slowly his terrible bulk moved higher and higher, and the crosshairs moved with him, moved to his heart. Mel had the sight picture, but she was breathing so hard she could not hold it still. *Please don't make me shoot you. Please don't make me shoot you.* He dropped to all fours again, flattened his ears back, popped his jaws. Why hadn't she shot him when he was standing up, when she had a shot? Her heart quaked. *Where do I go? Where do I go?* She couldn't think. She had to move, stood up, fell out of the canoe.

The fast current grabbed the craft and shot it downstream. Mel tried to clamber to her feet, slipped, dropped to her knees in the water, squeezed her eyes shut, flung her arms around her head, floundered around waiting for the bear's jaws to puncture her skull. Seconds passed and nothing happened. When Mel was finally able to look up again, the bear was lumbering off into a thicket, its great flanks rolling from side to side as its fair bulk was swallowed by the brush. She had actually scared him off, but not before his teeth had torn the side out of her canoe. God was a stand-up comic: "Take my life. Please!"

Mary Ellen Madden, known as Mel to her friends, didn't have very many.

It wasn't that she didn't like people. She did, and they in turn liked her. What she had to offer, right off the bat, was a double-wide smile and grey-green eyes that lingered like the haze of cigarette smoke in a friendly bar. Was she beautiful? Her nose, broken in a collision with a softball while she was on the mound in a women's fast pitch game, gave character to a face that looked like it would laugh long and hard at a good joke. If the light were harsh it would reveal the faint beginnings of slender lines, but was this merely history, or a map to the secrets stored in the sacred regions of her heart? Her teeth were large with dime-thin gaps between them, but so white they pretty near glowed in the dark. If you had to be eaten, you wanted those teeth to do the chewing. All in all, Mel got your attention. In return, she was a very good listener. She was by no means a politician, but she shared a trait in common with the most successful of them: she made you think that, at that moment, there was no one on Earth more interesting than you.

Then why were friendships so rare? She was a drifter, had been literally half her life, just couldn't stay put, so there had never been the time to invest an attachment with more than passing meaning. Her grandfather back in Mudsuck, West Virginia (so called because of a giant sinkhole that opened up near the tailings of the #10 Tug River coal mine, swallowing a steam shovel, two dozers, and a jackass used to haul the man cars in and out of the tunnels), had been a wanderer, always hopping freight trains to somewhere else. One morning he'd be eating breakfast, and by lunchtime he'd be gone, but he always came back, except for once, and that happened not long before his final demise.

The man was in his eighties then and suffering from dementia, so somebody had to keep a watch over him at all times to see that he didn't wind up hurting himself. But the old man was clever, could see through the darkness of his own mind, and one day he slipped away, disappeared like smoke up a chimney. A day passed, then a second, and still nobody knew what the hell had happened to him. The worry really set in when Mel noticed Gramps's shotgun had gone with him. All Mel and her mother could think of was that the daft old man had gone traipsing through the woods, tripped over a tree root, and accidentally blew his head off.

On the third day, the telephone rang. The ring sounded unusually rude and persistent. Mel was certain it spelled trouble. Mel's mother answered the phone, said, "Yes, this is where he lives." It was the state police.

"Anybody git hurt?" she stammered.

"No," was the answer, "but you'd best come get him before somebody does."

The old man had stretched a logging chain across the highway and sat himself behind it on a barrel with the shotgun across his lap vowing to anybody within range that he was there to "keep the furriners out."

Mel was barely sixteen when she and her mother left Mudsuck. Another year passed and she was out on her own. Mel waited tables and learned how to tend bar, transportable skills she could take with her as she gypsied around the country. At one point she dropped below the border into Mexico, but turned around before she went too far south, and came back. It'd been no insult to tell this Yanqui to go home because she couldn't wait to get there, though home did change every couple of years or so. She'd be someplace, and it'd be fine until it wasn't. No reason. Didn't have to be. Mel would wake up one morning and it would just be time to go. It was always the same: do a wash at the Laundromat, close her bank account, pack a box with easy-to-handle food so she could eat with one hand and drive with the other, fill the gas tank. The checkout drill. By afternoon she'd be gone, a duffel bag of clothing chucked into the back of her Dodge Ramcharger along with a Crock-Pot and Mr. Coffee.

There was, once, a point in Mel's travels where she clocked a personal best for Time Stayed Put. East of Phoenix, Arizona, in the desert, she was drawn to a remote strip of wooden buildings, the main street and only street of a dot on the map known as Apache Junction. Developers have since gotten their hands on it and cooked up a theme mini-mall, but back then, that's all there was: a bunch of sandblasted wooden shops in serious need of paint and customers. Mel pulled into an empty space, cracked a can of Country Time from the cooler, unfolded a map, and studied it against the steering wheel.

"If you lived here you'd be home by now," said a male voice outside her truck window.

"Maybe I should buy some property," she replied, and smiled at the young man who was smiling back. He was an Indian, the first one she had ever spoken to, Apache, she figured. Right now they were eye to eye, but he'd be taller if she stepped down from the cab of her truck.

"I've got the perfect plot," he said.

"Does it have a view?" she asked.

"I'm looking at it," he replied, his eyes never leaving her face.

"Are you serious?" she asked.

"As a crutch," he said, but he couldn't keep a straight face and neither could she.

"That is the worst pickup line I have ever heard," said Mel.

"Did it work?" he asked.

"Absolutely," she replied.

From inside the shop behind him, a telephone began to ring.

"Hold that thought," he said, turned, and rushed into the shop.

Mel hopped down from the truck and checked out the front of the shop he entered. A sign painted on the window said, "The Heeler," and, underneath, "Soles Repaired." A shoemaker's shop! He was a shoemaker? As far as Mel knew, shoemakers were all over fifty years old, and none of them were . . . Apache? Wait a minute, girl, Indians wear shoes, too. Somebody's gotta fix them, right? "Custom Moccasins," another sign said.

He was on the phone in the back, turned away from her. She walked through the front door. He heard the entry bell jangle, looked over his shoulder, smiled and beckoned "one minute." The sweet smell of leather and polish was intoxicating.

Mel looked at the bottoms of her shoes: the left one had a hole worn into it.

"You married?" she asked him, mostly mouthing it to keep whoever it was on the other end from hearing. He shook his head.

"Girlfriend?" No.

When he got off the phone they exchanged names.

"Gary."

"Mel."

"What's that stand for?"

"Mary Ellen."

"Nice."

"I don't use it."

"How long you here for, Mary Ellen?" he asked.

"Can I get back to you on that?" she answered. Mel was managing to shock even herself. She started back out the door.

"Where're you going?" he wanted to know.

"To get my duffel bag."

"I'll get it," Gary said.

"Thanks, but I'd feel better if I did it myself," she said. "You know what Smokey Bear says: pack it in, pack it out." She stopped at the door and asked, "Do you cook?"

"No," he said. "Do you?"

"Only between the sheets," she said. When had she gotten the balls to talk like this?

"Sounds like a gourmet meal," he said.

Afterward, after they had made ridiculous love a ridiculous number of times (or maybe in between, she was so lost in time and space she couldn't tell), she asked, "Won't they toss you out of the tribe for partying with the enemy?"

"I'm softening you up for the big feast, and then I'm going to eat you," Gary said.

"You wouldn't kid a girl, wouldja?"

"Tell me the truth," he said.

"Tell me no lie," she said.

"I bet your heroes have always been cowboys," he said.

"Things change," she replied.

Three years later, they had changed once more except for the Checkout Drill. As Apache Junction disappeared in the dust kicked up behind her pickup, she felt she could finally begin to think again, really, to breathe again. Mel had been on automatic pilot for too many days. Like the military manual at arms, she had practiced this exit routine so many times before that, once it was set in motion, it did what it did and nothing stopped it. Why? She and Gary, she had to admit it, were great together. She knew he would be when she saw him, and he had not let her down. There was lots to him that she would miss, but some things just could not be forgiven. Or forgotten.

She knew she'd miss his stories most. The reason Apache Junction's even on the map at all, he told her that first night, was that it sat only yards away from a trailhead leading to a vast and confusing mess of washes, boulder fields, drops, caves, mesas, and twisting canyons called the Superstition Wilderness. For two thousand years (some say three), Apache bands claimed that this poor excuse for a piece of real estate was the ancient domain of their thunder god, a fire-and-brimstone type, whose holy warriors guarded a sacred Indian burial ground. Somewhere else in that geological Babel, so swear many sober people, is hidden the legendary Lost Dutchman Gold Mine. No one knows where that crafty old bastard hid his mine, but he was seen to take a forty-pound nugget into the assayer's office. Somehow or other he still managed to die an old man's death without giving away his secret. Thus followed years of strange deaths, grisly murders, stolen treasure, madness. The lore of "the Supes" (that was how Gary spoke of the mountain).

Then, later, while he was still inside her he told her he had a real treat for her.

"What do you call what we just did?" she asked.

He told some of his best stories when he was still inside her. She'd put her arm over her eyes as if to shield them from the sun while she listened.

"We're gonna get rich," he said.

"Sounds good to me," Mel answered.

"The Lost Dutchman!"

"I'd buy the Brooklyn Bridge first," she said.

"Oh, ye of little faith," said Gary. "She's out there waitin'. Might as well be for us as anybody else. You're my lucky charm, I swear."

Oh, yeah, sure, Mel thought, but that really was the start of it. He got her into reading every word ever written about the Dutchman, which included not only various clues but tales of men who went mad or never came back, tales of desert rats and Indian burial grounds, and savage spirits. They scoured topo maps, aerial photos, satellite images, and one day Gary just announced that it was time to go. Three days later they were on horseback picking their way up a narrow trail over a rise that dropped them deep into the Supes on the other side. She rode a buckskin, Gary a blood bay. He led a packhorse behind him. They stayed in the mountains for a week that first time. He made the rocks as readable as a newspaper. In his mouth the cliff walls became stories of creation. She was living the dream, goddamnit! Livin' the mutha-fuckin' dream! Oh, yeah! After that, every chance they got they took to the mountains, sure that each time put them closer to the treasure. Basically, Mel hoped they never found any lost gold at all as long as she could have a guarantee that they would always go on looking for it. Well, shit, if you want to make God laugh, tell him your plans.

One Sunday, after a long weekend spent prospecting the Supes, the mailbox held a handwritten letter for Gary. Mel passed it to him on top of a batch of junk. He glanced at it and then tossed it in the trash can with the rest.

"You just threw a letter away," she said.

Gary opened the fridge and guzzled from a jug of cold lemonade. "Don't you want to know what it says?" asked Mel, astonished that he could trash a letter without even opening it, she who had to open every piece of junk mail that came through the door.

"I know what it says," said Gary.

"Okay, what?" She crossed her arms and stared at him with a Prove It To Me face.

"My long-lost uncle died and left me a billionaire."

"Come on, tell me."

"Mary Ellen, let's drop it." Normally, when he put her full name at the beginning of a sentence she knew he was annoyed with her.

"I never heard of anybody getting a letter and not opening it," she said.

"Well, you can't say that anymore, can you," he said, and took another swig. It dribbled down his chin.

"Gary," she said, "you're gettin' it all over."

That night, when Gary was asleep, Mel retrieved the letter from the trash, locked herself in the bathroom, and sat down on the toilet seat to read it. "Dear Gary," it began. "I hope you don't mind me calling you by your first name because 'Dear Dad' doesn't exactly sound right, either . . ."

The first thing Gary saw the next morning when he woke up was Mel sitting stiffly in a chair at the end of the bed, both feet flat on the floor. It took him another second to focus on the letter in her lap, and as soon as he did, he erupted out of that bed and grabbed it from her. "I could have you put in prison for tampering with my mail," he said.

"Reading is not tampering," she answered drily.

"What is it then? You sneaked behind my back," he shouted.

"You could've told me you had a kid," she yelled back.

"Why would I?" he asked.

"Because you do," she said.

"I got an address I send money to," he spat back.

"He wants some now," she said.

"No shit," said Gary. "That's the nature and nurture of our particular relationship."

"You sound so fucking casual," she said.

"Good," he shot back. "I've been working at it."

"You really don't give a shit, do you?" she said.

"His mother taught him to hate me. Do I give a shit? What good would it do me to give a shit?"

She continued to stare at him, unable to come to peace with this news, this revelation, really. A letter comes from your kid and you don't give a shit? What kind of a person would ignore something like that? Okay, maybe if it was a stepchild; maybe if it was some neighbor's kid. Uh-uh, nope, not even then, not even if it was some kid on the street. No fuckin' way. This was a crime against nature. One way or another you had to pay. It would not go unpunished.

"You can't believe I could be this way, can you?" he asked. "Well, I can't believe you'd sneak into my mail." Gary tripped over himself as he struggled to pull on his jeans at the same time he bolted out the bedroom door. Mel had never seen him this furious before.

"You fucked up, lady!" he yelled, and grabbed his shirt from a chair.

"When normal people get their fucking mail they fucking open it, goddamnit!" she fired back.

The front door slammed behind him. She started to yell something else, but suddenly the argument was over for her. Just over, like that. Mel had been so upset but now she felt practically nothing. For a while, she mistook that for feeling good. She wasn't aware of it, yet, but part of her was already out the door.

Mostly Gary avoided her, except for one point when he sat down at the kitchen table where she was leafing through an auto parts catalogue, scrawled out a check for $250.00, and shoved it right smack an inch away from her face. She couldn't tell the name on the check, Aidan or something like that, couldn't tell the last name, either.

"Happy?" he snarled as he licked the envelope and pounded a stamp into place. *Well,* she thought, *I'm not unhappy, nope. I'm okay.* That night, as she lay in bed reading a magazine, Gary got in beside her.

"I don't want us to go to sleep angry with each other," he said.

"I'm not angry," she said.

"What about that crack about normal people?" he asked.

"I'm not angry now."

"Tomorrow's a new day, right?"

"All day," she replied.

She could tell Gary felt better. That was good. Life's too short, right? He wrestled with his pillow and finally settled into position with his legs tucked up and his back to her, and fell asleep. Mel continued to read—an article comparing the different personalities of Chevy truck drivers versus Ford—until the magazine dropped over her chest and she fell asleep, too. That night she dreamed she was a woman accused of witchcraft in old Salem. The court sentenced her to die by having thick slabs of slate piled upon her chest. At each one she'd dig in her heels and heave or try to heave but the weight became too great. She struggled for breath. One of the judges suggested one more stone slab. Another said, "She's gone. She's already gone. Can't you see that?" Mel, in her conscious mind, knew that if she didn't do everything she could to wake herself up she would die, but she did not wake up, could not wake up, couldn't even move. She tried to scream, but the weight, she clenched her teeth, she could only moan. She sounded like the starter on a car when its battery was practically dead.

The next morning Gary got up early and drove to Tempe to pick up a new metal detector. He thought Mel was still asleep, so he decided not to wake her and went alone. He left a note that said he'd be back sometime early afternoon and bring Chinese takeout for dinner. Mel was gone before he reached halfway. She drove three hundred miles before she stopped for gas, and was well into Colorado by the time Gary got home. Three hundred miles in which she beat herself up for being so goddamn stupid.

She should've known better than to come back to Arizona after she swore she never would, but now it was years later, and Mel had found herself back there telling herself that as long as she stayed away from Tucson she'd be safe. But the ghost of Traumas Past tracked her down in the far reaches of a mountain range and tore the scab off an ancient wound. She was blindsided—but how could she have known what would happen?

Mel had always hated Tucson, right from the git-go, right when the old bitch told her they was gonna move there as soon as her grandfather was dead and donated to science so she wouldn't have to pay a single cent to bury him. She was a hard woman, Mel's mother was, viperous, mean, always bitching about wanting to move someplace that was always warm, bellyaching about putting up with this sack-of-shit weather her whole damn life— the goddamn snow in the Winter and the goddamn mud in the Spring—and now she wanted out. Mel's grandfather wasn't in the ground a week when her old lady sold the place to some people from Pittsburgh, packed the two of them into the Ford pickup, and followed the yellow line on the AAA map to Tucson. They arrived on a day in mid-July that was the hottest Mel ever felt on Earth. She looked over at her mother behind the wheel: the old lady had a smile on her face like Mel hadn't seen forever.

Mel remembered staying at a motel that had cable television and an air conditioner. Her mother mercifully let her stay put instead of dragging her along while she went out to find them a place to live. Each was relieved at being away from the other. One afternoon, after she'd been searching for a couple of days, the old lady came back right in the middle of this group on MTV that was weird even for Mel, looked at her daughter and said, "Saddle up," which only increased Mel's disdain because the old lady was such a phony. Mel remembered getting in the truck and driving to a house with a flat roof and a bunch of cacti with their arms in the air that looked like Gumby. What she remembered most was sweating like a pig because her mother wanted it hot, but she also remembered the ache of longing for her life back home. She lay in bed with a notebook on her knees and made a list of everything she could think of that she missed: taking the empties back to Mr. Tinney's store, certain trees (especially the big oak in the front yard where, when she was little, she kept a secret, magic, bejeweled horse), the creek. Mostly what Mel missed was people, which really meant her grandfather, nobody else. They were always together, and at least once a day they met in their secret hideout deep in the woods under some chestnut trees. Years later, as she passed into Colorado on a blistering July day, Mel thought about those chestnut trees and wished right there and then that she were back in them.

Since leaving Gary in Apache Junction, Mel had worked as a waitress during the Summer and Fall at Yellowstone, one ski season waiting tables in Aspen, Colorado, back to Yellowstone, then another ski season as a waitress in Utah before making out for the Pacific Northwest. When tips were minimal during the off-season she took work as an exotic dancer. Mel actually liked the word *stripper* better because she always believed in telling it like it is. Hey, it was honest work. She wasn't robbing anybody. If she had some assets that could draw a crowd, well, hell, why let them lie fallow? She knew she wasn't drop-dead gorgeous, but that didn't mean she couldn't damn sure keep your interest. When her body talked it said, "Let me wrap myself around you like a warm roll. Let me cradle you and sing sweet rock-a-bye." Loggers, mushers, river guides; lawyers, doctors, and defrocked priests: they couldn't stuff ten-dollar bills in her panties fast enough. It sure beat waiting tables. That aspect of her life was soon history. Of course, that was the problem, wasn't it? Everything became history sooner rather than later. Everything. She still couldn't stop moving from place to place.

She'd been just about everywhere in the Lower 48, been on the go for what seemed a lifetime, so when she found herself in the village of Toehold, Alaska, at the far northern edge of the Brooks Range at the very top of the continent on a gravelly bend in the Hulahula River, she was shocked to realize that, sister, this was it: there was just no place else to go.

Toehold hadn't seen so much excitement since that time Edie Kokuk, from the Indian side of the village, home on a break from secretarial school in Fairbanks, mistook a passing canoeist for Al Pacino. When he wouldn't pull over, she sicced her father's murderous Chesapeake Bay retriever in the water at him. The evil bitch came at the canoe like a torpedo, and no amount of whacking her over the head with an ash wood paddle could put her down. It took a .44 between the eyes to do that, but that's another story and some time ago, way before Mel Madden showed up.

Everyone in Toehold was asking the same question: what was Mel up to? Summer Joe, the chief's youngest brother, had just come back from a two-year stretch in prison. Bigamy. Like all con men, Summer Joe was a charmer. He hadn't learned to do much that was useful during his twenty-five years on the planet, but he could talk like he knew something, and he could smile the stripes off a zebra. What did him in was that the blood had a hard-core jones for social workers, especially overweight Jewish ones who graduated from schools like Barnard with a major in Redemption. He married his first, a sweet, well-meaning, bookishly intelligent young thing two years out of grad school. She thought her heart was big enough to cope with all the suffering in the world. When she still lived with her parents, she was always rescuing birds and mice from the claws of her cat. She was quite possibly the only vegetarian in Alaska, and she was dead sure she had won the heart and soul of a wild man. Summer Joe repaid her by marrying his second social worker without bothering to divorce her first. One lived down in Sitka, and the other lived up in Hungry Horse. Joe figured, "How could they ever run into each other, being so far apart in different places?" But they did, at a conference in the state capital. Joe threw himself on the mercy of the court. Both women pleaded with the judge on his behalf for leniency. Instead, the judge tacked another year on to Joe's sentence, the judge's reasoning being that if this predacious son-of-a-bitch could flim-flam two women so completely, he could certainly delude two more. The judge said he wished they were in Singapore so Joe could be caned, especially if the sentence could be carried out on TV, but, barring that, he had to settle for the max.

People told Summer Joe about Mel's stunt right after they said, "Hey, Summer Joe, welcome back." Didn't take a breath. Folks also wondered how Summer Joe was going to take it when he found out Mel was living in his place. Of course, it wasn't really his—he only rented—but, you know, people are funny about things. Since Joe was known as a charmer more than a fighter, the other thing folks wondered was if the worm turned while he was in prison, like did he have to toss the bouquet after he said I do, assuming he had anything to say about his situation at all? Everybody wondered but nobody asked. Cosmic payback was strong medicine. They were curious, but did they *really* want to know? Really? Probably not.

Buddy Barconi was the one who brought Cody the news. It was their habit to get together in Cody's taxidermy studio for coffee every morning anyway. Cody made a great cup of coffee. Practically everybody in town stopped in for a cup at least once a day. He brewed it in your everyday Black & Decker, but he ordered gourmet beans special from a firm back in New York. He'd order one dozen twelve-ounce, vacuum-packed bags of Ethiopian Yrgacheffe (Viennese roast) at six dollars and thirty cents a bag, sometimes Asian Celebes at eight-seventy. Come the holidays it'd be Hawaiian Kona at twice the price, but this was Cody's one splurge in an otherwise ascetic life, and Toehold had come to depend on it.

Buddy would come over from his cabin first thing, regardless of the weather. Cody'd have hot coffee waiting in mugs the size of tankards. The two men were separated by many years and separate visions of how the world worked, but they shared a fundamental addiction to spirited debate, a belief in the ultimate goodness of the other, and the faith that the Alaskan wilderness would make them whole.

Buddy had been a Marine who fought in Korea. He then spent his working years as a fireman in Brooklyn. He wasn't a hero, and he didn't consider himself one, but in forty years of hard work he knew that he had done a thing or two every now and then that had made a bad situation turn out better, and he felt good about that. Unfortunately, he was better at being a firefighter than a family man, so at the retirement party that his wife Lurlene threw for him, she got up on a table and announced in front of all the guests that she was leaving him. She was tanked, but she meant it. From now on the son-of-a-bitch could wash his own damn dirty drawers. She climbed down from the table, handed him divorce papers, picked up the suitcase she had previously parked under the sofa, and walked out. For what was the first time in his life, Buddy was speechless. He was too stunned to move. If he could have found a hole he would have crawled into it. He could divorce her or not; she didn't give a rat's ass. There was a guy waiting for her at the curb in a new, silver-blue Camaro. He had long sideburns and an Elvis pompadour, and he held the car door for her while she got in. She slid all the way across the seat so she could snuggle against him with his right arm around her, his hand cupping her breast. Left hand on the steering wheel, the guy laid rubber all the way down the block.

Buddy tossed everybody out of the house, locked the door, pulled the phone wire from the wall, and stayed drunk for a week. He had long ago lost touch with his kids—three daughters who always sided with their mother, anyway—and he couldn't face the neighbors after what his old lady had done. On day five he staggered to the library and borrowed a stack of atlases and travel books. On day six he spread them out on the living room floor and pored over them like a general in his war room. On day seven, he decided to take his pension and move as far away as he could get and still be in the United States—Alaska.

He guessed he could've gone to Hawaii, but he got seasick drinking a glass of water. Anyway, Hawaii just didn't seem like America. Alaska had moose, wolf, bear, wolverine; Hawaii had sharks and funny necklaces. Oh, yeah, sure, Hawaii had wild boar, too—he knew that—but Buddy didn't eat pig. Jews didn't eat pork, not that Buddy was Jewish, but those Yids were smart. If they don't eat pig they must have a damn good reason. Whatever that reason was, it was fine with him.

Cody Rosewater, son of a child of the sixties. He was conceived in 1965 by his mother, Fantine, outside of Cody, Wyoming, on the plains under the stars with her high school lover the night of their senior prom, her first love, everlasting, except he went to war the next day and never came back. News of her lover's death came so quickly that Fantine wondered was he shot dead the instant he stepped off the plane? Did his feet ever touch the ground? Four months short of her delivery date. She found herself furious with him, though she hated herself for it. *How could you have gotten yourself killed in five minutes?* her mind screamed. *Didn't you learn anything at boot camp? Where was your head?* The boy's family gave her few details and barely tolerated Fantine at his funeral. They left her standing by the grave as the rest of them filed out of the cemetery. Her own family tolerated her not at all. Big as a whale with Cody, she was a pariah with no place to hide in her own hometown. She adopted "Rosewater" as their surname and took "Fantine" as her own. Instead of feeling lost and useless, her baby powered her with a sense of purpose. He ignited a tenacity she didn't know she had. Everything became clear. Fantine would love the life inside of her forever. Fantine would nourish and protect this life with the ferocity of a she-bear. Be kind or keep your distance.

Fantine assessed her skills and determined that she had one that could make money. She could sew; she could sew well, and what's more, she loved doing it. To her it was like Rumpelstiltskin turning straw into gold. Taking a piece of material from here, another piece from there, a third, some thread, and a simple needle, Fantine turned rags into raiments. They were fanciful things, unsuitable for a small town that postured with a frontier temperament. Wyoming was the stuff of leather—chaps, gunbelts, saddles. Those folks were just not ready for a pink T-shirt with the picture of a kitten stating "Chairman Meow." They weren't ready for Stetsons with pastel bands and streamers down the back, and they sure as hell weren't ready for a yellow chenille sport coat with a peace sign where the breast pocket ought to be. But Fantine didn't discourage easily. She hadn't even birthed her baby, yet. This was no time for dismay. Every day she grew bigger. She felt the weight of two in the world. She knew her priorities and stayed calm.

News, good and bad, eventually reaches the most remote corners of the planet, even if it often travels at the speed of a mineral leaching through rock. It was 1966 when whispers of a new world arrived in Wyoming, a world with its own music, its own colors and language, a world with dreams of peace and the conviction of its citizens that all things were possible. As soon as she heard its music, Fantine knew she had to go there.

But how?

She had no money, but she had a prospect, a vision. First off, Fantine needed a job. Life at what she used to think of as home had become untenable. Her father ignored her existence, averted his eyes, refused even to respond to a direct question. As far as he was concerned, his daughter . . . What daughter? I have no daughter. And her mother's only words to her were issued as sharp commands or not at all. It had come to this: Fantine was given seven days to come up with room and board, or else she had to leave the house. Period. There was no discussion and would be none. The two people she called parents were ashamed of the life inside of her. Fantine had two choices: she could let this shatter her, or she could go on. Was there ever any doubt of it? She would go on. She no longer had the luxury of being weak and powerless. She was no longer alone. Like a tonic, her troubles made her strong enough for two. Fantine would have her baby, and she would go on. Resolve was certainty.

On the evening she came to such resolve, Fantine packed a kit bag with a few necessities. She would not sleep one more night in this house, never sleep another night where she was not wanted. She would not even say good-bye. When her parents were asleep, she closed the front door behind her and stepped into the night.

The moon that night was as big and bright as she'd ever seen it: a gigantic communion wafer in an indigo sky. Fantine took this as a sign, just as the children of Israel did when they followed a pillar of fire through the wilderness. She walked three miles to the cemetery where the father of her child was buried, lay down beside his grave, whispered she would love him forever, promised that their child would always be safe, closed her eyes, slept. She got up at first light, wiped the dew from her face, and walked downtown to look for a place to neaten up and then to find a job. She found both at the Greyhound bus station, a confluence of omens for her.

In the window of the ticket booth, stuck there with Scotch tape, a hand-lettered, five-by-seven index card stated, "Part-time position available. Apply here." Hoping no one had seen her, Fantine whisked herself into the ladies' room, where she brushed her teeth, washed her face and hands, fixed a yellow ribbon around her hair, and put on an extra-large, baggy sweater to conceal her pregnancy. Fantine just looked fat, which was exactly what she wanted. She got the job—a custodial one—on the spot. She was to keep the bathrooms clean, mop the station floor, and spruce up the buses when they came in off the road. She checked her bag in a locker and began that morning.

One of the perks of the job (actually, the only perk of the job) was free passage for employees to anywhere in the continental United States. This was not lost on Fantine. That evening she checked into the Young Women's Christian Association. She had a little money, and paid for the room one week in advance. On the corner was a small mom-and-pop grocery store. Each day after work she stopped in and bought a buttered seeded roll, a half-inch slice of provolone, and a pint of milk. In the morning, on her way to work, she bought the same thing, sometimes adding a thick slice of bologna. The rest of her money she stuffed in a beige Wigwam hiking sock.

This went on for two months. Fantine could stand anything

as long as she knew it had an end. People who looked at her, if they saw her at all, saw an overweight teenager with a pimply forehead in a dead-end job. They did not see her as she saw herself: a woman with a soldier's heart, a mother brimming with love. At the end of two months, Fantine had saved a hundred dollars. She requested a long weekend to visit a sister in San Francisco, got her free ticket, and left Thursday morning. Fantine said she'd be back to work Monday afternoon, boarded the bus, and, with one exception, never traveled east of California ever again.

In the Summer of 1966, Fantine disembarked from the bus at the Greyhound station in San Francisco, a good walk from the intersection of Haight and Ashbury but doable. Her hometown radio station had said that's where it's at—the birthplace of the new order—so she knew to go there. She studied a map of the city that she picked up from a counter rack in the bus station and made her way street by street, turn by turn toward "Hashbury."

About halfway there the scene began to change. The derelicts gave way to a sextet of Hare Krishnas with tambourines and ankle bells chanting and twirling on the other side of the street, then a guy with the longest hair she had ever seen on a man—midway down his back, black as a whipsnake, flowing freely as he shook his head, a leather band twisted like a lariat around his forehead. His face and hands were painted clown white. His lips were large and bright red. His eyes were sad, a tear drawn underneath one of them. He carried a bouquet of daisies in his hand, ran across the street to Fantine, and pulled out his empty pockets with a forlorn face. She smiled and gave him a quarter. He gave her a daisy, even tucked it behind her ear for her.

"Come on," he indicated, and beckoned for her to follow him. Her parents would have been mortified, but she didn't feel that way at all. She suddenly felt lighter on her feet. Where would this strange young man with the long hair lead her? And, anyway, her parents weren't here, were they, and they wouldn't be, would they? She felt safe. Yes. She didn't know why, only knew that her feet followed him and her breath came quickly. Fantine had never heard of a "pas de deux," but she felt as if she were being led step-by-step to a large crowd in front of a big building chanting, "Hell no, we won't go!" with young men like those with whom she went to high school setting fire to cards they took from their wallets. Young women in flowery prints and gauzy dresses that twirled as they did, others in denim overalls with construction boots, held up placards which screamed "One, two, three, four, we don't want your lousy war!"; which screamed "War is racism!"; which screamed "No Viet cong ever called me a nigger!" under a picture of a Negro prizefighter. And facing them across the street, a phalanx of soldiers with fixed bayonets and acne. Fantine could tell they didn't want to be here. They were the ones who were scared. Fantine watched as a young woman holding a bouquet of daisies walked down the line of soldiers, offering each of them flowers. Their NCOs commanded the men not to break ranks, hollered that if any one of them moved so much as a single muscle, that soldier would be made to pay dearly, so they all stood stiff and still and didn't reach for the flowers offered them. Fantine felt an impulse and acted on it. It was as if she had been overtaken by a spirit not herself, or not what she had come to know as herself. She walked up to the line of soldiers, looked into the eyes of one whose face strained with fear, took her daisy, and stuck it in the barrel of his M-16. He was as shocked at having this done as Fantine was at having done it. Somebody took her picture smiling at the soldier who now had the daisy down his gun barrel, the petals sticking out the business end, and then the other girl, the one with all the daisies, followed suit. She walked down the line and put daisies down the barrels of the rifles, too.

Photos were snapped of the other girl as well, but the one that appeared on lampposts and walls all around the Haight, the one that showed up on the front page of the alternative press, the one the wire services and, finally, the television networks picked up was the one of Fantine smiling up at her soldier boy.

Fantine lingered on the fringe of the festival, for that was how she perceived it, continually mesmerized by the scene and drawn into it, but when the crowd's energy dissipated, her own ebbed as well. She faded back out of the scene as easily as she had faded in, as easily and with as little thought, the entire picture breaking up as it crackled to black.

When she would talk about this in later years with Cody, when she would tell him the tales of their journey, that first day and night on the street remained as vivid as the morning news. Fantine vowed to find a place of her own, but it wouldn't be today. It had gotten too late. The sun barely showed anymore, just a snip of it. There was a neon sign on a hotel in the next block that advertised, "Rooms to let. Daily. Weekly. Monthly." She adjusted the kit bag from her right hand to her left, and determined that she would sleep there for tonight, get up early in the morning, and find a more permanent place to live. Just before she crossed the street to get to the hotel, she passed by a furniture store with a young man wearing bright green bellbottoms in the window who was dusting the model bedroom shown there. It had a gold and white décor. He tidied a wrinkle in the spread, fluffed the pillows, and turned on a faux Victorian reading lamp above the bed. *One day,* Fantine determined, *one day I will have a bedroom like that,* then walked away with purpose, crossed the street against the light, and entered the front door of the Pilgrims Rest Hotel.

What happened next can be told swiftly. Fantine asked for a room, got one, and even signed the register, but when she went to pay, she found a long slash in the kit bag, probably sliced by a razor, and the Wigwam sock filled with all of her money was missing. That was the first time she felt any panic since she had left Wyoming. "Where is it? Where the fuck is it?" She was shocked at herself—she had never cursed so in her life. "Okay, okay, okay, but what am I gonna do?" The room clerk had already closed the register and turned his back on her.

"Somebody stole all my money!" she tried to explain.

"I got my own problems," he said, his back still toward her, riffling through a notepad on his desk.

"I had the money right in here," she said, searching through her kit.

"On top," the clerk said.

"Yeah. Right. On top," she said.

"Somebody saw you do it, cut your bag."

"I don't have anyplace to sleep, to go even. What am I gonna do?" She looked up at the desk clerk who was now back at the sign-in desk facing her. He took a key from its cubby and held it up.

"Got its own bath, fresh sheets, towels," the clerk said.

"Sounds great. You'll let me have it? I'm gonna get a job tomorrow, so payin' you back's no trouble."

"Let's talk about a you-do-me-do," said the clerk as he dangled the key slowly from side to side.

"I'll clean the room," she offered quickly, brightly. "Hey, I'll give you a whole day's free labor, spiff the place up." He held the keys out. She reached for them. He yanked them back.

"The key to my heart," he said. "Don't you think it's worth something?"

"Cleaning up the place is worth a lot," she said. "I'll make it shine."

The clerk smiled. "What I got in mind is so much shinier."

"Tell me," said Fantine.

"I'm going to give you the key to my heart, and you're going to take off all your clothes, lie down on the floor, and jerk yourself off while I pee on you."

He noted the look of disgust on her face. "Sign on the bottom line, or sleep in the street."

Fantine felt the bile rise in her throat. She barely made it out the door to the gutter, where she vomited. She gagged and gagged, for she had eaten so little that day that nothing much came up, something foul and bitter, but not much.

"I thought you people believed in free love?" the clerk hollered after her. "Fuck you, fatty!"

Still shaking from her encounter with the clerk—that most foul piece of shit—she tried to cross the street but immediately ran back to the gutter, where she heaved again. Fantine felt as if she had swallowed a naked, newborn bird, its hungry beak poking painfully at her insides, its wings flailing wildly in her chest, its heartbeats drumming as fast as her own. When she could once again walk without heaving, she found herself in front of the furniture store window, the one with the bedroom of gold and white, with the wrinkle-free bed and the fancy light above it. A feeling of peace came over her. *What a nice bedroom!* she thought. *I'll have one just like it one day.* She felt better and sat down in the doorway to figure things out. Once her eyes grew accustomed to the dark, she spotted a piece of rug rolled up on the curb to be thrown away with the garbage. Fantine got up and went to the rug. It was the same color and had the same pattern as the one in the showroom window. *Unbelievable,* she thought. Her good luck.

Fantine took out a pocketknife and cut the string that held the rug. It rolled out before her, a piece just large enough to sleep on. The hungry little bird went away as she dragged the remnant to the window and straightened it out. One day this bedroom would be hers, but for right now, this piece of rug would have to do. Fantine lay down on the rug, the kit bag as her pillow, the sidewalk her bedroom. It did not take her long to fall asleep.

Her room (when she had one) back in Wyoming had faced east, so Fantine had always slept on her back for the rising sun to warm her face. Though she was asleep on the street, she felt the sun rise and grow warm. Her coat had fallen open. Without opening her eyes, she adjusted it as you'd adjust a blanket that had fallen off. She imagined she heard distant sounds, whispered words, breathy, unintelligible.

"Wow."

"It's her. Look." A rustling of paper.

"My God!"

"It is her, isn't it?"

Fantine shifted in her sleep. Her coat fell open again, but this time, she could have sworn, someone else closed it and covered her up. She opened her eyes and saw the girl with the bouquet of daisies from the demonstration. It was she who had closed Fantine's coat, she who was smiling down on the sleeping woman. The window dresser, the one wearing green bellbottoms, flashed the peace sign with both hands from the other side of the window.

"Would you like some juice? Fresh squeezed?" A young man wearing a shirt made out of an American flag offered her a container of orange juice.

"Have a blueberry muffin," someone said, and that was when Fantine looked around to see that she was at the center of a small clutch of people who stood smiling above her. One of them, a young man wearing a Jimi Hendrix T-shirt, held up the front page of the morning paper. Fantine's picture, the one that showed her as she put the daisy down the young soldier's gun barrel, took up most of the page.

"You're famous," someone said.

"And a gift to all of us," said someone else.

"You can crash with any of us until you find your own pad," the girl with the daisies said.

"We basically all live at each other's pads anyway," said the young man with the juice. Fantine took a sip then offered it around. Everyone else took a sip, too.

"Nobody else is having a baby, so this is really cool."

"Another sip?" someone offered.

"A baby!" someone else exclaimed.

"Oh, wow!" said another.

Thus were Fantine and Cody welcomed to their new home. Two months later, six pounds and seven ounces of Cody

Rosewater came into the world. Fantine bore him at home. A midwife nursed her through the birth. The rest of the tribe stood around her bed singing the baby down the birth canal into fresh air. As Fantine went into labor, everyone, including her, drank from a jug of freshly squeezed orange juice laced with drops of crystal-clear acid, so by the time Cody was really on the move, everyone was tuned into heaven. Cody flew from his mother's womb on the great white wings of a trumpeter swan. That tiny baby boy had the bodacious lungs of a full gospel, African Methodist Episcopalian church choir. He started off with a peep like a pennywhistle then escalated up the scale until the holiness of his voice wrapped around all the assembly like the rings of Saturn wrapped around the body of the mother planet itself. "Here I am, here I am, great Godawmighty, here I am!"

For seventeen years, Fantine raised her son to walk gently in the world, free of anger, full of purpose. She kept their lives simple and unadorned, and she coaxed Cody into a world where every object seen and every sound heard, where every step and breath taken, and every thing touched was sacred and had consequence. She knew where she belonged, and she was happy there. Because she was such a gentle and unassuming person herself, it's ironic, but she was one of those rare people who operated without fear. Fear in her was replaced by love. Most of the worst had already happened. Trouble? She'd had it, but once the epiphany took place, love defined everything she would ever do again. Anything else was superfluous. Fantine believed that she must make her decisions from that kindly place. Future steps then became obvious. Anything else was to put herself at risk. She would not contribute to the bedlam. Her responsibility was clear.

The only time Fantine left northern California was when Cody was still a little boy, when she could still pick him up and hold him on her hip. The call had come, and if it was that important (which it was), she had to put personal issues aside and answer. On October 21, 1967, people from all over the United States would converge around the five walls of the Pentagon in Washington, D.C., and attempt to levitate it. The idea was to exorcise the demons of war, to drive out the evil spirits and end the war in Vietnam. The demonstrators intended to encircle the building and to sing and chant until the Pentagon turned orange, broke from its moorings, and rose up into the air. One of the songs exhorted the people, "Imprison the President, incarcerate the Congress, levitate the Pentagon, now we're making progress." When the building refused to budge, some 70,000 demonstrators focused their passion on the 2,500 federal troops who formed a human barricade that prevented any of the marchers from climbing the Pentagon steps. As it was before, Fantine found herself in front of the soldiers with a bouquet of daisies, but this time, there was a difference: she would hand a flower to Cody and guide his little hand to the gun barrel. One of the commanding officers reproached her bitterly for endangering her child. She answered right back that the only people endangering our children were people like him and the men they worked for.

People who remember "Hashbury" from the old days might also remember Fantine's shop, Fanny's Down Home Stitchin', where she made a living for herself and Cody as a seamstress. It was a local hangout, too. Fantine became one of those people you just love to be around. The neighborhood would drop in, talk some politics, play some music. There was usually a guitar or harmonica somewhere in the shop. Folks took pictures of each other and covered the walls with them. Fantine kept a scrapbook of those years called "The Chronicles of Cody," but she never actually, physically, got into much of this herself. She was happy to continue sewing, happy that her place was a pit stop for so many interesting people right smack in the heart of the Haight. Wyoming? Wasn't that a state or something?

Fanny's Down Home Stitchin'.

She would fix what you wore or make you something new. She did pretty well, too, though she purposely kept her business small and homegrown until her untimely death. Acid reflux had finally baked her brain to the consistency of apple crisp. She stepped off a curb and got pulverized by a bus. At the time, she was flush with the bedrock certainty that physical objects really could pass through her body. So much for harmony with the universe. Yet, isn't the goal to die happily? No questions left unanswered? Doesn't that certainty mean you've reached a state of absolute grace? Fantine had done well for herself and her boy. Not that she was ready. Not that any of us are ever ready. But there it is. You know the saying: "Live each day as if it were your last because someday it will be." That had been Fantine's purpose in life, and she had been really good at it. Mission: motherhood. Mission: accomplished. Almost.

After her death, the seventeen-year-old Cody dropped into a deep sadness. The trapdoor had sprung, and he had fallen through. But the rope broke, and he kept on falling. His mother had always been there, and now, just like that, just because fate was measured by a hair, she wasn't. Her life had been his, and now, her life wasn't anything at all. Her son was the child of her beloved, a very brave man, and this son, this miracle creature, had been her beloved, too. She was wise enough to have brought him up with the idea that someday he would have to make his own way in the world, but that she would be the roots of his tree, his still point, his anchor. He would always know that he was loved, and Cody was not ashamed by how much he loved her back.

Fantine may have been a hippie, but being a mother at the same time brought out her practical side. She took her mothering seriously, particularly when it came to education. Until her death, Cody had been home-schooled. It had been his mother's fervent belief that she could do a better job than the public system, and to her credit, she bent her back and brain to the task. There was only one rule in Fantine's classroom: that Cody learn, and Fantine was determined that they would learn together. She read in one of her teaching guides that the Latin root of the word *educate* meant to lead forth, and that suited Fantine just fine. She would lead her son forth into the light, nudging him toward it, then she'd show him how to look up and find the light on his own. She brought him up with a gentle hand, only smacking his bottom once and that was on a rainy morning when he squirmed away and ran against the red into heavy traffic. Her mantra? Question authority. Her method: keep on reading. Her religion? There is that of God in everyone.

Cody missed her.

Since Cody was a minor, the state stepped in and took over. Cody sensed there was a problem when a van drove up to the social services building where he had been taken, with a sign painted on each side panel of the van that stated in bright yellow letters, "This Van is Prayer Conditioned." A phone number was painted on both sides of the hood where it couldn't be missed, "Call 1-800-MEET-GOD." The man driving, Ben Ken Stravitoni, was going to be his foster father. Ben Ken and his wife, Maylene, owned a Christian bookstore called "Books, by Jesus." His hair was freshly cut a solid two inches above his ears; Cody's was to his shoulders. The boy took one look at the van and at Stravitoni, and knew he was in a world of trouble. Unfortunately, Cody was still six months from his eighteenth birthday, and so had no say about this or much of anything else.

Cody Rosewater spent the better part of his senior year doing time at a conventional high school, and living in a foster home with people who saw it as their divine mission to housebreak his soul. As far as they were concerned, he was a wild child born naked in the jungle, suckled by sin, raised by apes. God was to be feared; revenge nurtured; distrust encouraged. Punishment could be expected and was to be taken as a man. *Jig, kike, slope, spic, chink, towel head, faggot*—new vocabulary words to be tucked away and used whenever needed just to let off a little steam. Maylene kept a refrigerator magnet on her Kenmore that said, "Blessed by Jesus—Spoiled by my husband," although the whole time he was there, Cody never saw any evidence of either. The day Cody hit eighteen he got the hell out without bothering to complete his diploma. He'd had his duffel packed for weeks ready for the Checkout. Just as he was walking out of the house for the last time, Ben Ken came up to him and said, "I've been wantin' to do this for so-o-o-o long," and slapped Cody hard across the cheek with an open hand. "For all you do," Ben Ken said, "His blood's for you." Cody promptly kicked him in the nuts, and while Ben Ken lay writhing on the floor, Cody bent over him, smiled right smack into his face, and said, "Don't forget to thank God today," as he slammed the door on his way out.

There was nothing more the state could do with or to Cody. Cody was finally both free *and* a man, and the system was glad to get rid of him. The foster care social worker had informed him a few months earlier that when he reached eighteen he would become his mother's sole beneficiary, which meant an inheritance of $50,000 from a life insurance policy, and the deed to the real estate in the Haight where he was raised (Fantine had been savvy enough to buy the storefront building with the apartment upstairs). Cody Rosewater returned home to his old neighborhood to make some choices about the future. It was dizzying. He could do whatever he wanted to do, and he didn't have to go to school, either. Cody hadn't put much stock in that religion of the Stravitonis, but he had to admit that fate had given him exactly what he wanted.

Fantine's principles and teaching continued to guide Cody all of his life, but she had also brought him up to be independent, and so his dreams and ways were his own. It was time for him to quit the old nabe, to discover for himself what else was out there and where he ought to be. He knew he'd miss his neighbors, family, really, people who didn't lynch, didn't start stupid fights with people who spoke a different language, and didn't care whom they sat next to in school. He also knew he wasn't kidding himself about what was on the outside. After all, Stravitoni's favorite T-shirt read, "Happiness is a belt-fed weapon." He'd also met Ben Ken's friends with T-shirts of their own, like, "Kill 'em all, Let God sort 'em out." "Come the Rapture, can I have your car?" "'Don't make Me come down there'—God." "Death from Above." One of the imponderables in Fantine's life was that men like these would register their sons but never their guns. She had never even allowed Cody to get a driver's license or Social Security card. Fantine didn't claim to be reasonable: she did not birth her son to die with strangers at the bidding of morons.

Cody knew there'd be scumbags out there and times unpleasant. Nonetheless, he had to saddle up and see it for his own. His mother had a theory that she wisely kept to herself. Cody had been a particularly easy child to raise, even throughout his teens. Fantine noodled with the notion that maybe Cody hadn't rebelled like most teenagers because he saw the alternative and recognized it for what it was: one sad sight. Even so, the Haight was no longer the center of his universe. For now, he was just one more wandering cowboy.

One of his mother's customers had given Cody the ear of her lawyer so he could organize his affairs. Within a week, Cody had established a bank account and worked out a deal with a local handyman, his wife, and four kids, whereby they moved into his apartment rent-free in exchange for utilities and maintenance. Cody had often heard his mother and the man (one of their neighbors) talk about how much he wanted a workshop of his own in order to make and sell handmade furniture. Aw, what the hell! So Cody threw his mother's shop into the bargain, too. All Cody wanted in return, if he ever needed it, was a bed. He would check in from time to time, but for now, it was adios, amigo. Go with God. For starters, they could reach him at General Delivery, Cody, Wyoming.

Why Wyoming?

It was a start.

Cody's lawyer had gotten him a Social Security number, a driver's license, and a credit card, and also helped him with his first purchase of a vehicle, a Ford Bronco, low mileage. Once he finished signing all the necessary papers, Cody headed to Wyoming, stopping only when he had to refill the tank. He drove directly to Cody, got a street map, asked a few questions, and found himself, at dusk, parked outside the grounds of the high school where his mother and father had been students all those many years ago. As the last light faded, Cody walked around the grounds of the school. He didn't know what he expected to find, nor did he really even know what in particular he was looking for. In that case, how would he know if he ever found it? Hadn't he been raised to believe that it was the search that mattered? Still, doesn't a search imply an object to be found? Otherwise, wouldn't it just be meandering around? Put that way, it seemed kind of pointless.

Jesus, he could talk himself into a circle!

The light was almost gone. Cody had nearly circled the campus and stood staring out across the open prairie that abutted the football field. Nothing pulled at him. He tried to imagine a prom night eighteen years ago, but, of course, how could he? Tonight was nothing more than another few hours of darkness. A few fireflies. Some other insects. Not much of a moon.

It turned out that Cody Rosewater learned quite a bit in Wyoming. He hadn't ever decided to settle there, but one thing came clear: he preferred outside to inside, and once outside he preferred the mountains. Nothing else came close. The world seemed a more treacherous place to Cody than it had to Fantine. Mountains promised that he could rise above it all. Yearning got him there. Cody rented a little wooden house just outside the Cody city limits, but he wasn't there one day when the urge to roam hit him. He began spending more and more of his time in the mountains. He learned to ride, bought a horse (an athletic blood bay), and began packing into the mountains for days at a time. Cody became one of their creatures. He didn't need a weather report. All he needed was to look up.

Wonderful things happened in the mountains. One crisp, Fall day, when the aspen leaves shimmered like caches of gold doubloons, Cody rode to tree line, though he had to pass through some pretty thick scrub before he got there. He spotted a cow about ten yards in front of him, and started to think, *Somebody's lost their cow,* some simple shit like that, when his senses just exploded from the input of suddenly finding himself—that was no cow!—in the middle of an elk herd. In the middle! Maybe thirty elk. Cody realized with surprise that the animals never spooked. He must've had the wind and was able to simply wander into the herd because he was on horseback. The elk know that a creature on two legs is a danger to them, but his horse transformed him into a four-legged one.

As if being in the middle of an elk herd grazing peacefully wasn't amazing enough, Cody's horse suddenly snorted and did a little dance. She wanted her head, so Cody gave it to her. She had been a cutting pony. Her instincts sensed the bull, and she moved to cut him out of the herd. He went to his right; she danced to her left. He went to his left, she to her right. Cody was ecstatic. My God, who had ever experienced such a thing? Then his good sense shocked him back into the real world when Cody suddenly realized that a seven-point, eight-hundred-pound bull elk, if he decides to come at you, is a whole world of dangerous animal, and that he, Cody, had better stop playing around if he intended to live through this day and tell his grandchildren. So he took off his hat, slapped it against his leg, and hollered, "Saddle up! Get outta here!" Cody couldn't count to five as fast as these animals managed to disappear. How does a herd of animals that size—so many tons—manage to just vanish in single-digit seconds? It was as if they were never there.

Cody had this theory, concluded while climbing Wyoming's mountains, most of northern Colorado's, and a few of Utah's (primarily in the Wasatch range), that it was better to climb the same mountain ten times than to climb ten different mountains once.

He wanted to know one hill, his hill, as well as he knew the morning walk down the front steps to get his newspaper. Cody could tell by the way the paperboy folded it if the kid was running late that morning or not. He could tell by where the paper landed when the boy tossed it whether the kid had gotten enough sleep the night before. He knew when his next-door neighbor took a sneak peek at the headlines by the way the newspaper was refolded and replaced neatly against Cody's front door, a dead giveaway, since the paperboy never got it anywhere near the door. By picking up the paper Cody knew what the weather was going to be that day. He wondered what that weed was called, the one revealed as Cody picked up the paper, and saw the line of ants marching up to and all over a used gumball somebody dropped yesterday on the bottom step. . . . Would an overnight guest have been that observant if he went outside to bring in the paper himself?

The trick was in finding that one mountain, the one where Cody didn't need to be anyplace else. By this time, Cody had gotten his guide's license and was packing hunting parties throughout the Snake River basin and parts of the Laramie range. He took to it like a tick takes to a dog. Even the Indian guides and packers, the locals, said this guy, Cody, could track a panther over solid rock. Somebody suggested that somewhere in his family line somebody had married a squaw. Had to be in the blood, they said. Had to be. He was that good.

Cody also became known as a hunter of rare ability. He realized he was never as happy as when he was onto an animal, and was not so much shocked at this revelation as moved by it. Time would stand still. He had an uncanny awareness of where the game would appear. His senses gathered intelligence at maximum capacity, and the part of his brain that organized the chase processed this information into a plan. At no other time did he see so clearly. At no other time did he hear so well or sense such slight shifts in the wind. At no other time than this was he able to become both the animal pursued and the animal pursuing it. He believed the act of hunting, the life and death of it, was a profound act and never to be taken lightly. You took your game with a single shot. You did not shoot at a fleeing animal. To do so was to risk a wound. The prey should never have known you were there. You do not take what you do not use. Yet, who was to say what you could or could not do in the wilderness? Nobody to see you, right? What difference did it make? Well, it made an enormous difference to a man like Cody, who believed that good sportsmanship is what you do when nobody's looking.

Fantine had taught her son well.

Who?

Fantine? Cody's mother?

What did a flower child who stuck daisies into the gun barrels of soldiers have to do with all this?

She taught her son what life was like when we feel the world and every object in it as holy. Even a weed in dirt is a little world: home, shade, food to some creature. She taught him to walk through the sky, that if we understand that the sky starts where the Earth stops, and not just *up there someplace,* we are always, all of us, walking through the sky. To do so turns everyday life into a miracle. One sees and hears and feels things never before felt, or felt only in dreams. Fantine had her own way of looking at things. So did Cody.

The day came when he could not get the thought of Alaska out of his mind.

Alaska.

Cody thought the word itself was an oxymoron. On the one hand, wilderness instantly came to mind, on the other, a moth-erlode of refugees from the Lower 48, all with a bit of larceny and a lot of anarchy in their hearts. More people live in a New York City neighborhood than live in the entire state of Alaska. He began reading everything he could get his hands on about Alaska. He sent away for topo maps to study the terrain. Almost every animal indigenous to North America lived in Alaska. It was a kind of Eden, but it made you work for its treasures. A lazy man would get nowhere. Cody began to dream of living there, way out in the bush, just beyond the edge of things, living off the land. His hind parts may not yet have left Wyoming, but his heart was already checking out. He laughed to himself when he thought that his mother might rather have seen him in a saffron robe, head shaved, with tinkle bells around his ankles. But, really, he didn't think so. Alaskan life had a purity to it. The land had soul. Cody felt he had been offered a blessing. He made plans to receive it.

Cody worked his way into the country as a deckhand on the Inside Passage and then worked his way through it as a packer and guide. Along the way, he had a marriage that was mercifully short. He fell in love with a bluegrass fiddler when he saw her win a contest outside of Burnt Paw. She was as shapely as her fiddle and just as lively. Her name was Michaelene. Michaelene's fiddle made you want to dance, and then it broke your heart, just like the woman herself. Cody never gave love at first sight much of a thought, until it thumped him. In effect, the boy was sandbagged. He watched her ride that fiddle like a jockey in a steeplechase, and when she was finished, he walked up to her and asked her to marry him.

He made it sound like a joke, of course—what kind of a dummy ever marries somebody they don't know?—but he was almost serious.

She took a long look at him and said, "Do we have time for a drink?"

"Make it two," he said.

"You drive a hard bargain, cowboy," she said.

With that, they went to the refreshment tent and hoisted the first of many ice-cold beers. If only these two had stayed in courtship mode.

For a solid week the rubber hit the road. Cody and Michaelene were inseparable, never more than five feet between them. She went home with him four beers into that first night. Neither one of them emerged until the morning of the fourth day when they ran out of half-and-half. They resupplied at the nearest market, then rushed back to Cody's and raced each other inside. Whoever made it to the bed first won. First prize was sex. The consolation prize was sex, too. Not so humdrum a way to spend a week, eh? The month they courted stands as one of the best chunks of time in either of their lives. Then they got married.

That was the problem. It was the only problem they had, but it had true heft to it.

Judging by her behavior, Michaelene thought she found a loophole in the marriage contract. Not right away, of course, but this was a woman who did not favor being left alone. She felt safest of all when she was onstage playing to an SRO crowd. Cody was just the opposite. He relished time spent alone. Since it was hunting season, he was now packing parties into the Denali range. At one point, he stayed at the spike camp for a solid month. When he came back, she was out on the road. When she came back she had three affairs going at the same time along with her marriage, not all men, not all human. (It made Cody feel just a little bit better to tell it that way.) They took a poke at mending things, but really, the marriage was over for both of them. It had been fun, and it had been stupid. No hard feelings except for the ones Cody harbored.

As soon as hunting season was over, Cody gave Michaelene money for the lawyer, signed the papers, jumped in his Bronco, and sped north. He'd let her know where to send them. She promised to send him her next CD as well. "The papers will be fine," he said, and floored it. That was it. He and Michaelene were again free-floating particles in the universe. At heart, Cody knew he and Alaska were the real true fit. How many times had he flown over the land in a bush plane accompanying clients to a spike camp, and looked down and thought, *Damn, I live here!* He knew they wished they could be doing what he was doing. They often told him so. Cody felt full. Almost. Once again the urge to know only one mountain came upon him. When this happened, he shifted a little to the east and followed a notion he'd had for some time. Cody headed for a river called the Hulahula, named so by the native whalers who, in past centuries, shipped out to the South Seas. The Hulahula flowed through a massive entanglement of rock and river called the Brooks Range, which spread across northern Alaska like the fossilized spine of a prehistoric creature so big that it had long since disappeared from Earth.

Cody was not at all surprised that when he finally reached the

Hulahula River he knew he could stay there forever. He settled in to do just that. On the day he chose to live there, Cody climbed a bluff overlooking the river, the edge of the edge of the country, with the Arctic Ocean just beyond that. He shivered with exhilaration. The beating heart of this wilderness was in concert with his own. He was suddenly immensely wise and happy. *My God*, he thought. *This is what they meant!* and laughed out loud.

Maybe it was because he was raised in such a fervently egalitarian milieu (Wavy Gravy was at his christening), but Cody, while artistically inclined, didn't much like the fine arts. He thought they were elitist. His tastes ran to those guys who carved exquisite re-creations of wild ducks, each feather in delicate relief, or engraved custom-made shotguns inlaid with gold, hunting scenes worthy of medieval tapestries. Cody knew a guy in Montana, Aaron Pursely his name was, who created clasp knives of cherrywood inlaid with brass engravings the wonder of any unearthed anywhere. Why a Cellini saltcellar and not a Pursely knife? If Cody had known who Cellini was, he would have thought it a good question.

The thing was, Cody was only so-so as a craftsman himself, a truth he had learned to acknowledge and accommodate. Barely. Still, he wanted to do *something*. Some time after his move to Toehold, after a time of living off everything this rich land had to offer, the old question came up again and wouldn't go away: what could he do that would make a difference, that would bring something special into the world? He wanted to leave his imprint on something, to mix spit and ashes on the palm of his hand and press it against a cave wall, except that had already been done. Then it came to him: what if they had been able to preserve the animals they revered? Egyptians preserved their dead as a holy ritual, but they were pretty much all pruned out by the time we got to them. What if they could look like they always looked?

Cody taught himself taxidermy out of a book. He worked hard at doing mounts for local hunters at cost. At some point, the word went out and guys started talking about this wizard up in the Brooks Range, fella who could do miracles, make the dead live again. An interview in a trade paper quoted him as saying, "What I do, people bring me their dreams—that's how I look at it—which they've gone and shot full of holes. A lot of these clowns don't belong in the woods, but that's life, and there they are. They see a vision with horns or fur or wings—bam! They kill it. If they know what they're doing, one clean shot. If they don't, I get the rest. What I do, I make it right. I'm like that guy Buonasera, the undertaker in *The Godfather,* the guy who fixes Sonny Corleone up so his mother can look at him. I give my customers back their dreams in one piece, and they can keep them forever."

Cody got so he couldn't keep up with the demand. If he wanted to he'd work forever, though working forever didn't necessarily strike him as a plus. He'd heard that Buddy, the retired fireman in that cabin with the old fireplug out front (Buddy had "borrowed" it from a warehouse before heading north), was a pretty fair carpenter. Cody cut a deal with him off the books, and the two of them built a studio and warehouse framed out with wood they logged themselves from a parcel granted them by the Bureau of Land Management. Anybody could do it, but the work was hard tired to the bone, so very few did. It goes this way: a forester marks the trees to be cut with a red slash. Thus, the BLM gets a stand thinned out, and the guy who thins it gets the wood. Everybody wins. And that's how Cody Rosewater's Taxidermy came to be.

Cody considered that he occupied a space somewhere between a fine artist and a plastic surgeon. Most taxidermists ordered rubber and wire or fiberglass prefab forms from supply houses. Cody made his own. He didn't do small animals very much—chipmunks, rabbits, squirrels—but when he did, he made their bodies out of straw that he wrapped and twisted into shape. The larger ones he carved himself out of foam or balsa wood, or made exacting molds of their bodies. These were the ones that established his genius. Whenever possible, he requested that his customers bring him the entire animal. In some mysterious manner, Cody "got" the personality of each particular creature that way. Then he would skin them himself, and while he skinned them and for some time after, he'd study the individual muscle structure. He'd even go so far as to examine the contents of the stomach to determine the animal's last meal. As best he could, Cody wanted to know his subjects from the molecules on up.

Sometimes Cody would construct the body out of wood, then cover it with wire screening that he molded into shape. After this he covered the entire structure with clay and carefully shaped it until it became like sculpture. The next step was to cover the clay with plaster. When the plaster dried Cody would cut it off the form, giving him the plaster mold that he needed. The clay, the wood, the wire screening—everything but the plaster mold would then be discarded. After this, Cody would take a paintbrush and "paint" layers and layers of paper and glue inside the mold, thus creating a papier-mâché replica of the body. Once this dried, the tanned skin would finally be stretched and sewn into place. Glass eyes were inserted in the sockets, but the claws, ears, whiskers, and nose were the ones the animal had when alive. It was at this juncture that Cody's creations blurred the boundary between life and death.

Entering Cody's Taxidermy was like stepping into the private menagerie of a potentate. Full body mounts dominated the room. Ten feet of grizzly rose above the rest. Three wolves followed a blood trail. A cougar hung on to a bull elk's back, raking it with its claws, its teeth deep into the nape of the big bull's neck. A Canada goose in full spread soared from the ceiling. A sharp-shinned hawk, its wings tucked tightly against its sides, plum-meted down upon its prey. All these were exacting re-creations of the final seconds of the creatures' lives. And yet it was so silent, not hushed but noiseless, eerily so, not one growl of triumph, not a single shriek of pain.

Cody placed his worktable (which was about the size of a Ping-Pong table) on a slight rise off to one side. Hides lay stacked in piles or were strung from the walls. He kept a small refrigerator stocked with cold Olympia beer. You wanted one, it was on the house, help yourself. And let's not forget the coffee. You might want some a couple of beers later. Or you might not. Cody didn't mind that people from both sides of the village would often stop by to watch him work, as long as they kept their conversation to a minimum. That was the tradeoff. Free beer and coffee but you had to shut up. If you wanted his opinion, he'd give it to you, just not during work hours. Before Buddy barged through the door with news of Mel's scheme, Cody had been working on a caribou head with a magnificently shoveled rack of antlers. On an earlier form he had the ears a little more forward as if the caribou were listening, but he discarded that one. The form he was bent on fashioning would ultimately reflect the precise instant the shot took the animal. Nothing else would do. The bull would have heard the snick of the safety. It was the last sound he would hear. He'd have been poised to run, though he would never have taken that next step. There was a point in time, and Cody was driven to nail it.

Buddy went on about Mel's ad in the magazine. "She never hinted about nothing to you?"

Cody shook his head and went on with his work.

"And what's this gourmet meal crap? She cooked on the pipeline for a while. Know what they called her? Who was that lady poisoned all them people? What was her name? They called her that."

"Lizzie Borden," Cody offered.

"Nope. She was the ax," answered Buddy.

"So what'd they call her?" Cody wanted to know.

"Who?"

"Mel! Jesus, Buddy!"

"You could help if you remembered that lady's name," grumped Buddy. "What's it like being her landlord? She pay on time?" Cody didn't move his head but raised his eyes and stared at Buddy.

"I know that look," said Buddy.

"Then pay attention to it," said Cody.

"Not a problem," said Buddy, who was normally not so easily deterred, but this time decided it was the best of his choices. His friend, Cody, had two kinds of silences: one was a rich, fulsome silence that emanated from him in waves when the work took him to a place of total concentration. It gathered the watcher in, placed a shawl around his shoulders, brought him closer to the fire, shared the moment of creation. This was the silence that Buddy wanted. The second silence shut out everyone. It encased Cody like an insect in amber. It was impenetrable. Buddy did not want this second silence. It would be like running up against an electric fence. It would hurt. Instead, he watched his friend work and tried to keep his mouth shut. After a while he said, "Most guys don't take their time like you do."

"I'd like to get something absolutely right for once," said Cody without looking up.

"Your mounts are the best in the business," said Buddy.

"I mean perfect," said Cody. "Something perfect."

"To me," Buddy said, "you're like what's-his-name? Michelangelo."

"Something so beautiful it doesn't look dead at all," said Cody.

Cody continued working. Buddy continued drinking. Later that day, Buddy said, out of what seemed nowhere,

"Lucretia Bourgeois."

"What're you talking about?" asked Cody.

"That lady who poisoned people," answered Buddy.

"Uh-huh," said Cody, as he finished setting the eyes in the caribou bull's head.

Somewhere around the time she was seven, Mel's first real memory got etched in her brain. She remembered shinnying up the pole of a metal backyard swing set. Her grandfather had set the legs in cement so the whole thing wouldn't pull up and over when she swung for the sky. As she shinnied, she clenched the steel pole tightly between her legs. As she shinnied, her crotch rubbed against the leg of the swing. It wasn't anything she had in mind to do. It came as a big surprise: climb, squeeze, rub. Mel had no idea what caused the sensation that came over her, but it was enough to keep her shinnying up that metal pole, desperate to keep the feeling that was such a mighty escape from everyday normal. It was like having her own personal supernova inside. It lit up, traveled up her backbone, lightened her load, then rolled back out to sea. Mel couldn't wait all day 'til school was over so she could run home and do it again. Got her ass kicked but good by the old lady once she figured out what Mel was doing. That old lady was lethal. She'd whack Mel with the closest thing she could get in her hand: coat hanger, hot iron, wooden spoon. Once she threw a tire iron at Mel's head, but she ducked and it crashed through a cellar window. Another time she told Mel not to sit with one leg crossed over the other, and especially not to swing the crossed one back and forth 'cause that's how women do their selves. Mel always wondered what the fuck was that all about?

Once Mel hit her teens, the old lady couldn't handle her anymore. Mel did what she wanted and managed to mostly jump out of the way when her mother came after her. One time Mel was about to walk out the front door, and for some dumb reason, her mother didn't want her to. Mel let her know point-blank she didn't give a damn what she wanted. The old lady snapped. Her fist came up, and she charged across the living room to hammer her daughter. Mel backed up a step and cold-cocked her mother with a quick right. The woman went down, out, and stayed that way a good while. When she woke up she asked how her daughter could do such a thing to an old lady. Mel said it was to get even for all the times she clobbered her when she was a little girl and way smaller than her. The old lady never hit Mel again.

Mel could tell this story today without any sorrow in her heart.

Mel's scheme began without her even knowing it. Wherever these things were sorted and filed inside her head, certain of them—thoughts, images, emotions—began to come together slowly like river ice or fontanelles, fragments with no particular meaning or relationship to one another until suddenly they meant absolutely everything. By the time the idea finally penetrated Mel's conscious mind she perceived it as a plan fully formed like Athena bursting from the head of Zeus. Some people throw bones. Some people check the entrails of chickens. Mary Ellen Madden trusted her intuition. She told herself that she was hip enough to know that sometimes our desire sees meaning in random occurrences, particularly when we want something so badly it hurts.

First of all, there was the letter, not the one to Gary from his son, but another one. Hers. It was forwarded from a previous address, and arrived in a wrinkled, dirty envelope with jelly spots that looked like it had been used once before and fished out of the trash. It also came postage due, which really pissed her off. The former recipient's name was scratched out with black ink and Mel's name scrawled in its place. There was no return address, but Mel knew by the scrawl exactly who it was from. The postmark, too. That was first of all. She stuffed the letter unopened into the pocket of her parka and forgot all about it until two weeks later when she got a nosebleed, pulled the letter out, and pressed it to her nose like a wad of Kleenex to stop the bleeding. By the time she finally read it, coffee stains had joined the bloody ones. It was a mess, and the news was just about as bad as she thought it would be, though what it was, exactly, was different from anything she had imagined. Now there was that to deal with, too.

Cody had noticed a change in Mel's behavior: wasn't she a bit hyper lately? Short-tempered? Kind of driven? Maybe a little preoccupied? It had been going on for a while: she hadn't seemed very relaxed at all. Maybe the boonies were finally getting to her. The edge of the world ain't for all of us, but the simple fact that Mel was still here, was still well and alive and had weathered two mighty Winters north of the Arctic Circle gave convincing testimony to her pluck. She could hunt as well as most. She hadn't lost the tip of her nose to frostbite, hadn't broken any bones, learned a few things, hadn't starved, had, in fact, put on her own extra layer of protection against the long arctic night. It didn't look half bad on her, either.

Cody was near certain that he was the first resident of Toehold to spot Mel the day she tooled along the 'dozed road leading toward the village for the first time. It was sometime in May, after thaw and break-up. About six miles outside of the village, the fan belt to his Bronco loosened up and started whistling, so Cody pulled over to the side in order to tighten it. Mel hammered by in the Ramcharger while he was under the hood. The springs on the Charger were shot, he could tell that much, the way her vehicle stuttered through that pothole. Once word got around that Whoever-This-Lady-Was was in the market for a yearlong rental, locals started making book on how long she'd actually last. Her license plate was from Arizona, for Christ's sake. And she was a woman. And she was alone. And she didn't know one single soul. And. And. And. Buddy gave her 'til Thanksgiving, and he was more generous than most. George Nanachuk gave her 'til Halloween. Esther said, "Wait until she tries to T-bone a moose." Mel was definitely a long shot. Good thing nobody told her.

It wasn't that Mel got things right the first time. She never got anything right the first time. Sometimes she didn't get them right the second time, and sometimes she didn't get them right at all. Mel didn't pretend to be perfect. In fact, she didn't pretend to be anything, a trait both arresting and aggravating, depending on how many times she asked if she could borrow your tools. Down the road some she'd always get her own, but she had to use yours first to know what she needed, didn't she? Well, often it turned out that the tool was Cody's, but there were good reasons for this. For one thing, he had every tool you'd ever need. If you were on his good side (you had to stretch to be on the bad), he'd lend you anything from a backhoe to a backscratcher, and if he had a free hand, he'd lend you that, too. Cody was Toehold's go-to guy. You could depend on him. For instance, there was that trailer behind his place.

It was actually a sheepherder's trailer, but in excellent condition, well winterized. The old man who owned it died three weeks after he took delivery. Cody came across it at an estate sale over in Barrow. He thought he'd put it out behind his shop as a guesthouse, though right offhand he couldn't think of anybody he wanted to stay that long. He did know for sure that it'd be an easy seasonal rent to hunters, so he wound up giving the guy fifty bucks less than he asked, and the trailer changed hands. Cody got it at a price because most people didn't want to buy a dead man's house until they were sure he was no longer in it. Bush communities could be a superstitious bunch. Something else they could be: poor, subsistence-level poor. That led to all kinds of situations, one of which was that somebody often needed a place to stay for a few days. Somebody'd always ask, in such a situation, "Anybody at Cody's right now?" "Leave it better than you find it," was all he'd say if it was empty. They did, usually. Even Summer Joe stayed there a while, before he went away to prison, but he trashed the trailer the night before he had to hand himself over, nearly burned the place down, and wound up stealing the woodstove to sell for cigarette money while he was inside.

Mel's arrival in Toehold nearly coincided with Summer Joe's departure for the state penitentiary. If it were any closer they would have spattered gravel on each other's side panels as their two trucks passed on the road heading in opposite directions. But Summer Joe was the only one guaranteed a roof over his head. Mel sped by Cody and the dead Bronco that first day, but she slammed on her brakes a few yards beyond him and backed up to ask if he needed help.

"Not unless you want to buy me a new Bronco," said the man under the hood.

Funny guy. Nice smile. It was emphasized by the grease on his face.

"Does this state have a lottery?" she asked.

"Uh-uh," he answered. "Lousy schools, too."

Mel's assessment: cute, good values. "Kids always wind up getting it in the neck," said Mel. "No matter what. Well, hey, I'm just in the way. Sure I can't help?"

"You heard my terms." He smiled. Funny guy. Likable.

Don't, Mel told herself. *Don't even think about it, lady.* "Adios," she said, and gunned it on down the road. He saluted with a Stilson wrench.

That Charger needs work, he thought as he finished tightening the nuts on his fan belt. He put his tools neatly back in his toolbox, wiped the grease off his hands with a Handi Wipe, cranked the big engine over, and continued on his way southwest, nonstop five hundred miles and change to Hungry Horse, where he intended to eat a steak that was actually bovine, not moose or bear, and then spend the night enjoying the expert services of someone you called when only a professional will do. Cody thought of it like going to an amusement park for a great ride. Every once in a while you just had to treat yourself. Cody liked to think of it as his health spa, his Golden Door, his Canyon Ranch.

Mel, on the other hand, continued into Toehold.

Dirty Dodge Ram Chargers didn't attract much attention. Some people swore by Chevy trucks, damn well swore by them to the point of apoplexy, but just as many swore by your Fords, too. You had a mind of your own you went to Ramcharger, but that didn't guarantee anybody'd bother to look, so when Mel first drove through town nobody took notice, except for that Arizona license plate, a dead giveaway.

Main Street in Toehold could have been called Dirt Street, for that's what it was, a short dirt road just wide enough to accommodate two pickups side by side. It started as a Cat trail because originally it had been worn by a Caterpillar bulldozer. Years of off-road tires, which were all people up here bought, had packed it down into a road. The village looked as if it had been shaken from a box, an indiscriminate warren of military surplus Quonset huts, cabins, and ramshackle sheds lined up along one side of the road, the side facing the river. Most had satellite dishes attached. A couple of the cabins had dogsleds parked on the sides with kennels in back for a dozen husky mix dogs. Not one was without a snowmobile. Snowshoes hung on nails beside the doors.

One of the buildings had to be a bar, though Mel couldn't tell which one. Another had to be a church, but she couldn't tell that one, either. The bar might have been the one with the six-foot-wide moose rack that hung above the entrance like bone wings. Or could that have been the church, some kind of totemic thing? Nope, it had to be a bar because a sign under the moose rack said, "Pingo Palace." Had to be a bar, only what the hell was a pingo? Once, she remembered, in a public library in Seattle, she had leafed through a book of nineteenth-century photographs of Alaska—mostly Gold Rush stuff—thousands of prospectors climbing up the Chilkoot Pass, tossed-together plank towns. Toehold, she thought, as she coasted by, looked a little like they did, more or less: canoes on the river's edge, a couple of out-boards, truck shells on cinder blocks; salmon belly strips drying on racks in the sun.

Three young Indian boys were out in the middle of the river in a canoe pulling salmon from a net stretched bank to bank. They'd conk the struggling fish with clubs made of hammer handles and stuff them in a burlap bag. These fish were called "dog salmon" because mostly they were used to feed the dogs. Mel didn't know that yet, but she would. For the present, she shuddered a little. This was the downside: she really didn't like fish at all, maybe tuna from a can, maybe. All the rest of them made her gag. *Well, girl,* she told herself, *get used to it.*

All of Toehold couldn't have been more than a hundred yards. As Mel reached the end of town she slouched a little and saw the last shack scroll by through her suicide seat window. Mel shifted the Ramcharger into four-wheel drive and followed the bank of the river upstream until the brush thickened and she didn't see any point to busting through it. Mel parked parallel to the bank, got out, and stood looking out over the water. The rush of wild water always sedated Mel. It seemed to her that pictures always made rivers look the same kind of blue, but this one had an olive color to it, inching toward brown. Mel sat with her knees pulled up, her back against the front wheel as the sky darkened and the moon came up, ivory with a blood-orange corona. It lay low on the horizon so that its light shone in rays across the water. Mel watched, mesmerized, as the sky above the moon pulsed with color. She decided this is what the old hippies meant when they talked about acid flashback. She remembered something Gary once told her, that gold miners in the Arctic believed the colors from the aurora borealis rose up from the mother lode. A line of slender spruce trees along the far bank were silhouetted like minarets against an upper sky literally glowing with shifting mists of green, red, and amber light, morphing from vertical curtains to horizontal waves—ionic particles buffeted by atmospheric winds. Mel was still there in the morning.

Sometime during the night Mel retrieved a blanket from the cab of her truck, although she had no memory of doing so. She was surprised when dawn rose and she awoke to find the blanket wrapped around her shoulders. The display in last night's sky had left her with a vestigial sense of wonder. She tried to hang on to it. It made her think of that painter—Gary had once shown her a book of his stuff, guy with one ear—his night sky, his stars. Her night sky. Her stars. She shut her eyes against the day and tried to bring them back. The growling of an old engine in low gear destroyed any chance of that.

Someone else was driving up from the village, somebody in a, let's see, some kind of . . . old . . . Jeep. It was a Jeep, the kind you saw in pictures about World War II. The sun reflected off its windshield, so Mel couldn't see the face of the person driving.

The jeep itself was painted red, white, and blue, and then she remembered having seen it yesterday as she drove through Toehold. It growled to a stop in back of the Ramcharger, and Buddy got out from behind the wheel carrying two travel mugs with a small bag tucked under his arm. His T-shirt said "I eat roadkill."

"Welcome Wagon," he said as he held out a mug of steaming coffee. "I took the liberty of adding Splenda and Cremora. Chemical sunrise. Pure Alaska's a shock to the system. You want to go slow, get acclimated. Name's Buddy."

Mel drew a sawed-off baseball bat from under the seat in the cab of her truck.

"I'm not going to have to hit a homer off your face, am I?" Mel asked.

"Did I do something to you, maybe in a former life?" answered Buddy.

"Fuck former life. I don't want you messing with this one," said Mel.

"Howdy, neighbor," Buddy hailed with more than a little sarcasm.

"Sorry," Mel said. "Gotta be careful." She took the coffee from his hand. "Thanks. I'm Mel."

Buddy smiled. "I was beginning to think you were bad for the neighborhood."

Mel stuck out her hand and said again, "Sorry."

"That's one ugly piece of wood," remarked Buddy, referring to the sawed-off bat.

"It makes a nice sound," said Mel.

"Have one," said Buddy as he offered the paper bag. "Donuts."

Before another fifteen minutes had passed, Mel had eaten four donuts and told him everything she needed to, basically; that she planned on staying and was in the market for a place to live.

"You want to move here now? Today?" asked Buddy.

"Why not?" she asked.

"'Cause Winter's a bitch," he answered, "and you're not ready for it."

"Watch me," said Mel.

"However, I can be had," Buddy said, "for a price. Your call."

"You've got to be out of your mind, Bobby," she snapped.

"Buddy."

"Out of your mind."

She did admit, however, that she needed a place to live. Buddy made the obligatory offer, though this time Mel didn't deign to acknowledge it. "What's for rent?" she asked. "You got a community bulletin board back there?"

"This community has a high rate of illiteracy," said Buddy, but he did have a friend who might have something.

"He keeps an old sheepherder's trailer on his property, not too far from his house but away enough for a little privacy. You might want to invite somebody over for supper sometime. You never know. It's kind of a mess right now because the last guy in trashed it, but I bet you could bunk there, at least, get you under a roof for the time being."

Mel wanted to know, "Don't you think we ought to ask your friend?"

"He's away on vacation," said Buddy. "If you want to make it permanent, you can ask when he gets back."

In the meantime, Mel moved in—or tried to, anyway.

Good God, the place was a sty! When Mel first opened the door to the trailer a raccoon practically bowled her over on its way out. You'd think that would account for the mess, and it did, some of it, but not the part that consisted of a quart of Jack and a case of Oly. Somebody'd had a party with a lot of nasty to it. Stale air—a blend of tobacco, cannabis, sour mash, and foreign matter of uncertain origin—belched out along with the raccoon. If she spent the night in that trailer she'd feel dirty for the rest of her life, the kind of grit-behind-your-eyeballs, cat-hair-in-your-nose feeling. Mel had slept in her truck plenty of times before. She could handle another night and refused to dwell on how much she'd been looking forward to sleeping in a bed. At least she was safe from parasites that bored their way through the soles of your feet and grew to two-foot worms inside your bowels. You're part of the goddamn ecosystem, that's for sure. You'd take a dump and all these worms would wriggle out your ass, and some would wriggle back, and, oh, my God, how hideous! The idea was blood-curdling. "This hooch should be torched," said Buddy.

"Talk about your pollutants," said Mel. "Got a mop I can borrow, Bobby?"

"Buddy."

"Maybe some Janitor In A Drum?"

Because she didn't have anything pressing to do, and be-cause with some work this might be an okay place from which to launch phase two of this part of her life, Mel spent the next few hours scouring and scrubbing, scraping, mopping, disinfecting, really disinfecting. She took no chances. If Mel cleaned it once, she cleaned it again. She found a custom chopper catalogue with a bleached blond babe in a lavender bikini straddling the tank of a midnight blue '55 Harley, and taped it over the hole in the wall where the stovepipe went. The babe in the lavender bikini had a world-class body—you had to be blind not to see that—but her face was pure honky-tonk, pure "Stand by Your Man." You'd never find it on the cover of *Vogue*. Some hours later Mel finally deemed the place clean enough, lit a clump of sage, purified the air, and said, "Amen."

Cody saw the Ramcharger with the Arizona license plate parked back up near his trailer, but he didn't care to check on it at the moment. It wasn't going anywhere, and if it did, then what was the problem? He remembered the driver, some lady, a funny one, something about a lottery, good energy. Right now he needed to tap his bladder badly, then a beer, a bath, and another beer, in that order. It was the end of a long drive, worth it, that's for damn sure, but wearing. He smiled at a thought, sucked air through his teeth at a memory, grunted with pleasure. He changed the CD, a little Jim Morrison. Cody had also loaded up with a new batch of CDs: Hendrix, the Stones, Olatunji—African drums—which he bought because of a suggestion from the lady he was with. Her father was a black sailor, her mother an Inupiaq—a pleasing combination in her case, but also one that really pissed her off at times. A friend of hers suggested a group he had never heard of, which made him feel older than he wanted. He didn't know how to feel about the fact that he actually liked their stuff. Cody also picked up some Bonnie Raitt and an album of bagpipes. Bagpipes. They chilled him to the marrow of his bones. He knew they were instruments of war, but, still, Cody loved to drive to the wail of the pipes. Funny thing about music, though, much as he loved it, he could rarely get himself to play it in the house, even when he worked, because he liked the silence so much it felt like a violation. He was sure that if he played a CD it was in the Bronco. This was not his intention at all. Sometimes he'd open the door to his house with a firm plan to play some bootlegged Rolling Thunder Revue, all cranked about playing it, and by the time the door banged shut behind him, he didn't want to anymore. No intent, just the way things turn out.

With two beers and a bath behind him, Cody sat on a hassock in a red chamois robe, his feet stretched toward the fire, smoking some homegrown, a look of beatitude on his face, a man glad to be exactly where he was.

An idea began to emerge from the haze like film of the pieces of a broken cup played backward and in slow motion. It might be that he'd have to play a little loose with what's in the Bible, but he didn't really think anybody'd much mind. Of course, you've always got your crackpots. Anyway, he thought about clearing a couple of acres out back and building a giant ark right down to her inner decks, wanted to build it with the wood he'd cut down to make room for it, though he was also thinking how nice the hull might be made from teak. It wasn't meant to be moved. It would stay where it was, so Cody didn't have to bother with making it float. He would forge his own nails to match the ones used by biblical ships' carpenters, and he would design brass fittings that he would cast himself. He'd put entire families on the ark, one family for every creature mentioned in the Old Testament. There'd be a male and female and one or more little ones, the best mounts anywhere. They'd be like real life. Cody would make them content and relaxed in each other's presence. Visitors could wander all around and belowdecks, and everywhere, even in the rafters, there would be families at peace. Eden on water, except there'd be no water, and it'd be absolutely free. Nobody'd have to pay a nickel. The whole thing would be Cody's contribution. It would be available to anyone who managed to get there. It didn't matter to him that his ark would remain so isolated that most people would never get to see it except in pictures. It would be there, and everyone would know it. The ark in the wilderness.

Ayers Rock. Victoria Falls. Old Faithful. They were all there before anybody knew they were. Back in San Francisco, Cody was close to a family friend who'd been a quadriplegic for years but still belonged to the Sierra Club. The guy knew he would never get to the heart of any wilderness area, but he needed to know that it was there. That way he still felt free.

Cody sat there stone-still for several minutes imagining that his arms and legs were useless. He thought about the family friend, Arthur, who had joined the navy as a young man and became a cripple when a truck on base at San Juan lost its brakes and pinned him to a wall. To get it in combat is one thing. It's awful, awful, just horrible, but the fact of how it happened and what you did it for could sustain you, give you something to hold on to, not much, maybe, but something. But an accident, something that could happen to anybody on a street anywhere? That gives you nothing! Jesus, where do you go with that? How did you live with that? You can't even kill yourself. How do you keep from going totally nuts? Is there something beyond the boredom? Maybe the boredom is a test? If you get through it, you come out the other side into some state of blessed stillness, somewhere where you'd be free because you could go anywhere you wanted and not have to worry about your body anymore. Cody thought it was just about time for another beer.

"Jesus Christ," he said out loud. When Cody was into his thoughts he often spoke them aloud, not for himself, not really for anyone else. The words came, that's all, of their own accord, and they stopped when there had been enough of them, and then he laughed at his own foolishness.

"I really get into some shit, don't I?" he asked himself as he took a third beer from the fridge. Being paralyzed sucked.

Mel must have fallen asleep because a Bronco was there the next time she looked out. She thought about getting up and knocking on his door, but it was late, and he obviously hadn't seen the need to knock on hers, yet. She was sure that it was the same Bronco she had passed a few days earlier on the side of the road. Yeah, that guy. Small world. Nice smile. There didn't seem to be any urgency in the air. Tomorrow, in the morning, she'd get on it first thing. If they could cut a deal on the place, she could make it livable, at least for a time. Eventually, she wanted to build her own place, but this would be okay for now. She'd get some decent furniture, curtains. The outhouse was a problem, and she'd have to bathe in a bucket, but what made her so high and mighty? Most everybody in the bush was in the same boat, or canoe. Buddy, quite handy with a wrench, was one of the few with indoor plumbing. He bragged that there were only three things you needed to know to be a plumber: shit runs downhill, payday's Friday, and the boss is a prick. He let her use his facilities to shower and do what she had to do, and then he stood right on the other side of the door the whole time. He said he wasn't there but she knew he was. "Anyway," he said, "I don't date women with hairier legs than mine."

Let him think it, she thought. What she said through the door was, "Your name, mine, and the word 'date' wouldn't be caught dead in the same sentence."

Cody was feeling good. He'd had his ashes hauled, his thirst slaked, his hunger satiated. Now it was back to moose meat, home brew, and five-fingered Mary for a stretch. Life in the bush. He chuckled. Y'hadda love it. He stepped out the front door dressed only in his red, white, and blue boxers. The morning air had some bite to it, not much but enough to let you know that Summer was on the way out even before it got all the way in. Cody glanced over at the Ramcharger. It hadn't moved. He guessed its driver was still asleep. Fine. It was early; Cody didn't feel like talking to anybody yet anyway. He'd catch up with the Ramcharger later. Right now he had a cup of fresh-brewed to enjoy. He was trying out some Tanzanian Peaberry this week. The name was a little fruity, but it was from Africa so he figured it had to have some oomph to it.

"Hey, check it out," he said to himself as he turned back to the door. His Winter garden beside the cabin was coming on strong. Lots of squash and brussels sprouts. Before the door slammed shut behind him Cody spotted a Hubbard that he guessed ran a good thirty pounds. Cody was neutral on the taste of Hubbard squash. What he really liked was growing something so preternaturally large in his yard.

That must be him, the guy with Old Glory on his ass, Mel thought when she peeked out the window of the trailer. She, for one, missed the old tighty-whities, never having been particularly crazy about underwear with a point of view. *That's gotta be him, right? Looks like him. There's the Bronco.* She threw on her robe and grappled for an instant with the unfamiliar door, only by the time she got it open he was back inside. *All right, now, to pee or not to pee, and where to pee?* The plumbing wasn't hooked up in the trailer, and out back behind was out of the question. Bobby was probably hunkered down somewhere eyeballing her right now. *Okay, couldn't be a better time to meet the new landlord,* she thought, pulled her beige chenille robe closed around her, and prepared to cross the few yards that separated her front door from his. The robe was an impulse buy at a garage sale she happened on as she made her way through Maine. She left the belt somewhere since, but managed to hang on to the robe as it gradually wore in the elbows and frayed at the hem.

Shit. Ouch! She was barefoot, goddamnit. She retreated to the doorsill, but when she reached for the handle it slipped away from her and locked shut with a terminal snick. At that instant it struck Mel that everything between the Big Bang (and Even Before) and this exact nanosecond had conspired to bring her right here right now. She could be nowhere else facing in no other direction. Fortified with this thought, she turned and trudged forward. Mel shuddered as she passed the garden. What the hell was that thing? Some kind of giant wart? Nobody would grow something that big and ugly on purpose, would they? Even up here? Ouch. Shit. She wished she'd remembered her mocs.

Cody had just finished his first cup of coffee when he heard the knock on his front door. "It's open," he yelled, and Mel walked in.

"Hey," she said.

"You must be the Ramcharger," said Cody.

"You were fixing your Bronco on the side of the road about a week ago. New fan belt?"

He nodded and said, "Your shocks were shot."

"Still are," Mel said. "It's been a bumpy ride."

"Lemme put on some jeans," said Cody. "I'm not used to talking to strange women in my underwear."

"You said, 'Come in.'"

"I said, 'It's open,'" he answered.

"Should I go out and we start all over?" she asked.

Cody picked up a cup and tossed it to her. "Grab yourself some coffee while I get my jeans."

Mel snagged it easily.

"Nice catch," he said.

"Teamwork," she said, smiled, and began to adjust her robe when she cut it out, dropped the smile, and angrily warned herself against her own worst self. *You want to be here for a while, girl. You've been stupid. Don't be stupid again.*

Cody took a well-faded pair of jeans from a hook on the wall, hopped on one foot and then the other as he put them on. It was hard to tell how old he was. Past thirty but not fifty. A bit worn, like old jeans, but it looked good on him. No double chin, no jowls, lined and weathered and a little ruddy as if he had just come in from the wind. Hard to tell. It was nice, though, but once again Mel had to warn herself about not getting stupid. She needed a friend, that was it, and something about this man made her believe he might be one.

"What can I do you for?" he asked. "You just passing through or what?"

"Or what," she answered. "You interested in renting that trailer?"

"Got any money?"

"Some."

"You got a chainsaw in that truck?"

"Nope."

"Ever chopped wood?"

"Uh-uh."

"Ever kill an animal?"

"I'm lethal with a fly swatter," she said.

"That's a start, but you'd have to swat a lot of those little buggers to make a soup."

Nice sense of humor. "I used to hunt squirrel with my grandfather. A couple of rabbits. Turkey once."

"Then you're not squeamish, right? Don't mind the sight of blood?"

"Long as it's not mine," she said. "What's the rent?"

"Two bills a month, first and last," he said.

She put out her hand. "Deal," she said. They shook on it.

This is a good man, she thought.

He thought, *She has a lot to learn and not much time to learn it.* Another few weeks and the place would be locked under ice and snow for the next twenty-eight.

So it was Mel would not have made it through her first year in the bush without Cody's help. She probably wouldn't have made it through the second year, either. Each day she learned something new, did something a little bit better.

If she'd had teachers at school like Cody, maybe Mel would have paid some attention. She rated him right up there on the riveting scale, thought him charming but no bullshit, and damn if he didn't know a lot of stuff. There was no lecture to take notes on and apply same at some later date, just the real thing, OJT, on-the-job training.

What Cody had was a strong belief in skills. He knew a person needed specific skills to survive in this country. You could hug all the trees you wanted. None of them would hug you back. No amount of chanting and waving in the wind was going to put meat in the pot and wood in the stove. Skills. Cody taught her how to set traps and run a line because trapping gets to feed you while you're doing other things. Trapping was cruel, but no more cruel than freezing to death or existing on dog food, which was what would happen without the pelts. A wolverine was an especially valuable pelt because wolverine fur sewn in the hood of your parka didn't ice up. If a local bragged he "got a Wal-Mart," it meant the guy bagged a moose, a good year's worth of meat. Cody taught her to hunt, field-dress, skin out, and butcher, how to store fresh-killed meat in the creek so the wolves and bears wouldn't catch its scent. He was impressed. She learned quick, and she wasn't squeamish. He wondered how she'd be when a large-caliber rifle slammed back into her shoulder, but she proved steady and didn't wince. When they went out to hunt she watched and followed as he maneuvered into position using wind and cover. He told her to keep the wind in her face, and when she asked him what'd happen if there was no wind, like, for example, right this minute, he reached out and plucked a hair from her head. Her first thought was that it must've been gray. She watched as he tied it onto the tip of her gun barrel, amazed that it picked up a hint of breeze.

As a tracker, Cody possessed the uncanny ability to keep on an animal's path, ability honed by hours of sitting still in the woods. He instructed Mel to sit beside him and listen, just watch. He asked her to remember that the world is in color, wanted her to see all those colors, discerning patterns, and when those patterns were broken looking for a glint, a flicker, a twitch of hide. When she learned to see as he taught her, animals seemed to materialize from what an instant before was an empty field, a quiet woodlot, scree. Once, high on a rocky outcrop overlooking the Porcupine River, she sat so still for so long her self-winding watch stopped.

Mel listened as Cody told her she had to know the animal to know what it would do, that the seeker becomes the sought, and he believed fervently that a hunter needed to understand how to track an animal way before he ever attempted to kill it. The ideal kill is a single shot, but that might not always be possible. Once an animal is wounded but not down, the hunter is obligated to follow and find it. Mel knew her survival depended on his advice. Cody Rosewater made her want to perceive his world as he did. It was like hearing sound the way a musician hears it, or seeing light the way an artist does. It was a dance with death of the utmost elegance. Do not ever let death lead.

Mel had put in the pot. Now she had to fill it, that or it'd be oatmeal straight up for the next seven months. Cody had Mel take the lead. The great annual caribou migration had passed with the herd now on its Winter grounds, but there were always stragglers, usually a young bull, isolated from the rest, following its own plodding compass. The trick was to find that one young bull, first; with enough cover between you and him to allow a stalk close enough for a clean shot, second. Third was you had to be able to cart all that meat back home.

They canoed upriver maybe three miles, beached on a gravel bar, then hiked inland another mile or so to where the spruce population ended and became the border of a vast plain. Cody imagined legions of classical Greek light infantry, those called hoplites, as they sprinted into battle. He liked to read military history, especially the ancient wars and tactics. Hunting was a campaign that also ended in death, but it had its own tactics and considerations. Cody waited to see what Mel would do. His best guess was that she'd gauge the darkening sky and quickly shifting wind patterns, and work her way slowly, just within the tree line, along the plain's near border. The trees would break up her silhouette, the breeze would make it difficult for an animal to pick up her scent, and the dark would tend to keep an animal in place or force it to drift toward existing cover. The tree line was that cover, so Cody figured she intended to ambush a caribou as it edged closer.

Cody guessed right. Without having to look to know that Cody was behind her, Mel began to pick her way along the tree line while keeping her eyes trained on the open plain. Every so often she would stop and lean against a tree and remain absolutely motionless for up to an hour at a time, give the squirrels time to get used to her, to stop chattering and treat her like another tree. It also gave the seeker time to see, to sort out shades of light and random shapes. Then, once she'd decided there was nothing left worth seeing, she'd check again and then move on. Cody was always a few yards behind her.

Given the time of year, the days had grown shorter. Mel could see the darkness nibbling away at the already dim light, knew it would soon be time to pack it in for the night. Cody watched as her body lurched forward and froze. He couldn't see what it was that caused Mel's sudden stop. Hunting was an opportune thing. You never knew what was going to turn up where, not really, not if you told the truth. Cody hunkered down and watched. Something Mel had first dismissed as a bush was . . . what? Did the wind move it, or was that a step something out there took? Mel barely allowed herself to blink. Something out there stared back. Now she was sure of it. Something didn't move when all the brush around it blew in the wind. That something, she realized at the next gust of wind, was an antler. Only one. The other hidden. But it was there. She knew it. And now she saw it. It moved a step out of the shadows and stood head-on to her. The young caribou bull sensed that something was there, but as long as Mel had the wind and didn't move, he couldn't tell what. Mel did have the wind, but she didn't have the shot. The young bull had not yet presented itself as a target. It had to move forward a little more and quarter to the side for that. Mel wanted her shot to go in just behind the shoulder to take out the lungs and heart. One shot. A kill shot. And then the young bull wheeled abruptly, no shot at all, unless Mel was willing to risk tearing up an awful lot of meat in the hindquarters. No damn sense to that. She'd wait. Maybe the bull would turn back. Maybe. Except it didn't. It began drifting toward the opposite side of the great field. Mel would have to stalk it while its back was turned and hope it offered her a shot before it spotted her. She knew what she had to do. She cautiously let herself down to a prone position and, military fashion, began to slowly wriggle forward. Gravel bit into her elbows and knees. When the caribou stopped, she stopped. When it moved, so did she.

Cody admired her grit as she crawled across the cold and clammy ground. She had no scope to gather more light, only iron sights, so maybe she had another few minutes. Not much, though. She never took her eyes off her prey, continued to move only as it did. The light was low now. Cody couldn't see either Mel or the bull anymore. He strained to hear but picked up nothing. What does she think she's doing? Why in the hell is she . . . ? He never got to finish that thought as a shot and a flash of muzzle fire cracked out of the darkness like a flashbulb at a crime scene. An instant later a miner's headlight switched on, so Cody could see Mel was up and slowly moving forward. The beam of her headlight swept the ground in front of her as she moved. Then it stopped moving forward but continued to swing side to side, left to right, and then the beam stayed in one place on the ground somewhere out beyond Mel. Seconds later Cody heard Mel's voice. "Cody," she called jubilantly. "He ain't Wal-Mart but he sure beats the corner grocery."

"There is no corner grocery!" Cody yelled back.

"You catch on quick, amigo," she said.

Cody flicked on the light he wore around his head. "About two years old, don't you think?" she said. "My shot took his heart right out."

"Dead on its feet," said Cody.

"Had to be," she said as she finished up. "But he still ran fifty yards. Send it to Ripley's, babe."

"Hold on a minute," Cody said in a tone that signaled some importance.

She turned and faced him, her flashlight still in her hand. "I think I got blood on this thing," she said, wondering what he wanted.

"Be still for a second," said Cody.

"I haven't moved, Cody," she said. In fact, since she first knelt beside the downed caribou she had scarcely moved at all. It was a strange moment Mel had with the animal as Cody crossed the meadow to meet her. As she touched its beautiful flank and watched its eyes glaze over, her elation became tempered by an unexpected sadness. It was an enigma that people who did not hunt would never grasp, that you kill a creature you love.

As Cody came closer, Mel didn't know what it was exactly she now saw in his face—a sense of appreciation, of admiration, maybe, of acceptance on a whole other level—an expression she hadn't seen before, or certainly had never seen so clearly. *Can a face beam without smiling?* she wondered. Cody's did. Look at it.

He knelt down beside the carcass. "Come here," he said. She did what he asked and knelt facing him from the other side. He dipped his thumb in the caribou's wound and anointed her with its blood. "Welcome to Alaska, Mel," he said, and daubed a sticky, red smear in the middle of her forehead. It left her breathless, like she'd won something huge and great, although she couldn't put a name to it.

"What did you say?" she asked.

"Welcome to Alaska," Cody said again.

That was it, she thought. *Alaska.*

Mel and Cody quartered the carcass and shouldered the quarters over to the tree line, where they hung the meat high off the ground to keep the bears from getting it. A black bear wasn't a problem; it was the grizzly that was the problem, and since grizzlies rarely climb trees, the meat would probably be safe. Probably. Grizzly could fool you. The next morning they'd hump the meat back to the canoe and float downriver. There wasn't anything more they could do before then. Cody made a fire while Mel laid out a caribou hide on the ground and placed her sleeping bag on top of it. She watched as he shaved some slivers with his knife off a larger piece of wood he'd picked up, set them on fire with a Bic lighter he took from his pocket, and kept adding bigger and bigger pieces of wood until the fire got going good.

"I figured you to rub two sticks together like they did in the caveman days," she teased.

"I don't know much," Cody replied, "but I do know one goddamn thing: a caveman would've bashed heads to get his hands on this truly outstanding piece of contemporary equipment." He held it up in his hand as if for a television commercial. "The cigarette lighter. Thank you, ladies and gentlemen."

She laid his kit out without his asking. By the time she finished, Cody was hot into cooking slices of bacon in a frying pan. Mel watched him slice up a chunk of caribou, deftly turning flesh into meat, then frying it in with the bacon. He looked at her and winked. "Don't tell anybody my recipe," he said. "I'll hunt you down, the secret gets out." Cody twisted an imaginary moustache. "Watch the wizard at work," he said as he pinched the fold of a tinfoil envelope between his thumb and forefinger, flipped it out of the fire, and unwrapped a stack of heated tortillas. Flour ones. More flexible. Easier to roll. "And now," said Cody, as he grandly plucked slices of meat from the pan with the tip of his knife and rolled them up in a tortilla, "the pièce de résistance," he continued in a faux French accent and handed it to Mel with a flourish. Who was this guy? Was he real? Cody wrapped a second tortilla and bit into it. "Food tastes better when you eat it outside," he said. "Something about it," he thought aloud.

She wondered if he'd have dessert, but Cody went her one better. When they finished their caribou wraps, he pulled a big, fat joint from his shirt pocket. "My hero," she said. Cody smiled, reached into his pack, and pulled out a gallon Baggie full of bite-size Oreos. Mel laughed and said, "We're talking prepared here." Cody lit the doobie with his Bic. She watched as he inhaled, held it 'til he might burst, and blew it out in a long, slim stream of smoke.

"Oh," he said in mock surprise, "did you want one?" He passed her the joint and lit another one.

"Candy man," she said.

"It's a celebration," he replied. As the herb reached his brain his eyes twinkled, or was that just a reflection of the campfire?

The fact that Mel hadn't jumped into bed already with Cody was testimony to . . . what? She'd never been shy about sex, who she had it with, or even where, but this didn't feel the same. Mel didn't have a word to go with what it felt like, but she knew it wasn't the same. With every relationship she'd ever had, Mel knew going in that she'd be going out. She might not know when, but the endgame was a given. Even with Gary, that had been true. Mel had long since accepted the fact that when it came to sex she was a predator, and that was fine. She was happy with herself as long as she stuck to her rules: women were out unless it was Angelina Jolie, and no men under eighteen need apply. She knew she needed a certain amount of sex to keep all her chemicals and hormones in balance; that was simply a fact of her life, like vitamins or protein or fresh air or natural hair color. No fuss, no muss. That was her MO. Until now. Whoops. Something about this guy. Watch it. He didn't feel . . . temporary? *Careful, girl.* He felt like a friend, more like that.

Listen good, Miss Mel Madden. Do not mess this one up.

Mel and Cody passed a third joint back and forth between them now. They sat there around the fire swapping stories under a star-filled sky. He asked her how she came to Alaska, and she answered that she couldn't think of anyplace else to go. She asked him, "How about you?" and Cody told her his odyssey. He felt like she gave him permission to talk, strange as that might seem, and it was true, for all Mel cared to do right then was listen. He'd never strung it all together before, but he saw now that there had been a strategy of sorts. He always headed north. Each move brought him closer to Alaska, though he hadn't ever thought of that as a final destination, until it was. It had drawn him without his knowing it. As Cody followed the rivers north he went through his Willie stage—"Momma, don't let your babies grow up to be cowboys"—and his Waylon stage—"Ladies love outlaws like babies love stray dogs."

"That was Montana, and then I got serious," he told her. Headed for the coastal rivers and estuaries of Oregon and Washington, following the salmon runs where he saw the great bears for the first time and was mesmerized by their power. Cody cut west a little bit and worked fishing trawlers up and down the Aleutian Islands, but it was cold, drab, and dreary work, plus he wanted to be back on dry ground, ground that generally stayed where it had been put.

Mel liked the way he put things, not always the same as the next guy. She liked listening to him, the sound of his voice, something soothing there. But he was also a smart one, and she knew a guy who could tell a good joke when she spotted one. One of the nice things about him was that he didn't seem to be talking to hear himself talk. What he was doing was sharing his excitement, his delight in almost everything he saw.

He went on to tell her he spent some time on Kodiak Island, territory of the Alaskan brown bear, the big ones, the biggest of the big, monsters topping nine hundred pounds, and from there how he odd-jobbed his way up the Cook Inlet, stopped in Anchorage for about two minutes (too many rules, too many people), worked his way up the Susitna into the Denali Range, took some R & R in Fairbanks. There he also took stock of things, wondered whether or not he ought to be a little open-minded, maybe suss out the south. Drive to San Diego, cut across the desert, check out the Confederacy . . . Overruled. The call of the wild, that's what Cody wanted, not "Ol' Black Joe," and he knew he wouldn't find it in the Lower 48. He pitied people who only saw their meat shrink-wrapped in a Styrofoam tray, felt sorry for them because the great connection had been severed. He wanted to live in a land that didn't give up its bounty graciously, that made a man earn his worth. Cody took work with a pack outfit out of Fairbanks. He worked 'til he got licensed as a guide in Alaska, then he took off and headed north again, earning some cash along the way, learning the territory. The farther he got from civilization, the better he liked it.

"You never get lonely?" asked Mel.

"As in women?"

"That's a start."

"Sometimes," he admitted. "But I don't miss the mess."

"Tell me your ideal woman," said Mel.

Cody laughed. "Let's see. Uh. Able to pilot a raft through Class Six rapids. Reads Tolstoy on her break . . ."

"Have you read Tolstoy?" asked Mel.

"Nope," quipped Cody, "but we weren't talking about me. Okay. Your turn. Ideal man."

"'Taint none," she said. "You just got to find your way through the mess."

He hadn't expected that.

Know what they say in Vegas? Whatever goes here stays here? Mel found herself wondering if that could be true of the tundra, too.

She'd been in love before. She'd even been in like. This was more like that, but it felt different. *Mel,* she asked herself, *what in the fuck are you talking about?* She didn't know. What there was was this incredibly attractive guy in a black and green buffalo plaid shirt, generous with the homegrown. So? She'd been there before. As Shania would say, "That don't impress me much." But, wait, not exactly. Not exactly. What would it be like to kiss this man? Mostly she didn't care much for kissing. Not her favorite thing. But she really wondered, What would it be like to throw a lip-lock on this guy? One problem: Mel prided herself on her ability to shut it down whenever she wanted, call a halt at any time, though she couldn't honestly tell you if that'd be true with Cody. They'd hoisted a lot of beer together, the two of them, since Mel's arrival, but that had been in town, and none of this ever came up. Always a pleasant evening then hasta mañana. Okay. Fine. But what would it be like to kiss him now, here, in this place? What would it be like to rock beneath him gently like a rowboat, all those stars up there? Be a damn shame to waste all this.

"Cody," she asked, "you know what they say in Vegas?"

"Uh-uh. Tell me."

"What goes in Vegas stays in Vegas."

"That right? That's what they say?"

"You think it's true for here, too?" she asked.

"Where? Alaska?" he asked.

"This little piece of it."

"Here?"

"Right here. This spot." She drew a circle with her finger that took in their immediate campsite.

"That what goes here stays here?" he asked.

"What about it?"

"What about what?" he said as he kissed her. "I already forgot." She laughed, but what she didn't want to tell him, what she would prefer to have forgotten by morning, was the feeling of their first kiss. It scared her.

Dwayne's Air, the bush plane, with Toehold on its bimonthly run, landed on the dirt strip just outside the village and dropped off a load of mail, a case of Seagram's for Sweet-ass Sue's Pingo Palace, two cartons of Snickers for Mel, Buddy's monthly copy of *Hunt 'n' Sport Alaska,* and two passengers: Edie Kokuk, who decided she didn't want to be a secretary in Fairbanks or anyplace else, and Summer Joe, looking pale and a trifle pudgy, fresh from his stay in the slammer. Another three to four months and Dwayne's plane would have to come in on skis.

"What do you know about this Golden Bear Lodge?" Dwayne asked Buddy.

"What d'ya mean?" said Buddy.

"Check out the classifieds."

"You been reading my magazine?" asked Buddy.

"Browsing," answered Dwayne, and took off for his next drop at Bettles.

Buddy checked the classifieds, hopped on his ATV, and raced to show Cody. The screen door hadn't banged shut behind him when he said, "Are you ready for this?" and shoved the ad under Cody's nose. "What the hell is this Golden Bear Lodge bullshit? Want to hear something rich? Listen to this: *Golden Bear Lodge. Grizzly Hunting At Its Best. Trophy Bear. Seeing Is Believing. Gourmet Meals. The Ultimate Wild Country Adventure. Contact: Mel Madden, Toehold, Alaska.* Did she tell you she was gonna do this?" asked Buddy.

"*Da nada,*" answered Cody.

"Speak English," said Buddy. "We're still in America."

"Not a word," answered Cody.

"Toehold's the size of a midget's left nut. Ever seen a Golden Bear Lodge? You couldn't miss it if it was here, right? So, you tell me, where is this Golden Bear Lodge?" asked Buddy. "You know where? Nowhere. It's figment. I don't know what the hell that woman thinks she's doing. She's bending backward to blow smoke up her own ass."

"I'm gonna take a wild guess," said Cody. "Her trailer?"

"Huh?" asked Buddy.

"The Golden Bear Lodge."

"You mean your trailer," said Buddy.

"She pays the rent," answered Cody.

"Sometimes."

"Don't push it," Cody shot back.

"What about gourmet meals? She kiddin'? Jesus! Ever eat her cookin'?"

"My birthday," answered Cody.

"What?" asked Buddy.

"Poached salmon."

"Poached is right," said Buddy. "She probably stole it from a restaurant. Jesus Christ, that woman oughta be prevented by law from buyin' raw food."

"I'll look into it," said Cody. "Just don't ride her about this."

"I ain't gonna ride—"

Cody cut him off. "Maybe she's tryin' to do something for herself, okay? Don't fuckin' ride her!"

It took an act of will for Buddy to keep the rest of his thoughts to himself, but he fished an Oly from the cooler and managed. He sat backward in a chair and leafed through his magazine chuckling to himself.

"Cut it out," admonished Cody.

"What'd I say?" Buddy replied. "Nada, right? Last time I

looked there was no laws in the United States sayin' you couldn't laugh a little. Ease up, Fidel."

"You weren't laughin'."

"What was I doin'?"

"Butting in," said Cody.

"That'd be hearsay in a court of law," quipped Buddy. "My case rests." He took another slug of beer and continued leafing through his magazine. "Check the Bill of Rights, amigo."

Buddy was on his second beer when Mel walked in with a mouth full of Snickers. "Want one, Cody?" she asked, running her tongue behind her teeth to get that last gooey little bit.

"I'll have a bite," said Cody.

"I'll have a bite, too," said Buddy with a wink.

"Bite this, Bobby," said Mel, and pointed to her ass.

"Close but no cigar, sunshine," said Buddy. "Tell me, Mel, does the Golden Bear Lodge have an 800 number? I'd like to make a reservation."

"You couldn't afford it," snapped Mel.

"Fuck it, people! Do I need to sit you two in opposite corners?" growled Cody.

"I'm serious, Mel," said Buddy without being sarcastic. "What's the Golden Bear Lodge?"

"It's for hunters," she answered.

"You got one?" asked Buddy.

"Not yet."

"What're you gonna do with one once you get him?" asked Buddy.

"I'm gonna guide him on a hunt, jerkoff," she answered. "What d'ya think I'm gonna do with him?"

"Play carnival," said Buddy.

"What's that?" she asked, though instantly she wished she had kept her mouth shut.

"Sit on his face 'n' let him guess your weight," he said.

Buddy cracked himself up. Mel stared at him stone-faced.

"Don't turn your back," she snarled. "You heard it here first." Buddy turned and waved his hind parts back and forth like a pole dancer. Mel snapped. She dragged him to the floor and straddled him, her knees pinning his arms.

"How much do I weigh, Moose Pellet?" she yelled. Buddy couldn't keep from laughing at his own joke. "Come on, fatso," she hollered. "Guess my weight!"

"Hey, hey," yelled Cody, "I'm running a business here. Let him up, Mel."

Reluctantly, she clambered to her feet. "You're lucky, hard-off," she said. "When's the last time you got this close?"

"Yesterday," Buddy said as he stood up breathing heavily.

"Liar. Jerk," she said.

Cody was disgusted with the both of them.

"Go answer your phone," he told Buddy.

"What phone?" asked Buddy. "I don't have a phone." Cody picked up a pot from the shelf and began banging on the bottom with the butt end of a knife. "That phone," he said. Buddy left the shop muttering something about Cody always taking her side. "We oughta enter him in a contest for prize assholes," Mel said.

"He's okay," said Cody. "He's a veteran."

"So's Himmler," she replied.

"Mel," he said, "level with me."

"What about?"

"What kind of scheme are you up to now?"

"It ain't a scheme," she said. "It's a plan, and this one's gonna work. Which reminds me: I'd like to make some improvements to the trailer, maybe put on a porch, somethin' like that. Be okay with you?"

"Why do you all of a sudden need a porch?" he wanted to know.

"It adds class to a place," she answered. "Is that a yes or a no?"

"It's a neither. What're you up to?"

"I'm realizing my total potential as a full human being."

"Which means what?"

"Which means I'll pay you back for the lumber when this is over."

"When what's over?" he insisted.

"The goddamn hunt that's in the magazine," she shot back.

"I didn't know you had a guide's license," said Cody.

"Lots of things you don't know," said Mel.

"Well, maybe you'd better tell me, Mel, especially since you want me to front you a load of lumber."

"Fuck it, then," she snapped. "Don't front me the fuckin' wood. I'll get it someplace else."

"Where? Even if somebody else in Toehold did have a nickel, they wouldn't lend it to you."

"Please," said Mel a little more softly. "I'll pay you back when the hunt's over. I swear. You got my word."

"You got to ease up, girl." Cody wanted to comfort her.

"Yeah. Christ."

"All right?"

"I will."

"You better," he said. "First thing a hunter looks for in a guide is to see if he's calm and collected."

"That's the first thing, huh?" she asked.

"Believe it," he said.

"That might not be the first thing he looks for when he sees me," she answered.

"You mean this gets worse?" he asked.

"I can handle it," she said with an attempt at bravado. "No problem."

Cody Rosewater didn't like the sound of this one little bit. His bullshit detector was on red alert but it hadn't homed in on anything specific yet. Noise, though, lots of noise, and somewhere in that noise lay something still to be determined. Ever since he'd known her, Mel was always coming up with some kind of scheme, some way to put a little more jangle in her jeans. Early on, when she first came into the country, he lent her the tuition to go to school to learn how to operate heavy equipment. There was steady work on the pipeline as well as the haul road, and it paid a chunk of money, but she fell off an Earth mover before she finished the course and wound up with two breaks in her leg and one in her wrist instead of a diploma. It took a while for her to heal, but she never went back and finished anyway because she was already onto a Mississippi State University Extension Service course on breeding chickens, but that didn't work out, either.

"Tell me somethin'," Cody said. "Is the Golden Bear Lodge what I think it is?"

"Bull's-eye," she said. "Pick a prize."

"How the hell are you gonna turn that trailer into the Golden Bear Lodge?" Cody wanted to know. "With a fuckin' porch? That's like puttin' a bow tie on a pig."

"It *is* a lodge, the *Golden Bear Lodge*," Mel insisted, and pointed to the name in the classified ad. "Says so right there." She stabbed her forefinger at each word. "'The ultimate wild country adventure.'"

"But you wrote that yourself," he yelped with frustration.

"So what?" she snapped. "Everybody makes stuff up, but not everybody makes stuff happen."

Cody wasn't sure what Mel intended to make happen, but he was fairly certain that whatever it was, exactly, was a bonehead idea. He knew she could hunt. Mel had proven that over the past couple of years, or she would never have been able to survive. She learned quickly, and she didn't flinch, was cautious and attentive to sign, came to understand the patterns of the caribou herd, to see moose as processed greens rather than Disney cartoons, came to love the game and grow familiar with it, and therefore became intimate with the mystery of the hunt. To kill an animal is to remove a living creature from the universe and so not to be done lightly. Life is taken so that life can be. This is the Great Paradox.

Cody often chewed on thoughts like these, and so, by osmosis, they became Mel's thoughts, too. But what was that woman up to now? Was she really after grizzly? Did she know what she was up against? Eight hundred pounds of pure fury. Cody must have said that last thought out loud because he heard Mel say, "A thousand."

"What'd you say?"

"I say one thousand."

"Pounds?"

"Pounds, but from the size of him it could be cubic feet."

"You know where one is?" asked Cody.

"More or less," Mel answered.

"Be specific," said Cody.

"How's this for specific, my man?" she asked. "I had the crosshairs on him, right on his great big sweet and tasty heart. Ka-blam!"

"You're lyin'," said Cody.

"He stood up he looked like a mountain with hair, then he dropped down and loped off through an alder thicket, and I swear, Cody, his hump was golden and his hide was golden, too. He looked like a fiery chariot moving through the tall grass. I ain't lyin' to you, Cody. I put the crosshairs on him."

"Why didn't you shoot?" asked Cody.

"I got plans for him," answered Mel.

"Maybe he's got plans for you," said Cody.

"Maybe we got plans for each other," she quipped. "That bear's gonna be my pot of gold."

"Ever smell a grizzly's breath?" he asked.

"Uh-oh, here it comes," said Mel.

"Mel, if you know what's good for you, you better take this seriously."

"Okay, I'm takin' it seriously. You, I gather, have smelled said breath," she said.

"Most evil damn smell in the world," he said. "It's like it don't digest nothin' it eats. Organic matter just stays inside its gut and putrefies."

"What'd you do," Mel wanted to know, "kiss one?"

Cody unbuttoned his shirt.

"Hey, Cody," she said, "what're you doin'?"

He pulled up his T-shirt. His chest and belly were crisscrossed with thick, fibrous scars. Mel, stunned, ran her fingers lightly over them. "God, Cody."

"They'll look a lot worse on you," he said. "Follow that map long enough, it oughta lead you to a dead man. Lookit this one here." He guided her fingers. "Straight up to my heart. Stopped just this side of hell."

"How come I never seen 'em before?" she wondered.

"Ever seen me without my T-shirt?" he asked.

She guessed she hadn't. "Why didn't he finish you off?" she asked.

"If he'd been hungry," he said, "I'd've been grizzly turds, but he wasn't. He just wanted to teach me a lesson."

"I believe you're givin' that bear more credit than he deserved," she said. "You got in his way. He attacked."

"Uh-uh," Cody continued. "I wasn't in his way. I *was* trackin' him, but I wasn't in his way. I was hunkered down checkin' out his print when he come right up behind me. Damn near half a ton of bear, and I never even heard him. Then the breeze shifted, and I feel somethin' hot 'n' wet on the back of my neck, and the air suddenly smells like the bottom of a coffin, the stuff mummy experts call coffin liquor. I knew what it was right away, and if I'd had any sense I'd've dropped to the ground and hugged myself like a fetus, hands over my head to protect the scalp, kept that demon away from my vitals. Instead, like the dumb bastard that I was, I spun around in a panic. He was just sittin' there at my heels starin' at me like a big dog with a thyroid condition. It was almost comical. For a second, neither one of us moved, and I thought maybe he wasn't gonna do a thing but stare. Christ, I swear the bastard read my mind. 'I ain't gonna just stare at you, you puny little joke. I'm gonna tear your guts out.' His mouth opened up like he was smilin', and his big-as-a-goddamn-shovel paw started to move, and I don't remember nothin' after that but pure raw pain."

"Jesus," said Mel.

"Yeah," said Cody.

"But you don't really think that bear read your mind, do you?" she wondered.

"The Indians say if you're huntin' griz, the big bear knows it," said Cody. "Ever seen one skinned out?"

"Uh-uh. Why?"

"Looks just like a man," said Cody.

The week Mel spent building her new porch turned out to be the hottest one of the Summer. Cody fronted her the lumber for the planks of the roof that had to be ferried in by helicopter. Mel swore on a stack of Bibles that she'd pay him back. He looked on the job as a capital improvement. Buddy looked on the job as an exercise in futility, pretty much the same way he viewed all of Mel's activities. But even he had to admit that she built a pretty fair porch: nice railings, built-in benches on both sides. The posts and rails she logged herself. Mel knew that the growth rate of trees in the Arctic was infinitesimal, a centimeter, maybe less, a year. A tree eight inches around after scores of years was considered a good size. In some places it was so cold the spruce trees didn't even bear seeds. They propagated by dropping branches to the ground that then developed root systems. If a fire ever burned the trees down, the resulting bare patch would never grow back because there were no seeds. So what Mel did for posts and poles was to harvest only one or two from any given stand. It would have been a lot easier to cut down an entire stand nearby and get it all over with, but that wasn't the way she worked. *Do the right thing or don't do it at all,* was what she thought. She guessed she sounded like she was turning into a female Cody.

Plank by plank and post by post the porch and roof came together. Mel especially liked working up on the roof. She loved to look down upon the brilliant red patches of fireweed and river beauty, common weeds but wonderful to see. Sometimes, in the heat of the Summer, she'd take a beer up there, and simply sit, sip, and stare. She was almost sorry when the last shingle was nailed down because now she had no real excuse to go up there anymore, not that she really needed one, she reminded herself. Wasn't that what the Alaskan bush was all about anyway?

Mel finished the roof on a Friday when the temperature was actually ninety degrees and the sun was blinding. She rested for a minute feeling good about her work, and then she climbed down to treat herself to a beer. When she opened the door to her trailer she was shocked to see a man inside at the refrigerator with the door open helping himself to one of her beers. Mel could tell he was an Indian—who couldn't?—maybe twenty-seven, twenty-eight.

"Who the fuck are you?" she asked.

"They call me Summer Joe," he answered.

He wasn't bad-looking, she had to admit, in a feral sort of way, though Mel guessed all that starch in prison food had softened him up some. Still, he was not without a certain charm. "Oh, yeah," she said. "The guy who's got the hots for social workers."

"Liberals turn me on, what can I tell you," he said.

"Not much," she answered. "Did I invite you?"

"No," he replied.

"I didn't think so," she said. "Get out."

"I used to live here," said Summer Joe.

Mel took a pistol from a kitchen drawer and leveled it at him.

"You left the place a pigsty," she said.

"That's no reason to kill a guy," he replied.

"Janitor In A Drum didn't make a dent," said Mel.

"Write the company," he answered.

"Scram!"

"Can I finish my beer first?" He took another sip. "I was curious what you were doin' with the old place. Fixed it up, huh?"

Mel cocked the hammer. "Good-bye."

Summer Joe put the beer down and his hands up. "Okay, okay," he stammered. "I know when I'm not wanted."

"Very astute of you," she said.

"*Astute*. Nice word. Can I come back and visit you some time?" he asked.

"Why?"

"You know," said Summer Joe. "Kind of a man-woman thing."

"I'm not a liberal," said Mel.

"I can work with that," he offered.

"Guess how many seconds you got to get out of here?" she asked.

"Five?" he replied.

"Four, three, two . . ." she counted.

"Whoa," he said, taking her seriously. "Take a breath. I'm history."

"You're damn sure gonna be," she said.

"I paid rent here," said Summer Joe as he walked to the door. "What do you pay?"

At that, Mel fired a shot into the wall above Joe's head.

"Jesus! You're crazy!" he yelled.

Mel pointed the pistol right between his eyes. "The only good Indian . . ."

Joe bolted out the door before she could finish the sentence.

"It's 'Native American,' you fuckin' cracker," he yelled as he ran away.

Even though Mel had gotten no hits on her ad, she spent the rest of the Summer getting ready as if she had. She pulled salmon from the river, cut their bellies into long strips, and dried them over a wooden rack in the sun. They would crackle and be gourmet tasty when heated over a campfire in the bush. She made a list of everything she needed on index cards, then she spread a rubber poncho on the ground and laid out all her supplies. She talked to herself as she methodically checked everything out. "Candles? Got the candles. Water purification tablets? Who needs 'em? Take 'em off. The client might want them. Put 'em back. You never know. Tent. One." That was enough. Mel always slept in the open. She'd roll a caribou hide out on the ground, burrow into her down bag, and that was all the cover she needed. If you were in a tent you didn't see anything, not the stars, not anything, though when it rained she did make a lean-to out of a tarp she carried. "Lemme see: rope? Enough to hang yourself. Bad attitude, Mel. Get it together. Do it. You gotta do it, girl. You are a pro. P-R-O. Lemme see: things I have, things I need, things I can forget, things I could do without but would rather have . . . Mel, you're crazy. Stop it. Where's my pencil? Behind my ear. I'm losing my mind." She pressed down too hard on the point of the pencil and broke it. "Shit. Where's my knife?" She sharpened the pencil, slipped and cut her finger. "Ow. Shit." Mel wrapped her finger in a handkerchief, then unwrapped it and stared at the blood dripping to the ground. She seemed hypnotized by it. She turned her hand over slowly, took the blade of the knife, and rested it against the vein in her wrist. "Oh, God, it would be so easy. Stop it right now, Miss Lady, that's stinkin' thinkin'. You got more important stuff to do."

Like learning how to bake bread.

Mel thought that would be a dandy treat to serve her hunter with his first meal at the Golden Bear Lodge. Fresh home-baked bread. Maybe make a batch of cookies, too. Call 'em "tundra nuggets." Now all she had to do was teach herself to make these things. How hard could it be? People've been baking bread for thousands of years. Cavemen made bread, didn't they? Well, maybe not, but she would. A few eggs, yeast, flour, some dirty dishes—no big deal. Maybe she'd better check with Esther Nanachuk, see if she had a recipe, but then Mel remembered how, when she was a little girl, she used to help her grandfather back in West Virginia bake biscuits. Her grandmother died before she was born, and the old man never remarried. Everybody knew she was the only girl in granddaddy's life, a fact that made Mel's mother smolder with rage and seep with jealousy. Her own husband, Mel's father, had lit out long ago. Mel got a little homesick thinking about the gravy that went with those wonderful biscuits, but she shook that off right quick. That was someplace she refused to go. No way. Uh-uh. Granddaddy was long since dead, died soon before she left, and nobody else back there was worth thinking about.

Mel spent an entire afternoon in the "kitchen" of the Golden Bear Lodge experimenting around until she concocted something that actually looked and smelled like a real loaf of bread—smooth, round-topped, sweet—looked just like a loaf that came fresh out of the bag from the corner bakery. She had truly hated cooking on the pipeline—three thousand eggs before breakfast was anything but her idea of jump-starting a day—but this was different. Nobody hollered at her to hurry it up. Nobody went, "Yuck! These 'thangs' is runny." All Mel needed now was to test-drive it on somebody. "Who y'gonna call, Mel?" she asked herself, and the answer came back as it usually did: Cody Rosewater.

"Mel, you decent?" Cody hollered from outside Mel's door.

"Not the last time I looked," she called back.

"My kind of woman," he said.

"Come on in," she said.

She'd stopped by the taxidermy shop to invite him an hour earlier, but hadn't told him why. Now, here he was, stepping into the trailer with a bottle of Christian Bros. brandy in his hand.

"Needed the boys with you, huh?" said Mel, referring to the bottle. "Scared to come in here alone?"

"Why?" asked Cody. "You in attack mode?" She put her hands up in a gesture of surrender. "What's goin' on?" said Cody.

"Sit down," she said. "Take a deep breath."

"Okay," he said, and sat down. "What?"

"Deep breath," she said, and waved her hands as if to push air into her nose.

"Smells like you've been cooking, Mel."

"Baking, Cody, baking. There's a difference." A timer dinged from the wood-fired stove. "Don't go anyplace," Mel said, then pulled open the oven door and took out a pan of newly baked bread.

"Hey, looks great," crowed Cody. "You make that?"

"No, my Aunt Sadie made it," she quipped.

"Well, damn, girl, let's have us a slice!"

"You sure?"

"Hell, yeah!"

"I don't have any butter or margarine," she said. "Just bread."

"Probably better without it. Be kinda like sprinkling sugar on a chocolate cake."

"What makes you so goddamn good-natured all the time?" asked Mel.

"Why'd anybody in their right mind want to walk around kickin' hisself in the ass all day?" Cody said.

"How 'bout kickin' somebody else in the ass?" she said.

"What's the percentage in that?" asked Cody.

"This conversation is starting to sound subversively touchy-feely to me," said Mel. "Eat the bread." He started to cut himself a very thin slice but changed his mind and cut a huge one when he saw the look on Mel's face. It was painfully obvious how important this was to her. *Damn, Mel*, he thought, *it's just a piece of bread.* He chomped down and took nearly half on his first bite. Mel watched him anxiously to see his reaction. Cody chewed . . . chewed . . . and chewed . . . and chewed again.

"You hate it," she said.

"Lemme finish chewing," he said.

"You hate it. I can tell you hate it," she said.

"Don't go jumpin' to any conclusions," said Cody. "It's got a taste to it I don't quite recognize is all."

Mel said, "Bacon fat."

"You put bacon fat in here?" he asked.

"I told you I didn't have any butter," she said.

She looked like she was going to cry.

"Don't get all wrinkly on me," he said. "It's unique, isn't it?" He fished something out of his mouth and examined it. "Chocolate chip? You got chocolate chips in here?"

"Gimme that goddamn thing," she yelled, grabbed the slice practically right out of his mouth, and chucked it out the door.

Then she picked up what was left of the loaf and heaved it through the door, too.

"What'd you do that for?" asked Cody.

"You didn't see your face," she said. "Looked like you had a turd under your nose."

"Did I say I didn't like it?" asked Cody.

"I repeat: did you see your face?" she answered. "A picture says one thousand words, or did you not already know that?"

Mel wasn't giving Cody much wiggle room. He'd blown it, and she'd known it. He racked his brain trying to come up with something positive to say, and finally came up with "Character. The bread has character," but it was too late.

"Let the weasels choke on it," she snarled. "Little peckers."

Once Mel started going downhill there was no stopping her. She was like an eighteen-wheeler that lost its brakes on a steep downgrade. Nothing's going to stop it except a dozen of those yellow rubber crash barrels filled with sand. All Cody could do was sit in the suicide seat and watch the crash come up to meet him.

"I can't fuckin' cook worth a good goddamn," Mel yelled, crashing around the trailer, kicking a chair, heaving the empty bread pan against the wall, stomping down hard on some imaginary monster that only she could see. The walls rattled on that one. "Fuck it, goddamnit, fuck it."

"Jesus Christ Almighty," said Cody. "You got the worst mouth I ever heard on a woman in my whole damn life. Clean the fuck up, Mel!"

"That's bullshit, Cody, and you know it. A woman up here can't afford a clean mouth. Lemme tell you something, amigo: when I was dancin' topless in Fairbanks, when I first came into the country, before I knew you? My mouth was so clean it shined in the dark. I figured I was doin' this for the scratch 'cause there wasn't any other work and it's what I could do. I made more money than a high school gym teacher, believe it. But just because I was dancing topless don't mean I can't maintain my dignity. So all the time I'm flashin' my hooters and swingin' my ass, I'm not cussin' and I'm not doin' any heavy drinkin' to speak of, and I'm sayin' 'No, thank you' very politely when guys ask me out. I'm sayin' 'Thank you very much' when they appreciate a particular move, and so forth. Wanna know how many times I almost got raped? None of those bozos believed me when I turned 'em down nicely. I'm looking at all the other girls yellin' 'Get the fuck off me, asshole!'—shit like that—and guys got the fuck off 'em. They had mouths you wouldn't feed to pigs, but they didn't have to fight nobody off. So, one night I'm dancing—I had a toke; I wasn't feelin' half bad—and some sailor yells out how he'd like to suck on my jugs. So, I take one in one hand, one in the other, and I say, 'Hey, swabjockey, you put one in your mouth and one in your ear you can talk to yourself!' The house came down, and after that nobody ever fucked with me again that I didn't want to fuck with. So, you tell me, do I need somebody to take care of me? I say, 'Hell, no, Jack! I just need the cash.'"

Fall is like a big old dog you've had for a million years. Every day you look forward to seeing him, and every day you feel the pull of his passing. Joy and sadness; equal measures. He is still robust with a shiny coat thickened for Winter, but his eyes have become cloudy, and now he groans when he lies down. He still chases rabbits through the field with an abundance of enthusiasm, but the joy of watching him is tempered by realizing he is one step slower than he was yesterday. He is beautiful, and he will die. Terrible joy; exquisite sadness; equal measures.

For Mel, Summer was to be endured until Autumn came in.

Yes, it was fine to see the sun and have a run of warmth, but the mosquitoes were horrid and the warbler flies worse. Word was the mosquitoes were so damn big they had to decide whether to eat you on the spot or carry you back to their nest. You went broke on insect repellent, but it was either that or suffer, and even 100 percent Deet, the strongest repellent on Earth, wasn't always strong enough. You'd swat your forearm and come away with a couple of dozen blotches of bright red blood. Cody once told her about the time he was hiking across the tundra and walked into a new hatch of black gnats that covered his face like tar. Got in his ears, his nose, and eyes. There wasn't anything he could do about it but grit his teeth and walk through the swarm. He had this idea that they bit all his skin off down to the bone so that he was just a skull wearing a watch cap on top of a body. Mel had a thing about her eyes. She couldn't stand them to be touched. If a bug flew in them she'd go nuts. Didn't even like to have them kissed, not that anybody was about to try.

Mosquitoes may have been invented by God, but warbler flies were the spawn of the devil. Mosquitoes by the millions torture every living creature in the Arctic, but warblers make mosquitoes seem benign by comparison. These grisly creatures about the size of bumblebees lay their eggs on caribou hair. The eggs become maggots that furiously burrow under the skin of the animal and tunnel their way up to the spine, where they cut breathing holes into the skin of the back. The maggots thrive off the caribou's body, seriously weakening the poor deer until the ghoulish things become full grown, at which point they emerge and drop to the ground to begin the cycle all over again.

And if warbler flies were the spawn of the devil, a demon far worse created the nose bot, arguably the most repulsive parasite of them all. The bot fly, huge and hairy, hatches its maggots inside its own body, then deposits them in the caribou's nose. They migrate through to the back of the caribou's throat, where they form a big lump and clog the already tortured beast's breathing passages. Caribou riddled with these maggots cough and sneeze to get rid of them. Eventually they do, but that is part of the demon's plan. They cannot be dislodged until it is time for them to begin the cycle again, at which point they, too, fall to the ground to start all over. Neither warblers nor bots have mouths because they have no need to eat. The maggots feed so gluttonously that they store up all the food they will need for the rest of their lives. If you ever saw a caribou raging like a wild horse, shaking its head, and running around maniacally any which way, it had most likely been driven mad by murderous flies and millions of mosquitoes.

So Mel was no big fan of Summer. It was a season that couldn't be avoided and therefore was to be enjoyed as much as possible, but she was always waiting for the chill wind and changing colors that signaled the onset of Fall. About the only thing she did miss from West Virginia was the brilliance and variety only the foliage of a hardwood forest could offer: maple, ash, beech, oak, black cherry, chestnut—each with a palette all its own. Balsam poplar, trembling aspen, paper birch—these were the hardwoods of the Arctic. But they were survivors, not beauty queens, small and stunted. Because of the cold, leaves and roots were necessities. Wood, the stuff of trunks and branches, was a luxury.

She remembered walking in the woods as a kid with her grandfather, kicking through the cover of leaves that had fallen to the ground. The smell of good, fertile Earth would rise from the spot where she kicked the leaves aside. For Mel, to walk through the woods in Fall was to experience something transcendent. Though she had no concrete thought of it, and would never have considered it in those terms, anyway, because she was gun-shy of anything that even remotely smacked of religion, she knew when it was there. It enveloped her and whispered to her, though she never quite caught the words. What was that, that something she almost remembered, a sad thing and a happy thing, not birthday party happy, astonished happy, and not terrible sad but longing?

She felt both at peace and a piece of the puzzle, tranquil and untroubled, and yet there was something she urgently needed to know, just out of reach. How could it be that with every breath she was both aroused and at rest? How could that be? She remembered leaving the woods of her childhood at dusk—she was thirteen—and above her the moon was full and bright, serene, imposing: Buddha. How could that be?

Fall and her grandfather pretty much came in the same breath. Mel pictured themselves together more then than any other time of the year, even Christmas. Holidays there were other people around. Fall was their time. She remembered when he taught her that if you studied on it and had two tons of patience, you could put meat in the pot and eat like royalty. It took some doing, but you could do it.

One October morning when it was chilly and still dark and before the stove was lit, he woke her up and told her to put on all of whatever warm she had. Mel was about ten years old as she remembered it. Could've been eleven.

"Where we going?" she asked.

"Gonna go talk to a turkey," he answered. He had his old shotgun with him, the kind with a hammer that nobody even makes anymore.

They left the house and walked across the back field, crossed a section of fence, and entered the woods, all by the light of a slender sickle moon. Mel thought only Superman could see in the dark, but her granddaddy could as well. He spoke to her in a low voice. "I turned the hogs out just a couple-three days ago, so we got to get us beyond where they is rooting. They'll be browsing on chestnuts and whatnot, so see if you can find some sign of 'em." She tried hard to do what he wanted, but her eyes hadn't adjusted yet, so she felt kind of stupid even though he would never have wanted her to feel that way. Mel wanted him to brag on her, to tell the folks in town that him and his granddaughter both together got theirselves a big old bird.

Suddenly the old man stooped and tore a small branch off a bush. "Can you see it?" he said, holding it out for her. "Look right there where's it's been gnawed on. See how fresh and white it is? Ain't been more'n a day. We'll be beyond them hogs sooner'n I thought. It's gonna be light soon, and they don't do much moving during the daytime."

Somewhere out there in the thick of it Mel could hear the faint, hollow sounds of the bells around the animals' necks, so she knew they were still moving, that she and her granddaddy hadn't passed them by yet. She could hear faint grunting sounds, however, and when he pointed a few yards out beyond a thicket, she could see moving shapes, though she couldn't see them clearly nor tell how many. She knew he had ten or maybe twelve of them, but she couldn't tell how many pigs were actually out there now.

Mel followed her grandfather as he carefully picked his way through the woods around the perimeter of the herd.

"There might could be a wild one out there with 'em, so we'll just take it easy," he explained. "Think of Thanksgiving," he said, "with a hog on one side of the table and a big fat turkey on the other." Mel's mouth still watered when she thought of it.

The thicket ended and the two of them emerged into a clearing that was beginning to lighten up from the first of the morning sun.

"Look here," said her grandfather. She kneeled close to the ground next to him as he pointed out some scratch marks in the dirt. "Been right here," he said, then, again, "Look here." He pointed out a pencil-thin, fish-hook-shaped piece of something. "That's his shit," he said. "It ain't white, is it?" he asked.

"No, sir," she answered.

"Means it's fresh. Yep, little girl, he's been right here. Gimme a hand."

They set about the business of collecting some large branches and placing them in front of a small clump of mountain laurel for a makeshift blind. When they were done they crouched behind it.

The old man looked at Mel, winked, then put his index finger to his lips. "Shhh. This old guy can hear you think, believe me."

He took a rag from his pocket, unwrapped it, and took out his call bone.

"What're you gonna do?" she whispered.

"Gonna make him fall in love," he said.

"How's that?" she asked.

"If he thinks I'm a female, he'll throw all caution out the window and come running. Now, shhhh."

Her grandfather cupped the call bone in his hands, raised it to his lips, and let out a yelp. If Mel didn't know her grandfather was right next to her she'd've sworn he was a turkey. He yelped again and whispered, "Y'don't want to call that old bird too many times and make him suspicious, and you don't want to make any little kind of bobble when you call him, either. He don't fool easy."

The next time he called he let out a series of yelps that sounded like rusty barbed wire scraping against a wooden fence post—boy, if he didn't sound real!—then he turned to her and again put his finger to his lips. She strained to hear something through the silence, and when she did, she could hardly believe it. Way out there somewhere a turkey gobbled back.

"If we wait real still he just might come close enough to peck the brass eyes out of your boots," he whispered. A few minutes passed and then some more, but they didn't hear anything else except a gray squirrel skittering through the trees. Yet, there was something else, another sound, soft, rhythmic thuds, like somebody far away thumping a mattress, and it was coming closer.

"That's him," said her grandfather. "Good Godamighty! That is him." He put the bone to his lips and called again. The turkey yelped back, and this time he sounded like he was right out there on the front porch.

"He's heading for Paradise," said her granddaddy with a huge smile on his face.

She strained to see through the brush, but he motioned for

her to keep still. He called one more time, and just like magic, like it came out of nowhere, a magnificent turkey cock cleared the wood line and stopped on the edge of the clearing. Good God, what a bird—bright red head, long, dangling beard, two-inch spurs sharp as arrows. When he beat his wings against the ground, Mel knew what that sound was. Then, as if he were a magician fanning a deck of cards, his great tail fanned out, and he began to strut from one side of the clearing to the other. When was her grandfather going to shoot? When? The turkey stopped mid-strut, folded his fan, and stared toward the blind. Had he heard her think? Once more, so slowly, her grandfather put the call bone to his lips and let out a low, soft, short purr. Oh, my God, that old tail fanned out and shimmered coppery in the new light! He took a step toward the blind, then another, beat his wings, and ran straight for the blind, whereupon her grandfather, lightning quick, shouldered the shotgun and fired. The big bird went down as if on a tripwire. The echo of the shot reached out through the woods like ripples of water, and then silence set in. Mel didn't move until her grandfather did, then she followed him to where the turkey fell. They looked down at the bird that, big as it was, looked smaller now than it had in life.

"Been a bad old booger, but he's come and gone," said her grandfather in a voice tinged with sadness. He didn't smile, and he didn't gloat. He stood in the clearing and simply bowed his head.

The problem was that Mel's grandfather got to where you couldn't know from one minute to the next whether he was going to be a three-year-old or thirty or eighty-five. That stunt he pulled by barricading the highway went beyond being a nuisance to a public danger. It was just the stunt Mel's mother had been praying for so she could commit the old man to the state. When the social workers came to examine him, the old man climbed up on the roof and refused to come down. "Come and get me, copper," he yelled, and peppered the man and woman below with his pea-shooter. For the old lady it was a blessed moment: proof her father was demented and had become a hazard to himself as well as others. "Had to hide his shotgun," she said, and bit her lip to keep from smiling.

The next morning Mel's mother pitched Grandpa's beat-up suitcase full of his personals into the back of the old pickup and got behind the wheel. Mel sat next to the window, and her grandfather sat in the middle. He wanted to know, "Why'd I have to pack my suitcase, Mommy?" and what Mel's mother told him was it was a special surprise and when they got there he could have any flavor ice cream his little heart desired. That made him happy. Then she told him to write down all the different flavors he wanted, he could have them all, so the old man sat there smiling with a notepad on his lap and a blue crayon in his hand writing down stuff like "chocklit," "sawbery," "pisstasho . . ." He stayed happy long as he was doing that. He also got his tongue all blue from sucking on the crayon.

The place they were going was called Warm Springs and was a long three hours away, so Mel and her grandfather were pretty antsy by the time they got there. You had to drive about two miles from the gate to get to the main building. The grounds were nice and green with lots of hills. What Mel thought was awful strange and even a little scary was to see all those old people pulling each other in Radio Flyer red wagons, tumblesaulting down hills, swinging on swings like they were but six or seven years old. God, Mel thought, this was so weird: old people acting like they were kids, except they weren't acting.

Finally, Mel's mother stopped the truck in front of a big brick building with a lot of wide, front steps. The old man was busy sucking on the blue crayon and didn't seem to notice much of anything else. That's when Mel spotted her: an Indian lady (like the ones who live in India where they don't eat cows) wearing a sari that was purple with gold threads.

She came down the steps with the biggest smile on her face like she was real happy to see them. Grandpa didn't seem to notice her until she opened the door for Mel to get out and reached in to help him. She introduced herself as Dr. Gupta. The old man screeched like a rabbit caught by an owl, grabbed on to the steering wheel, and hung on. "I want my ice cream," he cried, "but I ain't gonna be waited on by no gypsy!" All the fight left in him didn't do him much good, though, because right behind Dr. Gupta were two huge guys in white suits who pried the old man's hands off the wheel and carried him kicking and screaming inside. Mel called out, "Grandpa!" and tried to kiss him good-bye, but the men were carrying him so fast she couldn't reach his cheek. The last words she heard him say were, "Let go, you goddamn son-of-a-bitch!" and then they dragged him through the door, and she never saw her grandfather again even one more time.

First thing the next morning the phone rang to tell his next of kin he died in his sleep. An orderly went to get him for breakfast, and he never did wake up. Mel's mother said, "Right. Now for plan B."

Alaska had taken Mel a lot of getting used to. This country was another kind of playing field, and it would either kill you or drive you away if you didn't learn the game. It was not kind; it demanded proof that you deserved to live there; it gave no quarter. It could be bountiful, but only if you accepted its bounty, and it gave up none of it easily. You took if you were strong and dogged enough, but it held on tenaciously with a force that would take you down the minute you thought you had it licked. And then, if you had it in you, you stored the experience away and started all over. Mel had always been a survivor, but here it had become elemental. She could have managed in Fairbanks or Juneau, but she didn't want to manage. She wanted more, and the farther she moved from town, the closer she got to the fringe of this marvelous land, the more she thought, *I want this. I could do this.* She was one for raw determination, because that's what it took to get through the day, any day, every day.

But when Fall approached, her heart beat harder, more than ever now that she had truly become a proficient hunter. That was the only way to survive in the bush. Mel surprised herself with how she had taken to it. Never again would she have to check the expiration date for packaged meat bought at a supermarket. The expiration date would be when she nailed it through the heart with a thirty-aught-six. Cody lent Mel the first hunting rifle she ever owned, taught her that a thirty-aught-six was enough gun for pretty much any situation she got into, that it wasn't the size of the gun but the placement of the bullet. "Don't shoot unless you're sure. One shot," he said, "is all you should need."

That first Fall in the bush, when she learned from the master: it was the season when living things could be killed. It was true that subsistence hunters did not hunt for sport but for survival. Still there was the thrill of pitting your intellect against a game animal's senses. You couldn't outrun them, outsmell them, out-hear them, or outsee them, but you could outmaneuver them, sometimes. Mel hadn't felt this alive since she walked through the woods with her grandfather.

Summer was not the bear's best season, either. He didn't suffer
from insects the way other creatures did, but his golden hide was
ragged and worn from the heat. There were places where the hair
was off in clumps as if a fist had yanked it out. His bulk was
down as well (though he was still the most formidable animal out
there). The winterkill he feasted on when the snows melted was
long gone, and the animals he preyed on still hadn't fattened up
for the coming Winter. One of the ironies of his existence was
that for the most part he was either a cannibal or a vegetarian.
Given a chance, he'd eat his own cubs if the female, in raging fury,
didn't drive him off. He picked his fights, and this was not one he
needed. True, he might take a young caribou or a moose calf if the
opportunity presented itself, but mostly he was content to graze
on grassy slopes and supplement his diet with ground squirrels
and marmots as he waited for the hillsides to burst out in the Fall
with his favorite food: berries. It was an odd sight, funny, really, to
see this huge beast, swift as a racehorse, chasing a ground squirrel,
a fraction of its size, across the tundra. The squirrel weighed what?
A pound? One one-thousandth of the bear? If you were hidden
well enough and the wind was right, you might well laugh as the
squirrel scampered midway up a hill and dove down a little hole
surrounded by boulders, some of which were as large as the bear
chasing it. Outrun, the bear slid to a stop and tried to widen the
hole to get to the squirrel by digging furiously with its shovel-
sized forepaws. Nothing if not determined, he flung aside one-
ton boulders like M&M's. His focus was on that hole, nowhere
else, so he never saw the squirrel scamper out a back exit and
scurry away, free and clear of him. He was still digging as it was
pounced on by a hawk and carried away screeching in the bird's
sharp and deadly talons.

Most of Toehold's citizens waited by the grass airstrip outside of town for the bimonthly mail plane to land. It was a Cessna 185 piloted by Dwayne Shalhoub, who chose to be a bush pilot instead of going into the family sausage business back in Green Bay, Wisconsin. Dwayne had nothing against sausage other than the fact that you couldn't fly one. He was too much of a maverick to sign up for any government service. Dwayne just loved the idea of flying lazily above the Alaskan wilderness, seeing Dall sheep, mountain goats, and caribou moving below him, as he coasted sometimes so close to the ground it seemed he could almost touch their magnificent antlers. When the caribou undertook their yearly migration, it appeared as if a virtual river of animals flowed beneath his fuselage. Dwayne also loved the camaraderie of the bush. He loved being the one who brought in the news from outside and delivered the little luxuries that took the edge off the harshness of bush life. Dwayne brought Buddy back issues of *Sports Illustrated*. Mel got her monthly carton of Snickers. This trip, aside from the coffee, he brought Cody a custom-made skinning blade for which Cody had carved a caribou horn handle. It was a beauty, deep bellied, well balanced, carbon steel, and scalpel sharp with a full tang. George Nanachuk got pipe tobacco, Esther knitting wool, Sweet-ass Sue two weeks' supply of Jack Daniel's. . . . You get the point. Dwayne Shalhoub was a vital and dependable link between bush communities. If he had to (and sometimes he had to), he could land that plane on a Baby Ruth wrapper in a blinding snowstorm.

While they waited, Cody and Winter Joe, Summer Joe's father, talked about Summer Joe's parole. "You must be real happy about that," said Cody.

"Long as he stays away from social workers," said Winter Joe.

"He just has to stop marrying them," said Cody.

"I didn't mind so much the one in Fairbanks," Winter Joe said. "It was the one in Juneau done him in. She got pissed."

"Yeah, well," said Cody, "I guess she didn't appreciate it when she found out Joe was married to another lady."

"He meant to tell her," said his father.

"Why didn't he?" asked Cody.

"He forgot," said the old man. "It's exciting when you get married, you know. You can forget things."

"Any way you cut it, Joe, that's bigamy."

"White man's law," said Winter Joe.

"Two wives, five years. Out after serving a third. Hell, he's lucky. Some guys only get married once, and they serve a life sentence."

"I know what you mean," said Winter Joe, glancing at the dour face of his wife still sitting inside their Ford pickup.

The Cessna 185 glided in over the mountains and landed smoothly. Everyone watching from the sidelines clapped as they always did at the artful simplicity of Dwayne bringing her in. Cody looked around for Mel but didn't see her anywhere. Her Ramcharger had been acting up, and it occurred to him that she probably couldn't get it started or else she'd be here with the rest of them. Lately, she'd been real anxious about the mail, so, yeah, it had to be her truck. Cody wasn't one for depending on a Dodge in the first place. Never had. Always liked Broncos.

"Where's Mel?" Dwayne wanted to know. "I got her Snickers."

"I'll take 'em for her," said Buddy.

"Bullshit you will," said Cody. "She'll never see half if you do. Hand 'em here, Dwayne."

"Give her this, too," said Dwayne, handing Cody a letter. "Who's she know in Hollywood?"

"Mel knows somebody in Hollywood?" said Buddy. "Who?"

Cody answered, "Marlon Brando."

"Marlon Brando!" exclaimed Buddy. "The *Godfather* guy? Wait a minute. He's dead. Ain't he dead?"

"Stone cold," said Cody.

"Let's see it." Buddy snatched the envelope from Cody's hand.

"It's addressed to the Golden Bear Lodge from a Ray Marks, First Look Pictures," he said, reading the return address. "What kind of name is that? First Look Pictures. What'd they ever make?"

"Would you know?" asked Dwayne.

"I might," answered Buddy. "Why? You think I'm illiterate? Disney made *Old Yeller*, Universal made that one where Mel Gibson's face was painted blue . . ."

"Hand it over," said Cody.

". . . and Wild Bill Hitchcock made the one with all those birds in it." Buddy finished his thought and handed back the letter. "I also got a bootlegged copy of *Debbie Does Dallas*. It's a antique," he bragged.

"I'll tell you true," said Dwayne. "I just saw a sight Hollywood couldn't touch. Biggest bitchin' bear I ever laid eyes on. Had to be ten feet from stem to stern. Maybe more."

"That's record book," said Buddy.

"He come up out of the willows on his hind feet and swung at my plane like King Kong," said Dwayne.

"What was the hide?" asked Cody.

"Like an old gold coin. Amazing color," Dwayne replied.

"I'll be damned," said Cody just about to himself.

"You sure will be if you tangle with that one," offered Dwayne.

"Just a minute," said Buddy. "I'm makin' a connection here. Gold. Bear. Mel . . ."

"Mind your own business," said Cody. "I'll see Mel gets this, Dwayne."

"Then my mission is done. There's some wicked weather coming in, so if you gents don't mind, adios," said Dwayne as he climbed back into the Cessna, took her airborne, and disappeared into a bank of darkening clouds.

If you took an old storage shed and filled it with broken and rusted tools, traps, toboggans, miners' lamps, personal artillery, snowshoes, gold pans, animal heads, and various purloined signs from STOP to IF YOU LIVED HERE YOU'D BE HOME BY NOW (there was even an old bumper sticker that said GORE VIDAL, U.S. SENATE, though nobody could remember where the hell that came from or even who he was), if you set off a depth charge and everything stuck to the walls and hung from the rafters, you'd have the décor of Sweet-ass Sue's Pingo Palace Bar and Grill. Actually, it was a lot more bar than grill. Toehold's regulars, which was most everybody in town, preferred their alcohol pure. One boozy night Mel decided not to fret that Sweet-ass would think her ignorant and asked Sue what the hell was a pingo.

"It's like a big cone with a core of ice," said Sue. "Looks like a volcano sort of. Something inside like a little lake freezes and gets pushed up by the permafrost. I've seen one damn near half as high as a goddamn pyramid."

"You been to Egypt?" asked Mel.

"No," said Sweet-ass. "You?"

"Uh-uh."

Sweet-ass Sue weighed eighteen pounds, six ounces at birth, larger than a polar bear cub. Her mother complained throughout her entire pregnancy that she felt like she was carrying a cow. Sue was a full-blood Athapaskan Indian with a frame like a refrigerator—big, very big, but solid. She was not Wal-Mart fat at all, just huge. If she had on a football helmet you'd mistake her for a nose tackle. She always wore her raven black hair in two long braids hanging down her back topped with a purple headband.

People have a tendency to believe, when somebody's so big, that deep down inside they're really just a pussycat. Sweet-ass Sue gave the living lie to such bullroar. She had a heart, but you'd have to dig halfway to China to find it. People knew one thing about her for sure: they didn't want Sweet-ass as an enemy. They weren't totally sure they wanted her as a friend, either, but she and Mel were buddies of a sort, an odd coupling, but one nonetheless.

Sue was in her forties, so she just missed out on the time when female athletes were coming into their own. Even so, she would have had a tough go of it because her sport of choice was football. So often Sue wished she had been born a boy, not because she wanted to sleep with other girls (which she certainly did not, high school gossip to the contrary) but because she wanted to compete in a man's game at a man's level. She considered it a cosmic misfortune that she had been super-sized at birth but handed the sex of a woman. By the time she was sixteen she was six feet three inches tall, weighed two hundred and fifty pounds with the sleek, muscular haunches of a draft horse, and she could bench-press three hundred. So Sue decided to right a powerful wrong and go out for the football team. She was bigger than any of the guys except for the star defensive end who had her by a hair. Still, the coach dug in and said no way. She was a girl; she'd get clobbered; he didn't want to be responsible for what he considered child abuse.

"Why not take up soccer?" he said. Sue pointed out that their school had no soccer team, to which the coach threw up his hands and insisted, "No can do." Then he pulled his sweatpants out of the crack of his ass, took a sip of his Diet Pepsi, and said could she excuse him, he had a practice to prepare for.

Sue never had been one to take no for an answer. She decided this called for drastic measures. How to prove that she had the stuff to play football? When she finally thought of a way, she knew somebody was going to get hurt, but she didn't think it'd be her. Whatever. Sue was willing to take that chance. This kid had guts for days!

"Stop thinking," she said to herself. "Get to it."

And she did.

At lunch the next period, in the cafeteria in front of the entire school, she knocked the tray out of the defensive end's hands and told him to watch where the fuck he was going. He didn't know what to do.

"Are you gonna apologize or what?" she demanded.

"You bumped into me," he retorted.

"You calling me a liar?" She went right up in his face. Then she pushed him.

"You better cut this shit out," he threatened.

"Why? You gonna hit me?" she said.

"You're a girl, goddamnit," he squealed, totally confused about what the hell was going on here.

"I think you're a pussy," she replied.

"What the hell are you?" he said.

"You calling me a pussy? Huh? You insulting my sex? Huh?"

He was completely bewildered, and then she smacked him across the face. "Does that feel like pussy, asshole?" she taunted. "Does it?"

"Let her have it," shouted one of his teammates. "She's asking for it."

"Yeah, kick her ass," yelled somebody else.

"He can't," Sue yelled back. "He's afraid of a girl. He ain't nothing but a pussy himself."

At that, the poor kid lost it and punched Sue so hard she fell backward into a table. The rest of the students expected to see blood and tears. What they got instead was a smile on Sue's face. "Is that your best shot?" she wanted to know. "You didn't kill me with it, and you're going to remember that mistake for the rest of your life," at which point she charged headfirst, speared him in the belly, and landed two hard shots to each side of his jaw before he hit the floor.

Later, in the nurse's office, he didn't remember anything after the charge. The school still refused to let her play football. In fact, the administration refused to let her continue as a student. They kicked her out and wouldn't let her back in the door. Not that she gave a shit. As soon as she came of age, Sue joined the

Coast Guard and struck out for what she hoped would be more interesting than watching TV and chewing whale blubber.

It was there that she got her nickname and met the love of her life.

The Coast Guard wasn't as interesting as she thought it might be. Sue found herself wishing she had joined another branch of the service, the Navy or Air Force, so at least she could have gone someplace exotic. Her first tour of duty was in the Aleutian Islands, which, as far as she was concerned, showed a serious dearth of imagination on the part of the bonehead who made the decision to station her there. Stationing an Alaskan Indian in the Aleutian Islands? Come on! Where's the brains in that? So, Sue put in for a transfer to Key West because she heard it was a happenin' town, only she got shipped to Mobile Bay off Alabama instead. Shore duty. Perfect. A six-foot-three-inch woman of color in the redneck capital of the world. Sue was in a world of misery. She thought of going AWOL, someplace in the Arctic that didn't have a name. How would they ever find her? She decided they wouldn't and was damn close to taking off when a chunk of pure, unadulterated happiness strode her way.

Each day when she got off work, Sue would head for the gym, where she'd bench-press herself into near catatonia. Then she'd go outside to the track and run for miles. After all that, it didn't matter to her where she was. She'd sleep until reveille the next morning. One day, after her workout, she climbed into the stands on the side of the track to stretch her tired legs out in the late-day sun. Hey, now! What was that? Hercules in a sweat suit? Oh, my God. There, walking into the center of the infield, was the biggest guy Sue had ever seen. Taller than she was. Heavier by seventy pounds at least. Bulked. Ripped. Gorgeous, so gorgeous she had to turn her head away. It was like looking at an eclipse of the sun. He *did* eclipse the sun. He eclipsed everygoddamnthing in creation. And he was a man of color, though she couldn't tell his country of origin. All she knew was that in about three seconds she wanted to go there. With him. Now. That very instant.

She watched as he took off his sweat suit and stood there in shorts and T-shirt. He made Mr. Universe look like a famine victim. Was he even real? Was he some kind of special effect? He leaned over, unzipped a ballistic cloth bag he had carried onto the field with him, and took out a steel ball the size of a cantaloupe. As he hoisted it in one hand to his right shoulder and drew a half circle in the dirt with the left toe of his Adidas, Sue realized what he was doing. She watched mesmerized as he tucked the shot next to his chin, held his left arm straight out and up from his shoulder, whirled his massive body like the Tasmanian devil, and launched the shot. It sailed like a cannonball fired from a frigate. My God, the torque in that man's body! The graceful immensity of it all. Sue watched him work out all the rest of that afternoon and the next, never failing to marvel that such bulk could move so fluidly.

The closest thing Sue had heard thus far in the way of sexual endearment was that fornicating with her was like hanging on to the steering wheel of a runaway eighteen-wheeler on a steep downhill grade with no seat belt. Men did not whisper sweet nothings in her ear. They begged for mercy. Ultimately, as far as Sue was concerned, they were a bunch of little itty-bitty things,

not worth the time or effort. If she had lived in Japan she would
have hung out with Sumo wrestlers, but it seemed she wasn't going
to get any further than Mobile. Okay, she was tough; she could
live without it until the day the man who put the shot walked
onto that field. She lost her breath; her heart crumbled like a
sugar cookie; her legs went weak. On the third day he walked
over to her and said, "Hi, sexy." By the time those three syllables
crossed his lips she belonged to him heart, soul, and all the good
parts in between.

He was a full-blooded South Sea Islander, a Samoan, which
accounted for his size. She didn't know it yet, but her lover-to-
be was hung like a whale. Once they were intimate, which was
two steaks and six beers after they met, she took to calling him
"Moby Dick," and he took to whispering "Sweet Ass" in her ear.
When they coupled from behind, he said her ass looked like a
big, beefy heart. He'd explode into her like a broke-loose fire
hydrant, which set off a chain reaction of orgasms that put them
both onto a new planet. When he came, he'd kiss her hard on
the spot where her ass met her spine, then he'd whoop and cry
out, "Oh, Lord, thank you! Thank you! Thank you!" His name
was Manny, and he was the love of Sue's life. They became inseparable, like a brace of matched Percherons in a field with no
fence.

Manny was the type of man who always went for the gold, no
matter what he did. The thing about the shot put was that he intended to compete in the Olympics, intended to break the record
and make his name, then open a gym, and eventually a chain of
gyms, in Southern California. He and Sue would be equal partners. Maybe they'd call their place "In the Buff" or "Buff It Out."
They discarded the names "Gym Dandy," "Butt Factory," and
"Venus Envy," though Sue kind of giggled with the idea of calling
it "Moby Dick's," maybe have a logo of a giant sperm whale on
their business cards, but Manny wanted to keep that moniker just
their little secret, well, maybe not so little, but only theirs none-

theless. He truly was a sweetheart, her sweetheart. "Old Faithful" she sometimes called him for a change of pace.

The thing about sudden death is: it's so sudden. One instant the person is there, and the next nanosecond he isn't. There's the body. It's still warm. There's sweat on the brow. Maybe the eyes remain open, but they don't see you anymore, those eyes that were always filled with you. Where did the person go so quickly? Why did he leave his loved ones so empty, so scared, so desperate, so all in an instant achingly alone?

Even though she adored him, Sue was not the type of woman to always sit in the stands and watch her man do his thing. Manny sensed this (and, if he hadn't, she would have eventually told him), and one day at practice he strolled over to where she sat and said, "Come on, doll, I'll show you how." He was having a little difficulty catching his breath, but he'd really been working out hard. The Olympic trials were coming up, and Manny intended to intimidate the competition from the first toss. He'd been beating the record all week long in practice, and he was ready for war.

They walked side by side to the throwing circle, bumping hips as they went, playing around. He picked up the sixteen-pound shot and was showing her how to hold it when, seemingly out of the blue, he said, "Sue?"

"What, babe?" she answered.

He fell to the ground beside her and was dead by the time she knelt down. The autopsy showed that his heart was simply too small for his body. It was congenital, always only a matter of time. Who knew? For Sue, the love of her life had come and gone. The rest was just marking time.

Sue's was a big-shouldered grief. Everybody thought she was really tough about it, but Sue knew that if she uttered even a single syllable she'd cut loose a black hole of Hell and sorrow. She'd swallow herself up. Grief kept her moving like a vagrant hopping freight trains. It took her to the end of the world but not beyond, for her sense of ultimate survival was as big as the rest of her. It stepped in at the right time. She stopped at the edge and settled. If ever there was a place with a chance that somebody big as Sue might pass through, that place was Alaska. She thought, *Toehold.* Some time or other you've got to take a stand, and where does matter.

Normally, Mel would have been alongside the airstrip with everyone else, but that day she was sitting at the bar in the Pingo Palace hung up in a world of worry, nursing a draft beer and a piece of microwavable pepperoni pizza that tasted pretty much like the carton it came in. She'd been there for the past couple of hours moping by herself because Sweet-ass had left for the mail plane like the rest.

Ever since Mel had gotten that letter, the one with jelly spots that she stuffed in her pocket and pulled out to wipe her nose, she had been worried sick. The letter had presented her with a deadline, and she could no more stop that date from coming due than she could stop an earthquake, which was just about how the news felt. It shook her world and put her in touch with memories she'd rather not have. That's what this whole Golden Bear Lodge scheme was all about. It could solve a whole lot of serious problems, but, so far, she had exactly zero takers. Her ad had run for the past two months with not one response. Zip. Most hunters checked up on their outfitters first. She knew nobody would have anything negative to say about the Golden Bear because she never yet had a single client. Mel knew she could do this thing. She knew she could pull it off. All she needed—please, please, please—was a chance. *Come on, Big Guy,* she thought, *I sure could use a nice, juicy break!*

Mel was still nursing her beer when Sweet-ass Sue walked in with a case of Jack under each arm.

"Feels like an early Winter out there," said Sue as she took the two cases behind the bar. "Hey, doll, who do you know in Hollywood?"

"California?" asked Mel.

"Uh-huh."

"Nobody. Why?"

"Somebody sent you a letter from Hollywood," said Sweet-ass.

"A letter? From Hollywood? For me? Mel Madden? Me? From Hollywood?" shouted Mel.

"You're the one with the Snickers, right?" said Sweet-ass.

"Give it to me," Mel demanded.

"Cody's got it," said Sue. "Your Snickers, too."

"Oh, Jesus! Oh, my God! Sweet Jesus! This could be it," screamed Mel.

"What?" asked Sweet-ass.

"It. It! *It!*" yelled Mel as she beat it out the door.

"So get this," Buddy was saying as he watched Cody mount a moose rack nearly six feet wide. "It's unbelievable. His wife left him a message on their answering machine down in Juneau, said she was humpin' some guy and if he didn't like it, tough shit, he shouldn't come home 'cause she was leavin' him anyway. Jesus. The poor chump calls to find out what's for dinner, and he gets that. Nobody deserves that. Maybe a mass murderer but nobody else, right?"

"Lemme get this straight," said Cody. "She didn't call in and leave a message. She recorded one like, 'Hi, I'm not in right now 'cause I'm out doin' it with a neighbor'?"

"I don't think he was a neighbor," said Buddy.

"Point is . . ." started Cody.

" 'Course, I could be wrong," said Buddy.

"So everybody else who called in that day got the same message, right?" asked Cody. "B-r-r-r-r, that is very, very cold."

"At least he didn't have to explain when somebody asked how's your old lady," said Buddy. "They already knew, so nobody asked. Hey, I got a good one. Did you hear about the elephant and the ant? See, this elephant 'n' this ant get married. Their wedding night they bang each other's brains out. Wham. Bam. Next mornin', the elephant drops dead."

"This a joke?" asked Cody.

"To some people," answered Buddy. "So this ant takes a look at the elephant and says, 'Jesus Christ! One night of passion, I gotta spend the rest of my life diggin' a goddamn grave!'"

"Where do you get this stuff?" asked Cody.

"I shoulda been a stand-up comic," Buddy bragged.

"You *are* a stand-up comic," said Cody.

"I am," agreed Buddy, "but who's buyin' tickets?"

Mel burst through the door like a little kid looking for a chocolate cupcake. "Cody, where's my letter?" He pointed to the envelope sitting on the edge of his worktable. Mel grabbed it and nearly tore it in two as she tried to open it.

"Who do you know in Hollywood?" asked Buddy.

"I'll tell you in a minute," said Mel as she took the letter out and read it. "Oh, my God! I did it! I got one!" she cried. "I got a hunter. Feel this stationery. Is that expensive or what? Says he's a movie producer."

"He send you a check?" asked Buddy.

"This is the answer to all my prayers. This is the end of all my problems. This is so hot shit." Mel was raving.

"Better check the calendar," said Buddy. "Make sure you're not on the rag when he's here."

Mel turned on him. "What the hell business is it of yours?"

"Just lookin' to be of service, your honor," Buddy answered. "Male grizzlies attack women when they got their visitor."

"Gimme a break," said Mel.

"Gospel," said Buddy.

"Male bullshit," said Mel.

"Bear fact," Cody chimed in.

"Whose side are you on, Cody?" she wanted to know.

"Yours," he said. "But it's true. They pick up the scent. Somethin' to do with hormones. Same thing they respond to when the female goes into heat."

"Yeah?" said Mel. "Well, I've been there before except this time I get to shoot the hairy son-of-a-bitch." She laughed as a roll of thunder broke over the mountains. "Sounds like a storm, doesn't it?"

"That's why you're a professional guide," Buddy said sarcastically. "You notice pertinent details."

"Don't push me, bat shit," she said.

"Somebody oughta talk to you about your mouth," said Buddy.

"Somebody already did," said Mel.

"You better go close your windows, Buddy," said Cody.

"What windows?" asked Buddy. "Oh. Those windows. You always take her side of it."

"I don't want another fight in here," he said.

Buddy started for the door but stopped just before opening it and said to Mel, "Wanna play sixty-eight?"

"What's that?" she said. Buddy had suckered her right in.

"You do it to me, and I owe you one," he hooted, and beat it out the door.

"Gotta learn to ignore him," said Cody.

"Tell me the truth about this period stuff, Cody."

"I did. You can laugh now, but I hope you're still laughin' later. Grizzly's no joke. You're gonna have a guy out there don't know what he's doin'. You don't know what's gonna happen. Guy might panic. Just remember what happened to me. It'll look a lot worse on you."

Mel checked her reflection in the window. "Maybe it'll be an improvement," she said.

"I worry about you," said Cody.

"I can handle myself," she said, looking out the window. "Wow, lookit. It's really beginning to blow out there. That ain't hail. That's baseballs."

"Better get away from the window," warned Cody.

"And miss the show?" Mel said. Outside sounded like a rack of billiard balls on a hard break. A hunk of the stuff broke through the window and splintered Mel with glass. She yelped with pain and grabbed her eye. Cody rushed over to help.

"What is it?"

"My eye!"

"Let me see," he said, and tried to take her hands down in order to get a look. She pulled away. "Let me see, you stubborn mule!" Mel let Cody pull her hands away from her face. He examined it carefully, tenderly. "Keep still."

"If I lose the eye, you can give me one of those glass ones you use for deer," she said.

"You're not gonna lose it. The sliver's in the lid. Hold still."

"What're you gonna do?" She was frightened, and she sounded like it.

"Pull it out." He led her over to his worktable, where he took tweezers and sterilized them with a match. "Hold still."

"Is it gonna hurt?" she whimpered.

"If you keep squirming it will." He took hold of the sliver with the tweezers and quickly pulled it out.

"Ouch!" she yelped.

"Got it," he said, and showed Mel the sliver. "Little thing like that. Another eighth of an inch . . ."

"You saved my ass, Cody," said Mel.

"Your eye," he corrected.

"My eye, my ass. What's the difference?" she answered.

"One sees what's comin' . . ." he began.

". . . and the other gets kicked anyway," she finished. "What a team!" she said, and leaned against him as he put his arm around her.

"Did I get it all?" asked Cody.

She gingerly felt her eye before answering, "Yeah."

"Let's see," he said, but Mel pulled away.

"You got it. I told you," she said.

"You're still shakin'."

"I'm fine," she countered, the moment over. Cody took a bottle of Wild Turkey from a shelf plus a couple of tumblers and poured each of them a glass.

"Looks like the house special," she said.

"I serve it every time somebody gets glass in her eye," he said, toasted her, and tossed it back.

"Here's spit in yours," said Mel, and tossed hers back, too.

"Good huntin', kiddo. Want a beer back?"

"Nah," she said. "Why put out the fire?"

"Anybody ever tell you you drink like a man?" he asked.

"Only other men," she answered.

"You've had a hard time of it," said Cody.

"Who hasn't?" she snapped. "I like you better when you don't go feelin' sorry for me. So don't. I like it hard." He turned away from her and went back to his worktable. "You don't approve of me," she said.

"You care?" he asked.

"Should I?" she countered.

"I don't pay your bills," said Cody.

"Sometimes," said Mel.

"You do all right," he said.

"You're a taxidermist," she said. "You know what things are supposed to look like when they're dead. How 'bout when they're alive? What are they supposed to look like then? I'll tell you. They're supposed to look like what they look like. When I'm dead you can mount me in white lace, okay? On the other hand, that sounds a little sick to me." Mel laughed at herself. "I'm sorry I got such a hen on," she apologized. "This hunt's gotta go gangbusters."

"You must want that bear awful bad," said Cody. She didn't answer him. "Mel?" She had a strange look on her face. "Mel?"

"It ain't the bear," she said, so softly he couldn't hear her.

"Come again?" he asked.

"It ain't the bear." This time he heard her, though she kept her voice uncharacteristically low.

"It ain't?"

"No," she answered.

"Weren't we talkin' about a bear?" asked Cody.

"We were, yeah," she said.

"Were?" He was confused.

"I changed the subject," said Mel.

"Then what's the subject now?" he wanted to know.

She mumbled something.

"Huh?" Cody didn't get it.

"My kid," she said.

"What kid?" asked Cody.

"*My* kid," Mel repeated.

"Where'd you get a kid?" asked Cody incredulously.

"From that Great Pecker in the sky," she fired back.

"All this time I've known you, you never told me about a kid," he said.

"You never asked."

"A kid?" Cody still found it incredible.

"Yeah, a kid," she said. "Runny nose, diapers, goo goo gah gah."

"Named what?" Cody wanted to know.

"Theresa Louise Patricia Elizabeth Madden."

"That's a lot of names for a kid you never said anything about," he exclaimed.

"Does that mean I don't think about her? Huh?" said Mel belligerently. "I think about her all the time."

"Where is she?" asked Cody.

"Tucson," answered Mel, this time more with sadness than belligerence.

"What's she doin' there?"

"My mother's got her there," she said.

"I thought you were from West Virginia?"

"I was," said Mel, "but it gets real cold in West Virginia. It rains a lot. My mother wanted to go where it's hot."

"How old's this Theresa Louise what's-her-name?" asked Cody.

"Patricia Elizabeth Madden. Theresa Louise Patricia Elizabeth Madden," said Mel.

"Why so many?"

"My mother wanted to call her Patricia Elizabeth, and I wanted Theresa Louise."

"So?"

"So that's her name. All of it."

"How old?" asked Cody again.

"Goin' on sixteen."

"She know you?"

"Sort of," said Mel softly. "She kinda thinks my mother's her mother, not that she really thinks that, really, but that's what it's like."

"What happened to the father?" asked Cody. Mel shrugged. "He run out on you?"

"About five minutes after he ran into me," she said. "Disappointed?"

"Huh?"

"In me?" she asked.

"What're you talkin' about, Mel?"

"You are. Disappointed. I can tell," said Mel.

"What you do on your own time is your business," said Cody.

"Uh-huh," she said sarcastically.

Cody was surprised at how angry this made him. "Don't start talkin' crap." His words came as a low growl, a warning.

"You upset with me?" she said, knowing that he was.

"Not unless you start talkin' crap. Why didn't you ever say something about your kid before now?" asked Cody.

"What was I gonna say? 'It's Mother's Day. I didn't get a card'? I don't send my own mother a card, not that she gives a rat's ass."

"When's the last time you saw her?"

"My mother?"

"Your kid."

"What is this," said Mel, "cops 'n' robbers?"

Every damn time Mel opened her mouth she annoyed Cody even more.

"You don't want to talk about it," he said, "don't bring it up. It's not the kind of subject you just pass over."

"What're you gettin' so pissed off for, Cody? You'd think it was your problem."

"How many years I know you now, Mel, huh? Two?"

"Three, Cody. Count 'em."

"Three. Three years. I think I know you, right, Mel? Except today you waltz in here with the big news, and I'm supposed to act like all you did was catch a nice fish? 'Hey, nice,' I'm supposed to say, 'How big? Did you use a worm or did you drop dynamite in the water?' Come on, Mel. What do you take me for?"

"When she was a little baby, a couple of months," Mel mumbled. Cody wasn't sure he heard her.

"What'd you say?"

"The last time I saw her," she said.

"Oh, Mel." His heart went out to her.

"Yeah. Well." She didn't know what else to say.

"You miss her?" asked Cody.

"I don't know. I must miss somethin'," she said. "That's what this goddamn bear hunt is all about."

"Whoa, girl. Back up a few steps."

"What d'ya think, Cody, I'm huntin' a grizzly bear for my health?"

"You're huntin' a grizzly bear for a kid you've never seen?" Cody asked, his tone of voice betraying his skepticism.

Mel was really angry now, although if you asked her what at, it'd be hard for her to tell you. "I seen her some! She was cute. But my mother got the state to declare me unfit, then she took my baby, and I took the fuck off. Now the old bitch tells me she's gonna send her to me 'cause she's too old to take care of her anymore, and if I don't take her she's gonna give her over to the state. Am I fit now? Well, I got no choice. I got to prove to her that I am. So I figure, I'm gonna make some good money and take her to Hawaii. She's probably mad at me—I would be if I was her, a lotta time's gone by—but I'm gonna show her such a good time she won't be mad at me anymore. She won't want to leave me and go back to someplace else. Then we'll come back up here and live together. How's that sound?"

Buddy came through the front door as soon as she finished speaking. "Ridiculous," he said.

Mel turned on him with a fury. "You were listening outside the door, you scumbag."

"Like I said," quipped Buddy, "pertinent details."

"What'd you hear, pigfucker?"

Buddy ignored her and said to Cody, "Holdin' out on me, huh? Where's the bourbon?"

Mel felt she could kill him. "I'm talkin' to you," she hollered.

"Ease up, Mel," cautioned Cody.

"Cody, back off! Don't tell me, 'Ease up, Mel'! I spill my guts and this maggot laps it up."

"I wouldn't go that far," said Buddy.

"What'd you hear?" she demanded.

"So you got a kid, so what?" he said.

"What's 'ridiculous'?"

"Did I say that?" asked Buddy ingenuously.

Mel was about to put her fist in his face. "Tell me, or I'll feed you to the hogs, dead man!"

"Nothin's ridiculous," he said. "You're a wonderful mother." Mel started for him, but he pulled away and grabbed an ax handle. "You come near me, I'm gonna put this where the sun don't shine."

"Both of you, cut it out!" yelled Cody. "I feel like I'm running a juvenile detention center around here."

"Mel?" said Buddy.

"Say whatever you want, pal," she answered.

"This hunter you got?"

"Yeah?" she said.

"He know you're a girl?"

Cody did not need to look at Mel's face to know the answer to that one.

Ray Marks couldn't wait for this guy to get out of his office. This was going to be his first trip to Alaska, and Ray was anxious to get out of Los Angeles and get started. It had been a good week. The funding for his next picture had finally come together. Disney, the cheap bastards, had kicked in their share of the deal (though not before making him feel as if he'd been dragged behind a pickup truck with a rusty chain around his wrists), and that had been all that was needed to green-light his picture. Ray would take this last big vacation and come back to town ready to jump into the trenches. If only this guy would hurry up with his pitch.

If you were sitting where the guy was sitting, it would seem to you that Ray was assiduously making notes on a yellow legal pad. In actuality, Ray was making a list of all the women he had slept with in the past five years. (Ray believed that sleeping with women as soon as possible was a good way to get to know them, kind of a social shortcut.) It really didn't matter what this poor fuck pitching his heart out said. The guy had written a book that was good—lots of action, very sexy, kind of a car thief thing—and, in order to get the option on the book, the guy's agent made a deal with Ray wherein his guy got to write the first draft of the screenplay. It wasn't that much money—two-fifty against five hundred if the guy did a rewrite and polish—and Ray knew before he read a word that after the first draft he would put one of his favorite screenwriters on the project.

In Ray's worldview, screenwriters and real writers were two different breeds. Those who did one generally could not do the other. Real writers wrote books and stories and essays; screenwriters wrote movies. The kinetics were the same—fingers on keyboards, etc.—but the take was different. A real writer would describe a car, but a screenwriter would cut to the car plunging over a cliff with a baby in the backseat whose mother had been shot in the head. Screenwriters were clearly the superior species. It was simple. They made lots of money and millions of people all over the planet went to the movies, not to mention the TV and DVD rights. Who could argue with that? Except they all wanted to be real writers, write books that ten people outside of their families would read. Ray didn't get it. Go figure. Not his problem.

The guy sounded like he was winding down. Actually, that last idea he had wasn't half bad, or had that been Ray's idea? Well, who knew what would ultimately make it into the final draft? There'd probably be a dozen other writers by then, which reminded him, who was that chick who wrote that great script Meryl never did? Ray put her name on the list, not the list of sex partners but the list of possible writers, although it was conceivable she could wind up on both.

Ray Marks grew up wanting power. He was the only Jewish kid in his entire high school in Fenton, Nebraska. There were relatives in nearby towns, and there was a small Jewish community in Omaha, of course, but Ray's was the only Jewish family in Fenton. His father owned the local fabric store, which was a good thing since all of the women in town made their own curtains and most their own dresses, too. So business was good. There was enough discretionary income to keep lamb chops on the table once a week and take twice-yearly family vacations to various points of interest—Gettysburg, Washington, D.C., the Jersey Shore, New York City—always east and north, never west and south. Every year Ray suggested to his parents that they put California on the list. Southern California, what Ray thought of as the real California. But what was so interesting about artichokes and freeways? they wanted to know. "Movies," Ray answered.

"Read a book," they said. "Listen to Rachmaninoff if you want passion." And every time after they'd had one of these discussions, within a week a package would arrive direct from Doubleday's bookstore and Sam Goody's in New York City with fine books and select recordings for Mr. and Mrs. Marks's boychik.

Which he did read and listen to, by the way. He was certainly no
dummy. He was no philistine. And he took no crap from anybody.
Usually, he ignored the few slurs that came his way like the friend
who told Ray, when he was negotiating for a used car, to "Jew
him down," or when somebody called somebody else a Shylock.
Ray knew this was ignorant, but he also knew that most people
used these phrases as nonchalantly as saying "I like your wheels,"
or "She bangs like a screen door in the Summertime," or calling
the opposing team a bunch of fairies. They weren't in touch with
the bitterness that gave birth to these words in the first place. So
Ray had a long fuse, but when it was finally lit, he could explode
and grab whatever was handy to cold-cock the bastard who of-
fended him.

The Summer between his tenth and eleventh grades Ray
worked for a housepainter. Although Ray, for obvious reasons,
didn't like to think about it too much, he knew his mother was
considered a very attractive woman. She adored his father and
would never have been unfaithful to him. But she was exotic
with her raven hair and azure eyes, and she enjoyed the attention she knew she got when she walked down Main Street. That
Summer, Ray heard this guy who was twice his age and a third
again bigger, he heard this guy say he'd like to ram it to that
Hebe cunt. Ray kicked him in the balls, and when the guy fell
to his knees, Ray clobbered him in the face with a huge paintbrush loaded with green paint. Ray's mother was horrified at
the whole episode, but secretly, quietly, his father was proud of
his son for fighting back. What he didn't understand was why
Ray just didn't leave it at the kick in the balls. The momzer was
down. Why the paint?

"Because I want him to remember me every time he looks
into the mirror," was Ray's answer.

Ray was a kid who, it seemed to his parents, knew his own
mind from birth and refused to conform to any stereotype whatsoever.

"What kind of a Jew pulls a trigger?" his mother wanted to know when Ray went deer hunting with his gentile friends.

"Why would you want to wrestle with all that sweat and body odor?" she wanted to know when he went out for the wrestling team. But she was in the stands calling for his opponent's blood the day he won the Nebraska Class A state championship at 145 pounds. Ray could be a mean muthafucker on the mat. He'd fake a wrist injury in practice so he could wrap it in an Ace bandage that he would then scrape across his opponent's eyes, and he wouldn't shave for three days prior to a match so he could grind his stubble like sandpaper into his opponent's cheek. He was not a poster boy for loving kindness. Winning mattered. Power mattered. There were no absolutes for right or wrong. What mattered was who had the power, and Ray grew up wanting to be the man in charge. He had his values and principles, but what difference did they make if he wasn't the one who called the shots?

By now everybody in town knew Mel had a hunter, a Hollywood hotshot who'd be flying himself up in his own plane. Apparently, so the word went, he was looking for the real deal. He wasn't looking for his guide to make it easy on him. Ray Marks wanted the biggest, baddest grizzly bear out there, but he wanted the bear on the beast's own terms, no snowmobile, no airplane, on foot, a stalk, the closer the better. Ray Marks was a lot of things, but he definitely was not a coward or, in his words, a pussy. His motto: Bring 'em on. Ray wanted to see the defeat and humiliation in his enemy's eyes when the schmuck went down. He was like a pit bull that locked its jaws on your throat and chewed and chewed until you were dead.

This was the first time Toehold had such a distinguished visitor. Not since Edie Kokuk mistook that other guy for Al Pacino had the folks been so beside themselves. If it had been a movie star on the way (Bruce Willis, or Tori Spelling, or even, um, a weatherman from cable TV), well, of course, the folks would have been even more excited. The truth was nobody really knew exactly what a producer did, but whatever it was, they knew it was important, glamorous, and reeked of money. How to be on the receiving end of that money was the question foremost in the minds of many. Sweet-ass Sue figured she'd be getting hers because the Pingo Palace was the only bar in town. There wasn't any place else to go except to sleep, but the answer wasn't as clear to the rest of Toehold.

Mel was in a frenzy. Everything had to be just perfect, and yet there had never ever been a time in her life when it had been, so what was she going to do about it now? What had she been thinking? How was she supposed to pull this off? But what were her alternatives—go back to West Virginia and serve coffee at the counter in a café in a town where the coal mine had shut down and nobody liked her anyway, or leave Theresa Louise to the state of Arizona? She cleaned the Golden Bear Lodge until you could eat off the floor, then she cleaned it again. The Golden Bear Lodge? Mel had started believing her own publicity. Was she out of her mind? If she weren't already, the way she was acting, she surely would be soon. Perfect perfect perfect until Mel thought she would scream.

To Mel, the great golden bear was the least of her problems. Mel envied him. He roamed his range unencumbered by fear, family, or conscience, his only care to fuel his vast appetite. The hillsides were ripe with Fall berries, and the grizzly hoovered through them with a carelessness matched only by an extraordinary capacity to fill his belly. His golden coat was once again thick and heavy for the coming Winter; he wore it like a royal mantle. He had the center of gravity of an anvil and incomprehensible strength. When he walked it seemed as if the Earth should quake. Nothing challenged him, nothing could, except the man that would be coming, and that was less than a whisper to him now, an awareness that simply didn't exist for him at all and would not until the instant it appeared. On the other hand, Mel these days was fearful whenever she was awake and fretful when she was not. When the end came for the bear, if it came, it would likely come quickly, but in the eventuality that the end did not come as quickly as Mel hoped, still he would not be tortured by it in the months and weeks and days before. For bears, like all wild creatures, lived and died only in the present moment.

The day Ray Marks was due to arrive in Toehold, the weather was raw and miserable. An icy rain had been threatening all week, and just this morning it cut loose. Thunder rocked the mountains; thunderclouds hid them from view. Lightning zipped, crackled, and flashed in the sky; the valley smelled of it. Toehold's one dirt road became a sluiceway. The river seethed. A duck wouldn't fly in this weather, let alone a small plane. Mel was convinced she was being made to pay for the sins of a former life. She was afraid to think of what would happen whenever she'd be called upon to pay for the sins of this one.

No way could Mel sit still. Her trailer made it seem as if she were inside a little tin cage without even a slot under the door for bread and water. She paced, puttered, dropped things by accident, tripped over a footstool. Mel had to get out of there. She grabbed a poncho and ran across the way to Cody's. Buddy was there, as usual, drinking a mug of coffee. Cody was in the middle of building a new cabinet. He put his hammer aside when he saw Mel.

"Cody," she gasped. "What the hell you think happened to my hunter?"

"Check the weather, chief," said Buddy sarcastically. "It's raining."

"I wasn't talkin' to you." She made it sound like a warning.

Cody handed Mel a fresh mug of coffee. "Maybe he figured he couldn't get in," he said.

"Did you hear anything on the shortwave?" she asked. He hadn't. "He'll be here," she said. "I know he'll be here." Though it sounded more like wishful thinking.

"Faith is a wonderful thing," said Buddy.

Mel stared at him stone-faced, took Cody's hammer from the unfinished cabinet, and without warning smashed it down in the direction of Buddy's hand. He barely got it out of the way as the hammer shattered his mug, and shards of glass and hot coffee splashed all over him.

"You're outta your fuckin' mind!" he yelled. "You're fuckin' nuts. They oughta lock you up."

"You were getting boring," she said. Her attack on Buddy helped Mel blow off a little steam, but she still didn't have an answer to her most pressing question: how was she supposed to get through the rest of this goddamn day? She hated to give him credit for anything, but this time Buddy was right. They ought to lock her up.

Then, faintly at first, so faintly they weren't sure they heard anything at all, they picked up the sound of a small-engine plane coming through the storm. Mel screamed with delight, yelled "Bombs away!" and ran back to her trailer, leaving Cody and Buddy listening to the approaching airplane.

"I guess he got through," said Cody. "That boy can fly, can't he."

Buddy was truly pissed off. "Just wait'll he sees what's waitin' for him," he bitched.

Inside her trailer with the sound of the plane overhead, Mel strapped on a shoulder holster with a .44 Magnum revolver. Then she put on an Australian bush hat and checked herself in the mirror. Her reaction: "Yuck." She removed the shoulder holster, pulled off her shirt, and put on a brand-new red chamois one that she took from an Eddie Bauer bag. Mel looked in the mirror again, and this time she liked what she saw. "B'wana, eat your heart out," she said as she grabbed the keys to her Ramcharger, rushed outside, and jumped behind the wheel. She was so excited she had trouble sticking the starter key into the ignition, finally got it into its slot, and cranked the engine. It growled back at her, growled some more, coughed, died. The next time she turned the key, the starter whined in that way it does when you know the engine is stone-cold gone. Icy panic filled her gut as Mel turned the key again, but this time the only sound she heard was the airplane coming in for a landing. "No! No! No! Shit! Shit! Shit! Don't do this to me!" she yelled as she banged her fists on the steering wheel.

Summer Joe sat at the bar of the Pingo Palace nursing his third Oly of the day when he heard the airplane pass overhead. He knocked over a stool as he rushed outside and stared up at the sky. The clouds hid the plane, but Summer Joe heard it loud and clear. He looked up the street at the other end of town and saw Mel stumble out of her Ramcharger, kick a tire, and bang on the hood. He watched her throw up the hood and practically crawl inside. He heard her curse and scream, smiled to himself, then went back inside and asked if he could borrow Sue's truck for a few minutes. "Sure," she said, and tossed Summer Joe the keys. "You put one dent in it," she hollered after him, "I'm gonna put two in you."

"No problem," said Summer Joe. The gods were talking to him once again. Sue's truck caught as soon as Joe turned the key in the ignition. He headed slowly for the airstrip. *Let the guy stew a little,* thought Joe as he did a steady twenty-five.

Ray Marks was proud of himself. He had brought the plane through high-velocity winds, driving rain, an electrical storm, and minimal visibility, but here he was, safely on the ground, taxiing to a stop on the dirt strip outside of town. *Who the hell thought up Toehold?* he wondered.

Ray cut the engines and checked his face in a palm mirror. He wore wraparound shades, a sheepskin coat, hand-tooled boots, Carhartt jeans, and a Stetson. He smiled. He looked like a hero. Perfect. A number of villagers—kids, adults, and dogs—stood alongside the strip to watch him come in. Yeah. The smile stayed on his face as he climbed down from the cockpit and gave a candy bar to the first kid with the nerve to approach him. Ray opened the baggage compartment and said to the group of kids now crowded around him, "Who wants to make five dollars?" He pointed to an L.L. Bean duffel bag and an aluminum gun case, and smiled as the kids crawled all over each other trying to get to his gear.

The problem was that there was nobody in a Ramcharger to pick him up. The instructions Ray received in the mail from Mel Madden assured Ray he'd be there to meet him. "I'll be waiting right there at the airstrip when you land," the letter read. Where the hell was he then? Ray looked up from the kids and spotted a two-tone Chevy pickup headed toward his plane. *That's got to be him,* thought Ray. *But what the hell kind of guide can't tell a Chevy from a Ramcharger?* Marks didn't have a good feeling about this. He worked from his gut and that same gut just put out a subtle warning. "You Mel Madden?" he asked the guy behind the wheel of the Chevy as it pulled to a stop beside the plane.

"My name's Summer Joe. Need a lift?"

"I'm supposed to meet somebody," answered Ray.

"They forget?" asked Summer Joe.

"Looks like it," Ray said.

"Hard to find a local you can trust," offered Summer Joe. "Hey, lemme get you outta this weather. We'll drive to town and find your party."

"If this is the way this party's starting out," said Ray, "I might have to goddamn well find another one. Put that stuff in the back of the truck," he said to one of the kids. "What'd you say your name was?" he asked.

"Summer Joe," he answered, leaned over the seat to open the door, and stuck out his hand.

"Ray Marks."

"You must be here to hunt, Mr. Marks," said Summer Joe. Ray climbed aboard, and Summer Joe turned the truck back toward town.

Mel finally managed to get the Ramcharger started and sped out toward the airstrip. Coming toward her on the other side of the muddy road she spotted Summer Joe behind the wheel of Sweet-ass Sue's pickup. It didn't take Mel a nanosecond to figure out who sat beside him. She slammed on her brakes, but the Ramcharger skidded out of control, plowed through some thick scrub at the side of the road, and got stuck in the mud. Mel slammed the gears forward and reverse, but no amount of rocking the Charger back and forth could get it out.

"Shouldn't we give that guy some help?" Ray said to Summer Joe.

"I got no winch," said Joe, and kept on going. Mel shook her fist at him.

"You shitbird," she yelled. "You son-of-a-bitch. You slimy, twisted, scumwad crap-artist." Mel stuck her head out the window and pleaded with the sky, "Why are you doing this to me?"

Ray Marks had heard all about Cody Rosewater—"The Rembrandt of the Arctic"—way back in L.A., and was anxious to meet him. After all, Cody would be the one to confer immortality on Ray's hunt. Ray's cohorts and underlings wouldn't just have to take his word for it; he'd have proof, life-size. He planned to mount his grizzly on its two hind legs right outside his bedroom door—a temple guardian of sorts—which was fitting, since he considered his inner sanctum a trophy room anyway. His custom-built bed was the altar on which wet dreams were consummated. His mattress, also custom-made, was buoyant enough to float a boat with lots of room to roll around. It could accommodate, if called for, a full squad of sexual enthusiasts. The maid changed his silk sheets daily (each day a different color), and Ray liked to brag that his bed had seen more traffic than the freeway on Thanksgiving. Ray Marks did not like to sleep alone, but on those rare occasions when he did, he entertained himself with home videos taken at different angles from discreetly placed, remote-controlled cameras. Eat your heart out, Larry Flynt.

Ray asked Summer Joe where he could get a good cup of coffee and then he said he wanted to see this guy Cody Rosewater's work firsthand. Summer Joe nodded and took Ray Marks to Cody's Taxidermy, while Mel was still trying to winch herself out of the mud. Ray had to admit to himself that he wanted to impress a guy like Cody, though he really didn't like the idea. But it was what it was. He took out his hunting rifle to show it off almost as soon as he set foot inside. "I had this baby custom-tailored like a Hong Kong suit," he was saying. "She's chambered for a .375 H&H."

"That'll knock a hole in your day," said Buddy.

"You said it, chum," Ray replied. "On top of that I shoot a hot load that reaches out there three hundred yards flat."

"You risk a cripple that way," said Cody, who had been working and looked as if he weren't listening.

"I use a partition bullet," Ray went on. "Excellent penetration, and then she mushrooms. Ever seen the hole you can blow in a beast with that son-of-a-bitch?"

"Yeah," said Cody, "I have. Be better to get close."

"Can't always get close," said Ray.

"I can," said Summer Joe.

"Can you fix a Porsche?" Ray asked.

"No," answered Summer Joe.

"I can," said Ray.

"You load your own shells?" asked Buddy, who seemed the most interested in what Ray had to say.

"Who's got time?" Ray asked. "A guy in the Valley does it for me."

"What valley?" asked Buddy, somewhat confused.

"The San Fernando Valley," said Ray. "Same guy that built this mother."

Buddy checked out the rifle's stock. "Black walnut," he said. "Good wood."

"Guy's a genius," bragged Ray. "Not good. Great! Check this

out." Ray demonstrated as he spoke. "If the scope fogs up—rain, snow—just snap it down and use the iron sights. Snap it up, it's back at perfect zero."

"Nice," admired Buddy. "Must've cost . . . what?"

"It was part of a deal," said Ray as he put the rifle back in its case. "I told the studio throw it in, we'll close. Hey, anybody know what the hell happened to my guide?"

"Mel Madden, right?" said Buddy.

"That's him," said Ray. Cody shut Buddy up with a look. Ray took off his Stetson and hung it on a caribou rack affixed to the wall.

"We didn't know if you'd be able to make it in," said Cody, "so Mel went off to take care of a few last-minute things." Cody took Ray's Stetson from the antlers and a beer from the cooler, and handed them both back to him. "Mel told me to make sure you're comfortable."

"I'm comfortable in L.A.," said Ray as he took back his hat. Right that minute, he felt distinctly uncomfortable. "I came here to hunt."

"Can't hunt in this weather, anyway," offered Summer Joe. "Have to wait 'til it lifts."

"Summer Joe's right," said Cody.

"Of course I'm right," said Joe. "I'm an Indian."

"Grizzly's the biggest animal out there, and the best," said Buddy.

"And the meanest," said Cody.

"We'll see," said Ray Marks. "You do nice work," he said to Cody. "We'll be doing business."

"Could be," Cody answered.

"If I know Mel . . ." Buddy started to say when a look from Cody stopped him. "If I know Mel"—he changed gears and continued without missing a beat—"Mel's got your bear all picked out. If you can shoot like you say, you might as well leave Cody your deposit right now."

Ray suspected he was being played with. "Gonna be that easy, huh?" he said.

Buddy shrugged. "I got it secondhand. Hey, Cody, tell the man about your black bear."

"He don't want to hear that," said Cody.

But Buddy went on. "The man's a movie producer, right, Ray? They're always lookin' for a good story. Tell him."

"Tell me," said Ray.

"You tell him," Cody said to Buddy.

Buddy protested, but he went on just the same. "He had a black bear used to break in his trailer, open the fridge, and drink all his beer."

"Not the bottles, just the cans," interrupted Cody.

"You gonna tell it?" asked Buddy. Cody continued.

"He'd been hangin' around the place for years. I'd hear him up on the ridge. He'd growl. His stomach would growl. Him. His stomach. That bear had a bad case of indigestion. I guess he was just gettin' old like the rest of us."

"Why didn't you shoot him?" Ray wanted to know.

"He made me laugh. All that belching and farting. I got used to him up there, sort of imagined his feet hurt, too. I guess I just liked having him around."

" 'Til he started bustin' into his trailer," said Buddy. " 'Til he started bustin' into your trailer."

"Yeah," said Cody. "One time, it was funny, but he lost his fear, kept doin' it. Problem was, this old bear knew my moves as well as I knew his. Better. So once I started huntin' him, he stayed out of my way. He had his eye on me, wasn't a doubt in my mind about that. I decide I gotta fake this guy out. Instead of huntin' him at dawn or dusk like usual, I go out about two o'clock in the afternoon. This time I take a bucket of bait along—peanut butter, molasses, rotten salmon, hog maws—a real cocktail for the old bastard. I put the bait under this tree at the edge of a swamp trail I know he's using, and I crawl up a hill about thirty yards away, take a seat in a stand of spruce, a good clear shooting lane. Well, it was a hot day. I fell asleep in about fifteen minutes. When I woke up an hour later, the bait was gone. I heard him laughin' up on the ridge that night."

"Did you ever get him?" asked Ray.

"Nope," said Cody.

"I did," said Summer Joe.

"Yeah," said Cody. "Summer Joe did."

"Caught him right in the middle of a can of Bud," said Joe.

"What d'ya say, Ray?" asked Buddy. "Think it'd make a good movie?"

"You ought to write that up, Cody," Ray suggested. "*Field and Stream* maybe."

"You got animal trainers could get a bear to drink beer, right, Ray?" said Buddy.

"In my business," Ray answered, "you don't take anything for granted."

"Jesus," exclaimed Buddy. "I thought you guys could do miracles. Whatcha call 'em? Special effects. Part the Red Sea. Make zombies."

"I been to Hollywood," said Joe abruptly.

"When?" Buddy was skeptical. Summer Joe ignored him.

"Nice town," he directed to Ray. "I seen *Jaws,* too, about eight times."

"Jaws 2, Jews 0," said Buddy.

"Excuse me?" Ray said.

"Come on," said Buddy, "you know that's a funny line. Go ahead. You can have it. Use it in a story."

"Did you make it?" asked Summer Joe.

"*Jaws?*" asked Ray.

"One."

"I wouldn't say that," said Ray. "Steve was at the beginning of his career, so he did consult with me on the script, and I slipped him a few ideas in post . . ."

"What's 'post'?" Buddy wanted to know.

"Post-production, but he got the credit, and he deserves it, God bless him."

"Nice town," repeated Summer Joe. "Good pussy."

"Grade A," agreed Ray. Summer Joe smiled conspiratorially.

"Tell me something, Ray," said Buddy. "What's a producer do, anyway? I mean, exactly . . . what? I been meanin' to ask and, well, we're here waitin', and as a movie fan, I'd like to know. What? You put up the money, right?"

"No," said Ray. "The studio puts up the money, sometimes private investors."

"Private investors. Right. Then what?"

"The man don't want to think about business, Buddy," said Summer Joe. "He's here to get away from it all, right, Ray?"

Buddy disagreed. "I can't get away from bein' retired. You can't get away from bein' a Indian. The man spots an opportunity, 'course he's not here to think about that, but if it comes his way, hey. So," he said to Ray, "then what?"

There was no way Ray was going to get out of this. "You find a property," he said.

"Real estate?" Buddy was confused.

"A story. A book. A magazine article. A concept."

"What's a concept?" Buddy asked.

"An idea," said Ray.

"You make it up?"

"Sometimes, yeah, sometimes I do." He was getting tired of this conversation fast.

"How 'bout the books and etc.?" Buddy persisted.

"There are people who specialize in that sort of thing."

"Like whatcha call 'em? Writers, right?"

"Right, but an idea might come from anywhere," Ray tried to explain. "You might have one, for example." Ray regretted the words as soon as they came out of his mouth.

"Yeah?" Buddy jumped on it. "Then what? We go fifty-fifty?"

"It doesn't exactly work that way," said Ray. "You'd give me the rights."

"Why would I give 'em to you?" Buddy wanted to know.

"We'd work something out," continued Ray. "Then I'd hire a writer to develop it, a director to get a green light, some actors . . . star power . . ."

"Who'd think up the title?"

"You ask a lot of questions," said Ray.

"Be glad you weren't my teacher in high school, Ray. I couldn't sit still. So what about the title?"

"We'd find one," said Ray, truly sick of this now.

"Then there'd be a movie?" said Buddy.

"Eventually."

Buddy still didn't quite get it. "And what exactly would you do?"

"I make it happen."

"He's the man, Buddy," piped in Summer Joe.

"Right!" said Buddy, though he still wasn't sure he got it.

"Right," said Ray.

"Jesus, have I got stories!" exclaimed Buddy.

"The man don't want to hear 'em," said Summer Joe.

"Why don't you let him decide that?" Buddy snapped.

By the time Mel winched herself out of the mud, she was covered with it. And as far as Summer Joe was concerned, she was feeling damn near homicidal. The situation called for a command decision: go home, take a shower, dress in clean clothes, meet Ray—who was probably at Cody's—and murder Summer Joe. Or go straight to Cody's, meet Ray as she was, and murder Summer Joe. Mel didn't know what that sleazy fucker was up to, but whatever it was, she knew she wasn't going to like it. As it happened, once she checked herself out in the side-view mirror she figured she could look worse. She pictured what interior linemen looked like after a hard-fought game in the rain. They looked like warriors and, goddamnit, so did she. Okay. Fine. Then she would act like one.

Five minutes later, pumping hi-octane, Mel blew into Cody's. Cody stared at her dumbfounded.

"Hey, Cody," she said. "How's it hangin'? Buddy, my man, gettin' much? Summer Joe, we need a powwow, sport." She crossed the floor of the shop to shake Ray's hand. "You must be Ray Marks. Mary Ellen Madden's the name. My friends and clients call me Mel. Welcome to Alaska."

"Glad to be here," Ray said. "They told me Alaska was full of surprises."

"Who told you? Them?" she said angrily, thinking he meant the "boys."

"Not them," said Ray. "Generic. A figure of speech."

"Gotcha," said Mel, still suspicious. "Rough flight, huh?"

"I've flown worse."

"With a little luck, you'll fly outta here with a thousand pounds of bear. We're talkin' record book."

"I'm ready," said Ray.

"We'll leave in the morning, before daylight," Mel said.

"You think you can handle a bear that big?" asked Ray.

"I thought you'd be handlin' him, Mr. Marks," said Mel. "But just in case you can't, and I can't, I got two friends who can." She took the .44 out of its holster. "Mr. Smith and Mr. Wesson." She reholstered the pistol. "Come on, Ray," she said. "Close your mouth."

"I heard that line in a movie," said Summer Joe.

"So what?" she snapped.

"If that bear is as big as you say he is, I'm glad two more men are coming along," said Ray.

"I thought you Hollywood fellas were class acts," Mel quipped.

"What do you mean?" asked Ray.

"I figured you'd be more open-minded about women than that," said Mel.

"No question about it," Ray said.

Mel came back with, "Good, 'cause you're a Jew, right? Don't take offense. This ain't prejudice. It's just what you are. Now, I've seen women hunt bear, but I never seen a Jew do it. I've seen 'em fish, seen 'em pull a sixty-pound chinook out of the river on a fly line, number four, silver doctor, but I've never seen 'em hunt bear. Catch my drift, Ray?"

"I don't think I could miss it."

"Great. 'Cause I'm gonna show you the time of your life, Mr. Marks. You just be ready to pull the trigger."

"Pow!" said Summer Joe. He had made his hand into a pistol, tracked and pointed it at an imaginary target.

Buddy got right into it. "Where'd you get him?"

"Broke his shoulder," said Summer Joe.

"He's still comin'," said Buddy.

"Pow!" went Summer Joe. "Broke his other shoulder."

"He's down but he's growlin'," said Buddy.

"Pow!" went Joe. "Heart shot."

"That's it," said Buddy.

"Only way to stop a grizzly," said Joe.

"You've done it, huh?" said Ray.

Summer Joe nodded. "Remember, Ray, both shoulders, then the heart."

Mel glared at Joe and growled through clenched teeth. "Wanna know how to stop an Indian?"

"Hey, Ray," Buddy jumped in. "Know what to do if a griz jumps you?"

"I know you're going to tell me," said Ray.

"Reach up and grab his pecker," said Buddy. "Give it a good wank."

"You swear by this?" asked Ray.

"I got it from a friend of mine. He was crossin' the tundra one day when a griz jumped him. He was panicked, right, so he grabbed onto that bear first place he could. Got the bear's pecker and gave it such a wank the griz let go, and my friend ran off. About a minute later that bear caught up to him again. Same damn thing. Wanked his pecker, bear let go. A minute later, goddamn if it don't happen time number three, but my friend grabbed that pecker and wanked it to save his life, and the griz let him go again. This time the bear didn't come after him. My friend looked back over his shoulder and there was that griz sittin' up against a tree, big smile on its face, one paw on his pecker and the other wavin' to my friend to come on back and do it again."

"True story?" said Ray.

"Gospel," answered Buddy.

"Then what did your friend do?" asked Ray.

"Shot it through both shoulders, then the heart."

"You don't wanna fuck with no grizzly," said Summer Joe.

"Be about the only thing you wouldn't fuck with," said Mel.

"You know the Moon Bar down in Fairbanks?" said Joe.

"Yeah," Mel said. "So?"

"Saw your name and number on the wall in the john."

"Great," flipped Mel. "I thought all those boys had me figured for a dyke."

Cody decided he had to put a stop to this. "Mel, why don't you get Ray settled in?"

"How'd you and Joe hook up?" asked Mel.

"You weren't at the airstrip," said Ray. "I needed a ride."

"Learn much about the indigenous population?" she wanted to know.

"Not too much."

"Mel," said Cody. It was a warning.

"Right," she said. "Hungry, Ray?"

"Starved."

"Caribou ribs sound good?"

"I'm game," said Ray.

Mel went on, "Medallions of muktuk . . ."

"What's 'muktuk'?" Ray asked.

"Dried whale, kind of a tidbit to get started. You'd call it a delicacy." Mel kept going. "Moose roast with gravy so thick a shotgun could stand up straight in it. Sweet potato wedges bubbling in bear fat. Tossed tundra greens. Fresh-picked blueberries. And all the hot coffee you can swallow. I gotta admit I had some trouble figuring out what wine went with whale, but I believe I got her licked. The cuisine at the Golden Bear Lodge awaits you."

"Got any Splenda?"

"I got whatever you need, Mr. Marks," Mel said with a wink, then she opened the door and held it back as she hefted Ray's gear bag to one shoulder and grabbed his gun case in her free hand. "Hombre, take a load off."

"You're the boss," Ray said as he went out the door. Mel shot Summer Joe a dirty look . . . "Stop hustlin' my hunter, asshole!" . . . and followed the man outside.

For a minute after Mel walked out, the three men left in the room were silent. Everybody wanted to say something, but nobody knew just what to say. Finally, Cody broke the silence. "She's tryin' to do something for herself, okay? And nobody in this room better fuck her over, hear me, Summer Joe?"

"I ain't gonna fuck her over," protested Summer Joe, though with minimal conviction.

"If you do," threatened Cody, "you better get your ass outta here right now."

"I wouldn't fuck anybody over in this weather," said Joe.

"Get out!" shouted Cody.

"It's pourin' buckets out there," resisted Joe.

"Out!"

"You got too much imagination, Cody," said Joe.

Buddy chimed in. "What's he gonna do, Cody? She's gotta have a deposit from the guy, right? He ain't gonna give up his deposit, know what I mean, Summer Joe?"

"I do," said Joe. "I see your point."

"Be better if you were inscrutable," said Buddy. "All right, boys. Let's smoke a peace pipe."

"What d'ya say, paleface?" said Summer Joe.

"I already said it," said Cody.

"Cody, come on," said Buddy. "We ain't gonna fight over some broad, are we? I mean, what the hell, none of us is gettin' any, right?" Cody didn't answer. "Right, Cody," Buddy said again. "But I gotta tell you, amigo, I think you're actin' a little, how shall I say . . ." He made a little wobbly motion with his hand. ". . . funny."

"What the hell is that?" Cody was really getting ticked.

"All right," said Buddy. "You don't want to talk about it, don't talk about it."

"I'm warnin' you," said Cody.

"And I'm warnin' you," countered Buddy. "As your friend, you're gettin' involved here, and it ain't healthy."

"Me 'n' Mel go back," said Cody. "I want to make sure nobody takes advantage."

"Cody, Cody, listen up, amigo," Buddy said. "You ain't thinkin'. You ain't seein' this the way it is. She'd be disappointed if nobody takes advantage. She'd think she had a bad day."

"You're drunk," said Cody dismissively.

"I'm always drunk," said Buddy. "Never stopped you from listening to me before."

"I don't listen," Cody burst out angrily. "I turn you off. You start in with your stupid drunken prattle, my brain goes to another planet."

"I didn't know that." Buddy's feelings were hurt.

"Learn somethin' new," fired back Cody.

"Nice to know who your friends are," Buddy went on. "Mel's

got a lot of friends. Half the guys on the pipeline was her friends. The other half had to pay for it."

Cody picked up a knife and said, "How'd you like this up your pipeline?" Summer Joe took one look at the knife in Cody's hand and bolted out the door.

"Chickenshit!" Buddy shouted after him. Cody stood there holding the knife and shaking with anger. "I wouldn't," Buddy said to him.

"I don't want to hear another goddamn word about her," cautioned Cody.

"You're treatin' her like she ain't what she is: desperate!" said Buddy, who didn't know enough to shut up. "Whatever she wants, she wants it bad. Mel's hustlin' the son-of-a-bitch. She'll do anything conceivable to man or beast, but no way do his shekels leave Toehold without her."

Cody reared back and threw the knife. Buddy made it out the door with about one half second to spare as the knife stuck in the wall where he'd been standing. Cody hollered after him, "Next time you're drunk in a ditch at forty below, I'm gonna leave you there, goddamnit." Cody pulled the knife and went back to his workbench. "Goddamnit!" He stabbed the knife into the wooden top. "God damn it!"

Cody couldn't focus. No matter how hard he tried to concentrate, he simply could not focus. Normally, he was so self-contained when he worked that a bomb could explode beside his head and he wouldn't wince. But right now his concentration was shot. Thoughts he'd rather not have were nibbling at the edges of his brain. He tried to tell himself he didn't know what those thoughts were, but he knew. He knew. There had been that night, or maybe it was the early hours of the morning, in the beginning, aurora borealis behind her head, something never spoken of again though not talking about it couldn't make what happened go away.

Still, wasn't it better to be good buddies than ex-whatevers? So why was all this seeping to the surface now? Hadn't time settled the matter? Wait a minute. Had there even been a matter to settle? Things sink to the bottom of a lake but even a lake turns over from time to time. What did that have to do with the price of moose meat? Or anything? Now Cody's muddle was turning to annoyance, no, to anger. He felt the bile rise in him like lava through the core of a volcano. What an asshole that Hollywood guy was!

Hold on, Cody, he thought, working it through. *You're annoyed at this guy, yeah, okay, he's an asshole,* but it came to Cody that he was really pissed at Mel. It was true. She was the root of his anger. Or, wait a minute, was it himself? What in the hell was that all about? Come on, what did he do to get himself pissed at himself? Cody couldn't figure out any of this shit, and that's what was really chapping his ass. He didn't even want to think about it, let alone suss it out. So why was he?

Cody heard a rifle shot from over near Mel's trailer. What a relief! It gave him something else to think about. The last time anyone discharged a rifle within the village limits was when a young bull moose wandered into Toehold at high noon and took over Main Street. Everybody jumped through the nearest door, but the enraged bull never got past the Pingo Palace. Sweet-ass Sue clocked him with a single shot, and Toehold had a barbecue that very evening of the finest game dinner anybody had eaten for a long time.

Cody went outside to see what the shooting was all about and saw Ray leaning across the hood of the Ramcharger with the barrel of his rifle resting on a rolled-up towel. Ray was sighting in on a paper plate affixed to a tree, making sure the scope was still at zero after traveling such a long way. He fired a second time and a few seconds later a third, then chucked open the bolt and laid the rifle on the hood before he walked to the tree and checked the target. Cody didn't realize Ray had seen him until Ray called out, "Hey, sport!" and held up the paper plate so Cody could see it. "Check it out. Tight as a nun's ass."

Cody walked over and took a look at the plate: three holes in a pattern so tight you could barely tell three bullets had pierced it. "I'd say that's zeroed in all right," said Cody. It was meant to be a compliment, but Cody's voice betrayed an edge that surprised him. " 'Course," he continued, "no bear I know's gonna let you hang him from a tree first. Where's Mel?"

"Inside mangling a whale or something," said Ray. "Tell me the truth, Cody. You honestly think she can handle this?"

"Can you?" asked Cody.

"That wasn't my question," said Ray.

"Except she's not the one who's worried, *sport*. You are."

"I think . . ." began Ray. "Call me crazy, but my radar just went on full alert. Any truth to the rumors, or are you two just good friends?" Ray held both palms up in a gesture of peace. "I know. I stick this nose where it doesn't belong. Bad habit. Been trying to break it for years."

"Either that," said Cody, "or somebody's liable to break it for you."

"There's always that possibility," said Ray.

Mel opened the trailer door and called Ray to dinner.

"Don't want to keep a lady waiting," said Ray. "You know what that's like." He winked at Cody as if the two men had shared a crude joke. Then Ray turned his back and went inside.

Mel had tried real hard to make dinner special. She didn't bother trying to bake bread from scratch again, but she had picked up a couple of recipes from Esther Nanachuk and did her best to follow them word for word. If she had to say so herself, Mel thought the moose especially delicious. Ray spent a lot of time pushing his food around the plate, but since he hadn't doubled over in pain or barfed or anything, she guessed she was ahead of the game. Sweet-ass Sue had pitched in with a couple of wines, but the white was too sour and the red too sweet, so Ray contented himself with two cans of room-temperature Mountain Dew.

"More moose, Ray? There's extra sweet potato wedges, too."

"I'm full up," said Ray.

"How was it?" She had promised herself she'd never ask, but the question just slipped right out.

"Unforgettable," he said.

"I guess that's pretty good, huh?" she asked.

"Absolutely."

"Great. I wouldn't want you to be disappointed. How 'bout some brandy?" Mel suggested.

"You're on," he said.

"I gotta go next door and get it," she said. "The only thing the Golden Bear Lodge can't offer is a hot tub. Not yet, anyway, but we got one on the drawing board. I can rig you a sweat lodge if you want—open your pores, loosen your bones . . ."

"My bones are loose enough for now, thanks. Why don't you show me where we're going?"

"No problem." Mel cleared the dishes and spread a topo map out on the table. "We'll canoe upriver to this point here, then carry our gear overland to this fork here. I've got an inflatable raft stashed at the campsite. We'll spend the night, start out the next morning when it's barely light, float a couple of miles, and begin the stalk right about here. Make sure you bunk in early tonight. You're gonna need your strength." Mel folded the map.

"Mind if I take a look at it?" asked Ray.

"Not a problem," answered Mel. "It's burned into my brain."

"Thanks," said Ray. "Now, where do I sleep?"

Mel pointed to her bed. "Hope it's comfortable."

"Where are you going to sleep?"

"Outside," she said. "You need somethin', I'm only one holler away."

"Promise?" asked Ray.

"Read the brochure," said Mel, and winked.

"I don't think you included one."

"We must've run out."

"I guess so," said Ray. "You were talking brandy?"

Mel said, "I'll be right back," and left to get the bottle from Cody.

"How's it goin'?" asked Cody, as Mel came rushing into his shop.

"He liked the fresh blueberries," crowed Mel enthusiastically. "No, I mean he really liked them. It's goin' dandy. And this guy is used to the best there is. Listen to this. He's been quail hunting in Georgia where these black dudes drive mule wagons to the field and serve you mint juleps right there. He's been dove hunting in Mexico where these little Mexican kids run out and pick up the birds for you. He's even been on a safari to Africa where they served antelope filet and *pommes frites* in the middle of the jungle. Know what they are?"

"French fries," said Cody.

"Fancy ones—skinny, curly, and oil-free," said Mel.

"Who served him?" asked Cody. "Pygmies?"

"Some tribe," she answered. "I can't pronounce it. Hey, Cody,

I need a favor. Your brandy, can I borrow it?" He took the bottle from under his workbench and handed it to her. "I'll buy you another bottle right after the hunt, okay?"

"Don't worry about it."

"Just keep the tab," said Mel. "I don't think my hunter liked the wine too much. Said the bouquet was okay but it didn't linger, or somethin'. So I want to whip a little of the good stuff on him." Mel studied the label. "This is pretty good, isn't it?"

"Well," said Cody, "it's from California."

"Great," she said. "Make him feel at home."

"What's he doing?"

"Relaxin'. Checkin' out the map. We'll be outta here at dawn, and Cody, I'll tell you what: I ain't stoppin' 'til I hit Hawaii."

"You got a deposit from the guy?" Cody wanted to know.

"Of course I got a deposit. It's standard procedure. Every guide gets a deposit. You keep it no matter what, like a good faith thing. Says so right there on the check: Mel Madden. But you know what? I got somethin' even better. I got this dude in the palm of my hand. He's gettin' a hunt and a half, Jack."

"How's that?" asked Cody.

"First class. Whatever it takes. That extra mile. He loves it I'm a woman, too. I mean, yeah, it took him some to get used to the idea, but once he did, whammo! He's used to Hollywood starlets hustlin' him for a part in his movies. Hey, this babe's takin' him to the jaws of death. It's different than what he's used to."

"Maybe he isn't interested in the jaws of death," said Cody. "Ever think of that?"

"I thought of everything," she said. "My dude's lookin' for the experience of a lifetime. Whatever he wants, that boy's come to the right place." Mel pointed to her head. "I got it here . . ." She put her hand over her heart. "Here . . ." Then she grabbed her ass. "And here. He's got twenty-five large; I got the bases covered."

"I'm not sure I heard what you just said," said Cody, an edge to his voice.

"Yeah, you did," laughed Mel. "What? You don't think it's worth twenty-five grand?" Cody scowled at her. He wasn't enjoying this even a little. "I'll settle for twenty-two-five. Plus your sales tax, your tip . . . That oughta bring it close enough. You ain't laughin'."

"What's funny?"

"Oh, come on, Cody. You ever seen those Hollywood types? The only thing me 'n' Jessica Simpson got in common?"

"Tell me."

"We both wear panties from La Perla."

"What's La Perla?"

"Only the crème de la crème of high-end lingerie. And I do mean high end. Capital H, capital E. Smack in the middle of 90210."

"What's that?"

"Beverly fuckin' Hills, my man."

"The mind boggles," said Cody.

"At what?"

"The thought of you in Beverly Hills."

"Is that a good boggle or a bad boggle?"

"Just a regular boggle."

"Like, what's wrong with this picture?"

"More like *Crocodile Dundee*."

"Crocodile Dundee in La Perla panties. Hey, whoa, now, that boggles the mind."

"You caught my drift," said Cody.

"I'm slick that way," she replied.

"Slick in a lot of ways."

"You don't know the half of it," she said.

"Maybe not," said Cody, "but I got the other half down pretty well."

"Think so, huh?" she asked.

"Know so."

"Know where I got 'em?"

"Have we moved to a need-to-know basis?"

"I thought you'd be curious," she answered.

"John Travolta gave them to you," said Cody.

"I've had my admirers," she said with a sweet, sleepy smile. "You're right, as always. Travolta was among them. He liked me to call him that. Just 'Travolta.' At special moments. You know."

"Green eyes," said Cody.

"Huh?" It was Mel's turn to be unsure of what was said.

"You both got green eyes," he repeated.

"Who?" Mel was confused.

"You and Jessica What's-her-name? Rabbit?"

What the hell is this all about? she thought. "All right," said Mel, "so we both got green eyes. Big deal. The whole point of all this is, why would Mr. Hollywood Big Shot Ray Fucking First Look Marks fork over five cents for a beat-up broad like me when he can waltz into a Tinselville party full of hotties and just point to the babe du jour of his choice?"

"So you were joking?" asked Cody.

"About sellin' my tush?" answered Mel. Cody nodded. "Sort of," she continued. "See, on the other hand, my hind parts are gonna look good compared to, say, a moose. You know how food tastes good on the trail no matter what you do to it?"

"No, I don't," said Cody obstinately. Oh, boy, could he piss her off!

"Well, you damn well should," she snapped. "You're the one who told me." Mel didn't like being pissed at Cody, and, really, never was for very long. "Come on, Cody, I'm not plannin' on doin' the horizontal cha-cha with this guy. I'm just plantin' the possibility in his mind—the tundra, the moon, the hunt, the woman . . . 'Maybe it's gonna happen,' he says to himself, 'and I don't even hafta shave.' See if the Indian can top that!"

"That's what this is all about? The Indian?" said Cody.

"I might trust Summer Joe if he was gagged with duct tape and cuffed to a tree. Other than that, this girl's takin' no chances."

"I don't like it," said Cody.

"Who cares what you like?" she shouted. God, this man could get her so damn angry! "I gotta get that money."

"Then go back to the Golden Bear Lodge and stop pestering me," yelled Cody. He was always putting up with something from this woman, and right then he was damn tired of it, of her, of it, of her. Jesus, she was exasperating.

"What the hell's your beef, Cody?"

"You want to know?"

"I'm in suspense." She meant to be sarcastic but not *so* sarcastic.

"Forget it." Exasperating wasn't even close to what she was. Irritating. Aggravating. Infuriating. There had to be a word for it.

"Tell me," said Mel. "Come on. Please."

"It ain't clean."

"That's why God invented towelettes." Mel could have kicked herself for being so sarcastic, but it just came blurting out, as if the words had a life of their own.

"You're pushing me," threatened Cody.

"You gonna throw a punch?" she said. Where the hell did she think she was taking this?

"Don't push me," he said.

"'Cause if you do, you better kill me with the first one, buster!" Mel had her right locked and loaded.

Cody stared back at her for a few seconds. He wanted to say something that would wither her at the roots, but all he could say was, "I don't like you today," and turned his back on her. He went back to his workbench without another word, puttered around, and tried to make it look like work, but his mood was black, and nothing good ever came from that. Why didn't she just leave, take her ass out of here? He resented the silence. It was awkward and uncomfortable, not the same thing as solitude at all. What he wanted to feel was nothing.

"Cody?" Mel said after a while. He didn't answer. "Cody?"

she said again. He refused to open his mouth. "What do you mean it ain't clean? I really want to know." She really did. "What?"

Finally, he turned and looked at her, and said, "Guy comes to hunt, you give him a hunt. You keep his mind on the game. That's what you do. Nothing else. You don't mix and match."

"Can't you understand?" said Mel in frustration. "I'm 'merchandising' the man. It's an accepted business practice in many leading stores, for Christ's sake. Make the customer think he's gettin' more than what he's payin' for. Now, if you'll excuse me, I got business to attend to." She turned to go but his voice cut through her bravado.

"You're scared numb the Indian's gonna ace you out."

"Then why do you blame me for hedgin' my bets?" she demanded.

"Because you oughta have more respect for yourself."

"I got so much self-respect I'm poor," she quipped. Some seconds passed, seconds in which Cody wanted to make certain of what he was about to say.

"How 'bout," he said when he finally let himself speak, "I lend you the money?"

"Huh?" It was more a gasp than a question.

"For your daughter," Cody said.

"Lend me the money? *You* lend *me*?"

"Yeah. Me lend you."

"Why do you want to lend me the money?" She was really curious.

"We're friends, right?" said Cody.

"You're friends with Buddy," Mel countered. "You wouldn't lend him fifty cents."

"Buddy gets what he needs from me," said Cody.

"And this is what I need?"

"That's all you've been talking about," he said, baffled. Cody could not understand why Mel was being so contrary.

"I mean, from you," said Mel. "Need from you."

Mother of God, thought Cody. *You give her what she wants and she still kicks you in the ass.* "Yeah, you do," he said.

"Where are you gonna get that kind of money?" she asked skeptically.

"I got it," he said. "My mother left a life insurance policy. I still got some of it."

"Twenty-five thousand dollars?"

"Enough to get Terry Louise up here from Tucson," he replied.

"Then what?" she wanted to know.

Damn, thought Cody, *what is her problem?* "She'd be here," he said.

"What about Hawaii?" Mel asked.

God, thought Cody, *we're talking bottomless pit here.* "Scratch Hawaii. She'd be *here!*" he said in frustration.

"It's cold in Alaska, goddamnit," exclaimed Mel.

"What's more important," Cody wanted to know, "being with your kid or the weather?"

"It's gotta be right," she said.

"You're the one's gonna make it right," he argued. Wow, was she a frustration! "No Eskimo kid cares about Hawaii. His mother's on an iceberg, he's on an iceberg, and glad to be there, too."

"Maybe you should have been the mother," she wondered softly.

"No tits," he replied.

"Seriously," said Mel.

"I used to like kids," said Cody.

"What happened?"

"Oh," he said, "I still like 'em. There just aren't too many around this place."

"No, I mean, what happened you never had any?" she persisted.

"Well, you know," he hemmed and hawed, "this 'n' that. I wasn't married that long."

"Long enough," she countered.

"That long?" he said.

"You're evading the issue," Mel insisted.

"All right," Cody said, giving in. "I was shooting with blanks."

"What's that mean?" Sometimes she could be awful thick.

"I went to the doctor's office for a test one time, saw my jissom under a microscope, looked a lot like little tiny tadpoles wiggling around, except not too many were wiggling, and the ones that were sort of raised their heads and coughed a lot before, um, they stopped moving, too."

Mel was quiet for a moment, then said pensively, "Everything everybody wants is out there in the world, except the wrong things go to the wrong people. If I was a writer I'd write a book called *When Good Things Happen to Bad People*."

"Do I get an autographed copy?" asked Cody.

"You bet. I'll even dedicate it to you."

"An honor bestowed upon me why exactly?"

"'Cause you're like the sky. You've got me covered."

"I accept."

"We're a funny couple, aren't we?" asked Mel.

"A funny couple of what?" asked Cody.

Mel laughed. "Yeah. Right," she said. Mel leaned back against Cody. He put his arms around her, a comfortable fit. "That was a nice night," she said, and she really meant it. "My God, what was it, how many years ago?"

Cody knew exactly what she was talking about, and it made him feel slightly awkward.

"About that," he said.

"Why didn't we do it again?" Mel couldn't leave anything alone.

"We didn't know each other then, not really."

"I knew there had to be a reason it was so easy."

"It was a good kill. You got high. I got high. It was dark. Who knows? We get along, right? Whatever works."

"Yeah," she said. "Whatever works. So . . . tell me," she said, "what would it be like if you lent me the money and I brought my kid up here?"

"How do I know?"

"You must have some idea," she persisted.

"The only thing I'm thinking is that maybe I could help you out some. A kid takes getting used to. I could, y'know, babysit once in a while, free up a little time for yourself."

"The three of us could go to a ballgame? Like that?"

"Name the night," said Cody.

"You 'n' me," asked Mel, "would we have some kind of understanding?"

"Not necessarily," he answered, not waiting for the end of a sentence that she did not want to finish anyway.

"I never was big on a nuclear family," said Mel.

"Who's talking 'nuclear family'?"

"But if I was to say yes?" she asked.

"I don't know," said Cody, quickly becoming more and more confused. He walked away from her and took a beer from the cooler.

"You wouldn't want to?" She was always pushing him.

"It'd depend."

"On what?"

"Us," he blurted, not one bit sure of what he meant.

"That's what I'm gettin' at," she said. Why did she always have to push it? "What about us?"

"It wouldn't have to change," he said. What were they talking about?

"A kid changes everything," she told him. Each word emphasized. Spelling it out.

"Jesus Christ, Mel," he stammered in frustration. "I'm not

offering you a house in the suburbs, just a chance to be with your kid, what's-her-name?"

"It ain't what I had in mind, tell you that," said Mel.

"The mind's a big place. Room for a lot of things in there," said Cody.

"We could still take a trip to Hawaii, her and me. Get settled in here. Put some cash away. Wait 'til they run a special. Off season." Mel gave herself a minute to think this over. "Would you wanna come?"

"Don't count on me," he said. "I don't like vacations. I'd spend all my time looking around for something to stuff."

"Maybe me 'n' her could talk you into it, two attractive available ladies like us," said Mel. "We agreed I'd be available, right?" she asked.

"Oh, sure," he said. "But still, don't count on me. You two go and have a good time."

"She might want you to come along," mused Mel.

"We'll see," said Cody.

"Wouldn't want to disappoint her."

"We'll see."

"That's all you can say?" pushed Mel.

"How do I know what's gonna happen?" He was really confused. What were they talking about? "I might not have the money even if I did want to go."

"If it was really important to you, you'd get the money somewhere."

"Let's just wait and see, all right, Mel?"

"It ain't easy havin' a kid, you know," she went on. "It's a big responsibility. You gotta be ready to do what's right. You don't bring a kid to a place like this without a clear understanding of this fact of life: a kid don't go away."

"Take it easy, Mel." She was really getting upset.

"Don't tell me, 'Take it easy, Mel'! We're talkin' about a

crossroads here. I want to know what's your place in the scheme of things. It's a simple-shit question, and you're slippin' around the answer like the captain of the goddamn *Exxon Valdez*. You want the kid, or you don't want the kid?"

"I want the goddamn kid," he yelled. "Do you?"

"What the hell is this all about if I don't want the kid? Of course I want the kid, but I want to do it right," Mel insisted. "If it ain't right, it's nothin'. It might as well be shit."

"Then make it right!" said Cody impatiently.

"That's what I was doin' 'til you got me all cranked with this other idea." How did he do that?

"It's just an option," said Cody.

"Yeah. Sure. Thanks," said Mel.

"You're making too big a deal out of it," said Cody. But it was a big deal, wasn't it? Hmm? Right?

"Uh-huh," said Mel. "If it's no big deal, what's in it for you? Huh? Let's be honest. We know I'm a rotten cook, so that can't be it. You ain't the first guy in my life, and we both know there's a good bet you won't be the last."

Cody tried to lighten it up. "But I'm the only one named Rosewater." Mel wasn't biting. "Seriously, Mel, you're putting words in my mouth. Who asked for anything?"

"Must be somethin' in it for you," she insisted.

"I see a chance to make a difference, all right? Do something nice for somebody I like. Make myself feel good, all right?" he tried to explain, but he couldn't think of what to say that wouldn't sound so stupid.

"You 'n' me 'n' my kid," said Mel, "we're not some sort of perfect specimens you're gonna mount for some diorama in the Museum of Natural History—'The Typical Contemporary Alaskan Bush Family.'"

"I never said . . ."

But Mel never gave him the chance to finish. She burst

out with sudden finality, "I've thought about it. Let's forget it. I'm takin' my kid to Hawaii. Maybe I'll get a job and stay there. Why should I put up with all this cold weather?"

"Fine." Nothing else to say.

"That's it, then?" Mel asked.

"Yep."

"You hurt?"

Cody shook his head. "It's your life."

"Right," she said, and started for the door, but the door opened before she got there and Ray Marks walked in. Mel had forgotten all about him.

"Am I interfering?" he wanted to know.

"In what?" Cody asked belligerently.

"Oh, Jesus!" yipped Mel. "I forgot. God, I'm sorry."

"No problem," said Ray. "At least, nothing a little brandy wouldn't solve."

Mel was rattled. "Here you fly all the way up here from Southern California, and I leave you sittin' in the middle of nowhere. What can I get you?"

"Brandy?" said Ray. The tone of his voice had a tinge of impatience to it.

"Right," said Mel. She practically thrust the bottle at him. "Oh. Cody. I need a glass."

"There's paper cups on the shelf."

She got them and poured Ray a drink. "Here y'go." The last time Ray Marks had a drink in a paper cup, well, he couldn't remember the last time. Preschool maybe? He lifted the cup to his nose and sniffed. Mel never took her eyes off his face. "Can you tell me where it's from?"

"Albania?"

"California," she said. *What did he mean, 'Albania'?*

"Why didn't I know that?" he asked.

"How's the bouquet?" She wished she could just settle down.

"Very ... um ... California," he answered. "Hey, doll, did you check the weather?"

"We blow this pop stand at daybreak," said Mel. "Better get some sleep."

"Gotta make a phone call first," said Ray. "By the way, how far are we from the Arrigetch Peaks?"

"That's not where your bear is," said Mel, with more than a hint of suspicion.

"Color me curious, sweetheart," said Ray.

"Dogsled?" asked Mel.

"That'll do."

"You can't walk it, and there's no snow," she said.

"Chalk it up to the intellectual curiosity of my people," he quipped. *What the hell is this all about?* she wondered. "How far?" he asked again.

"Two days by dogsled, if there's snow," she answered. "But I can't guide there, plus the obvious fact that there's no snow at all, of course." Wow, she sounded like such an idiot.

"What're you worried about, babe? You and me, we're joined at the hip. Wherever you go ..." Before Ray finished his sentence, Buddy and Summer Joe barged through the door, both so drunk it's a wonder they were still standing.

"Hey, compadre," said Buddy to Ray. "Still here? Lemme buy you a beer."

"Rain check," said Ray.

"Tell me the truth, Mel," said Buddy, spotting the brandy in her hand. "Is that brandy? Don't lie to an old pal." She handed him the bottle, though the expression on her face clearly indicated she wished Buddy were in Siberia. "Shouldn't hold out on your old friends. It ain't generous." He poured himself a drink and offered the bottle to Summer Joe. Summer Joe turned him down.

"I don't like that kind," he said.

"What's wrong with it?" challenged Mel.

"What do you care?" said Joe.

"First time I've ever seen an Indian turn down a free drink." Did she really say that? She wished she hadn't. This fucker brought out the worst in her.

"Ancient shaman say," signed Summer Joe sarcastically, "'Keep night eye on eagle eye, and sun eye on owl eye.' Suggest you do same."

"Hey, Charlie Chan," said Mel. "What the hell's that supposed to mean?"

"It means I don't like the bouquet," he said. Mel's stare was lethal. Summer Joe stared back. It was a standoff.

"So," said Buddy to Mel, "how's business over at the Golden Bear Lodge? Has success been kind to you?"

"Go pack sand up your ass," she said.

"It don't pay to be nice to some people," Buddy said to Summer Joe.

"Hey, Joe," said Ray. "Gimme a ride to the plane?"

"I can take you," said Mel, jumping on it.

"That's okay," said Ray. "We've got a big day tomorrow. You relax."

"What're you doin' at the plane?" she wanted to know. God, why did she have to sound so desperate? "It's dark out."

"Gotta make a phone call," said Ray. "Satellite's in the plane."

"Who're you gonna call this time of night?" What was wrong with her? *Girl, Jesus, settle down.*

"L.A., if you must know," said Ray. "See if the ship's still floating. I've got a picture shooting in Mexico with a fifty-year-old coke freak who says he's a movie star. He's fucking his leading lady—who happens to be fourteen—*and* her mother. I've also got a director who is so certifiable he'd be stashed in a padded cell if it weren't for the movie business. Glamorous, huh? Mind if I make that phone call now?"

"You're the boss," Mel said lamely.

"So I'm told," said Ray. "Joe?"

"Right with ya," said Joe, and he and Ray went out the door. Mel looked distressed. The door closed behind them, and she didn't know what to do.

"Fuckin' Indians," muttered Buddy.

"Why'd you say 'fuckin' Indians'?" she asked suspiciously.

"People've been sayin' 'fuckin' Indians' since time immemorial," he answered.

"You and him were drinkin' out in the pickup," she said.

"Me 'n' him were drinkin' out in the pickup. Right."

"What'd he tell you?"

"About what?" said Buddy.

Mel grabbed him by the front of his shirt. "About anything I might like to know about, you slob," she yelled.

Cody pulled her back before she clobbered Buddy. "Mel," he said, trying to calm her down, "take my advice . . ."

She broke free. "I don't need your advice." She was scared, and she was furious, a deadly combination. Buddy stared at her dumbstruck.

"Get outta here, Buddy," ordered Cody. Buddy didn't need to hear it a second time. He was out the door and gone. "Listen to me, Mel," said Cody as he tried to reason with her.

"I don't want anybody tellin' me what to do, includin' you, Cody, you understand?"

"Mel, come on," he said. "You're gonna get slammed."

"I'll handle this myself," she bellowed.

"Like you handled everything else?" he said.

"Back off, Cody!"

"You're playing it all wrong," he said, still trying to get to her.

"I know what you're thinkin'," she yelled.

"I'm thinking about you, goddamnit!"

"Yeah? Well, think about this: you mess my deal up, Cody, I'll cut your heart out!"

Who was this kid, this Theresa Louise Patricia Somebody, this distant creature, this teenage tangle of matter and impulse? How was it possible that this thing, this whatever-it-was could be headed for a collision with Mel's own life? Mel had scarcely ever seen this child, and then not since all she was was a poop and puke factory. Seen sixteen years ago, a thousand years ago, a million trillion years ago. It might as well be a creature from outer space, from Mars, from Pluto. Which planet was the farthest away? Uranus? Mel didn't know. And she wanted to know. She had to know. How could so distant a thing make such a claim on her? She felt like she was trying to shake something off her hand, off her fingers, something sticky, and she couldn't do it. She shook them and she shook them, and damn if whatever it was didn't just stick there, obstinate as hell. Was this love? Was that possible? How could it be? Love? Come on. She felt like a Little League catcher, a kid, trying to catch the hundred-mile-an-hour fastball of a major-league pitcher. She couldn't even see the thing hurtling toward her, let alone get a glove on it. What kind of protection could she possibly have against something like that? Oh, my God, my God, was she in trouble! But what if she did love it? Come on. How real could this be? How could you feel something so mighty for someone you'd barely seen and didn't know hardly at all? How could there be a connection so strong to something outside your own body? Was this what being a mother felt like? God help her if it was, because she was in deep, deep trouble. She was in danger. She was ready to die for this kid, this person who wouldn't know her if she tripped over her. So let's say this kid gets off a crowded plane in Fairbanks. Air Alaska, say. Suppose it was a bunch of kids getting off the school bus after a class trip to Valley Forge. How would Mel even know her in the crowd? She would, though. Mel knew for sure she would know this person of five thousand eight hundred and forty days as well as she knew her own troubled face.

Would someone somewhere please explain to him what just happened? Cody pled silently to whatever cosmic force might take the trouble to listen. Cut his heart out? What in the fuck had he done? Cut his heart out? His heart? Wasn't that a little extreme? All he'd offered to do was help, help out just a little, and for that this woman wanted to cut his heart out? And what was this shit about going to a ballgame? Where'd that one come from? Women! Can't shoot 'em, can't get three in a pickup. Now he was really getting pissed! Try to do something good for somebody. What the fuck did he think he was, the fucking Salvation Army? He expected to pay for his sins in the next life, but who the hell was she to make him pay for them right now? Just who the hell did she think she was? Ungrateful. Evil tempered. Flat broke. Needy. Greedy. Fucked up. Used up. That woman had busted his chops, and he hated her for it, right? Pow! "To the fuckin' moon, Alice," right? Right?

The brandy was all gone, and Cody needed a drink, right now, *right now,* goddamnit!

Summer Joe and Ray picked Buddy up in Sweet-ass's truck on their way back from the airstrip. He was plastered on the side of the road singing to a tree: "I like the night life, I like the bright lights, I like to boogie, too . . ." And then he'd howl at the moon like a gutshot dog. It sounded painful as hell, but he was smiling when they stopped for him. It was like he was laughing at a joke only he had heard.

"I don't know about you, Buddy," Joe told him. "Seems like you in your own world."

"You're invited," said Buddy. "Come on down!"

"What night life?" Ray wanted to know.

"Not too much," said Summer Joe. "We tend to be self-contained up here."

"There's this big contest we got," Buddy tried to explain. "We all sit on bar stools and drink as much beer as we can. Last one to fall off the stool wins."

"Wins what?" asked Ray.

Buddy was stumped. "What's he win, Joe?"

"He just wins," said Joe.

"Why'd I ask?" said Ray.

"Hey, Joe, take him by Sweet-ass Sue's," suggested Buddy.

"What's that?" Ray wanted to know.

"Y'mean who's that," corrected Buddy.

"The man was right the first time," said Joe.

"It's our after-hours joint," explained Buddy.

"Yeah," chimed in Summer Joe. "Like after an hour the house rules say you gotta go outside to pee."

"Instead of where?" Ray really didn't have to ask the question.

"Inside," said Summer Joe.

"Wonder if we could get Sue topless tonight," mused Buddy.

"Ugh," grunted Joe.

"It's somethin' the man oughta see," insisted Buddy. "Like Mount McKinley. You up for it, Ray?"

"Why not?"

"I don't mean to tell you your business, Ray," said Summer Joe, "but you got a large, mean-tempered mammal out there with your name on it. You might want to get some rest."

"After I see Mount McKinley," said Ray.

"Let's get on it, then," said Joe, as he gunned the truck through the mud and down Main Street to Sweet-ass Sue's Pingo Palace, where Joe then slid into the wall sideways.

"Your parking needs work," said Ray.

A group of five Athapaskan young men, more or less the same age as Summer Joe, came out of the bar just as Joe, Ray, and Buddy were getting out of the truck. One of the Indians, the one in front, had a gunbelt and holster slung over his shoulder. The revolver was enormous—.44 Magnum, seven-inch barrel, black. "Hey, Chief," said Summer Joe, greeting the man.

"Wha'd'ya say, Joe?" said the man.

"Hangin' in," said Joe.

"You like bein' single?" the man asked.

"I like bein' free," answered Joe.

"But you miss the pussy," the man said. He wasn't smiling.

"Always a problem, ain't it, Chief?" Joe answered.

"Gone the way of the buffalo," said the young man.

"Pussy?" said Summer Joe, not quite certain what the man meant. The man nodded.

"You think the white man had anything to do with this?" he asked, dead serious.

"Probably." Summer Joe nodded thoughtfully. The man nodded with him in agreement.

"See ya," he said, and sauntered away, followed by the other four Indian men.

"That guy really a chief?" Ray was curious.

"Sure," replied Summer Joe. "Beaucoup big medicine," and the three of them stepped inside.

"Hey, Meatie," hollered Buddy as he slapped his palm on the bar, "give us a drink!"

Like Jaws tearing suddenly out of the water, Sweet-ass erupted from behind the bar wielding a sledgehammer handle above her head. Swinging from the shoulders, she pulled at the last possible instant and stopped the handle an inch from putting Buddy's face into a forensics lab.

"Don't gimme another excuse, jerkwad," growled Sue.

"Hell of a swing," admired Ray.

"Buy a ball club, Ray," said Joe. "Bat her cleanup. Hey, Sue, meet Ray. He's here for grizzly."

Sue looked Ray smack in the eye. "You rich?"

"Rich enough," said Ray.

"I know that, Slim, or you wouldn't be here," said Sue. "What I want to know is: how rich are you?"

Ray went right back at her. "So rich," he said, "my shorts are custom-made. So rich my secretaries all drive Hummers. So rich I could wrap your titties in brand-new one-thousand-dollar bills and slap ten large on your ass."

Sweet-ass Sue and Ray stared eyeball to eyeball. Not a blink. The moment of truth. Summer Joe and Buddy held their breath. Her eyes wrinkled. Her face softened. She chortled. She chuckled. She threw back her head and laughed out loud.

"You're all right, Ray," she said, and clapped him on the shoulder for emphasis.

Summer Joe sighed with relief and asked for three beers. "Who's payin'?" Sue wanted to know.

Buddy pointed at Ray. "He is."

But Summer Joe jumped in with, "I am."

"There's a first," slurred Buddy.

"Stop droolin' on the bar, lug nut," cautioned Sweet-ass Sue.

"Yes, ma'am," he said meekly.

"Hey," said Ray, "didn't somebody say something about Mount McKinley?"

Sue fixed Buddy with a lethal stare. "You're dead meat," she rumbled.

"Why're you pickin' on me?" yelped Buddy. "I'm an old man. No teeth. Talk to him." Buddy pointed at Summer Joe.

"Be cool," said Summer Joe.

"They said you've got tits worth dying for," said Ray. "That true?"

"'They'?" yelped Buddy.

"Would fifty bucks do it?" asked Ray.

Sweet-ass cracked a smile. "You the man was talkin' thousand-dollar bills?" she asked.

"Yep," said Ray, "but not on me. How about a hundred?" Ray peeled off a hundred-dollar bill and placed it on the bar.

"That'll get you one," bargained Sue. Ray peeled off another hundred. "That'll get you two," said Sue. She put the two hundred-dollar bills in a big jar next to the cash register. Then, with a whoop like a war cry and an agility made more startling by its being so unexpected, Sweet-ass turned and vaulted up onto the bar. Her legs swung over Ray's head and crisscrossed around his back. Sue sat facing him, Ray's face inches from her chest.

"Behold," Sue announced, "the breasts of destruction!" Then she grabbed her shirt collar with both hands and, one by one, popped the snaps ... all ... the ... way ... down. Ray gaped in awe, as did everybody else, at two titanic tits with brunette nipples wide around as coffee mugs. Those two double D's were massive pieces of equipment—high, firm, and huge. They couldn't have been more perfect had they been advertised on a billboard. Their cleavage was so deep a man could fall into it and never be heard from again. Sweet-ass Sue leapt to her feet on top of the bar, raised her hands above her head, stomped and whooped in victory.

"We are talking wonders of the world," said Ray, truly dazzled.

"There's more where that came from," bragged Sue.

"I don't think I could handle it," said Ray.

"Ain't many could," she said as she closed her shirt and climbed back down from the bar. "Takes a big man to admit it," she said with a wink and a sly smile. "Grizzly bear ain't shit, Ray."

Nothing in this world Sweet-ass Sue liked to eat better than black bear, especially rump roast of black bear, naturally fattened on sweet mast, pounded with juniper berries, and served with mashed potatoes and applesauce. A few brussels sprouts wouldn't hurt any, either. Succulent ones, the size of Ping-Pong balls, grew right into November. *You can have your moose and your caribou,* she said. *I'll take a nice fat bear anytime,* and each year damn if she didn't manage to come up with one. The only thing you had to be careful about was not to eat it too pink. Had to cook it good or else you could wind up with a dose of worms. It was like pork that way, only it tasted better. Each year, just before she took her first bite of the season, she'd chant an old childhood ditty, one of the many things that she learned from her older cousin, Buck. "Through the lips, over the gums, watch out stomach, here it comes." Then she'd shriek with laughter, throw back her head, and stuff a juicy chunk of hot meat in her mouth. As far as Sue was concerned, there wasn't any finer eating in all the whole wide world. Nobody tried to tell her different.

Normally, she made something from the hide—the warmest blanket in creation, a full-length coat—or gave the hide to one of the old grandmothers to work with, but this year she decided to simply have it tanned and hang it on the wall of the Pingo Palace. She wasn't one for bragging, but this year's bear was the juiciest one yet, and Sue wanted to be able to look over at the wall and remember how sweet that rump roast really was. So what she did was to give the hide to Cody and ask him to cure it for her. Which he did. Now, Cody Rosewater was not a man to do one thing if he could do two, and he was not a man to do something in the first place unless he could give himself a pretty fair reason for doing it. He was thorough and thoughtful, but not exactly a spur-of-the-moment guy. If he was going to be spontaneous, he had to have a good excuse. So the night in question, Ray's first night in town, Cody decided to, one, get drunk, and, two, deliver the finished hide to Sweet-ass. She had whiskey; he didn't. He had the hide; she didn't. The symmetry was perfect.

Ray had just finished paying for the second round of beers when Cody walked in. "Make that four," Ray said to Sue, ordering one more. Cody took a stool at the far end of the bar and put the bear hide on the stool beside him. Sue popped the cap on a bottle and slid it down to him. Cody caught it and slid it right back, easy as a shortstop making the flip to second. Then he pointed to a bottle of rye and indicated three inches with his thumb and forefinger.

Summer Joe leaned in and said to Ray, "Old Indian custom."

"Drinking?" Buddy asked.

"Sign language," said Joe.

"Hey, Sue, put it on my tab," said Ray.

Cody put a pile of ones on the bar. "I got it," he said without looking up.

Just like that, the Pingo Palace got real quiet.

Mel did not want to be alone with the one person in the world she loathed more than anybody else—herself. She didn't want to talk to anybody, but she didn't want to be alone, either. After she slammed out of Cody's, she went back to her trailer and sulked, but that got her nowhere except deeper into a mess of emotions she didn't want to deal with—didn't *know* how to deal with was more to the point. Let's be honest, girl: what Mel knew was that if she stayed alone, the weight of all those stone slabs would just crush her flat. She had to settle down. She had to get it together. She had to go to Sue's for a drink. Maybe a couple shots of Jack would do it. Maybe a couple shots of embalming fluid.

Ray walked over to Cody's stool and stood beside him. "You're an interesting guy, you know that?" he said as he inspected the tanned bear hide. "Nothing second-rate about your work, either. How long have you been at it?"

"I came here to drink, Roy," said Cody without looking at him.

"Ray," said Ray.

"Not talk," said Cody.

"Man's got a hair up his ass," said Buddy.

"Maybe," said Summer Joe, "it's the full moon."

"Hey," Ray said magnanimously, "the man's honest, says what's on his mind. It's good for me to get out of the city for a while, get to what's real."

"We had a guy up here a couple seasons back," said Cody. "Said the same thing. He was in TV."

"Long form? Short form?" asked Ray.

"He got skunked," was all Cody said. "Didn't shoot a thing."

"That right?" said Ray.

"It was his moment of truth," said Cody.

Any minute now, thought Buddy, *somebody's gonna throw a punch.*

"You don't kiss much ass, do you, Cody?" asked Ray.

"No," said Cody. "Do you?"

Any minute now, thought Buddy.

Ray went on. "You got me for a genuine bullshit artist, right? But, hell, that's real in its way, isn't it?" Cody didn't answer. "Come on, I'm just a poor schmuck trying to make a movie or two. I ain't Mother Teresa. I ain't feeding refugees in Sudan. On the other hand, making a movie's no less real than these mounts of yours."

"What's the point?" asked Cody.

"I made it," said Ray.

Wham, thought Buddy.

Cody poured himself another three fingers. "What'd you say your name was?"

"Ray."

"Ray what?"

"Marks. I don't want to hear any more Jewish cracks."

"Why would you?"

"Those are the rules."

"Fair enough," said Cody. "Got a family? Wife? Kids?"

"Kid."

"No wife?"

"Divorced," said Ray.

"She mess around?"

"No way."

"Never?" asked Cody.

"Not 'til she caught me doing it," said Ray.

"Your wife got the kid?" Cody asked.

"Yeah," said Ray. "In Bhutan or Carmel or Sedona, wherever it is she went to find herself this month. I've got a housekeeper from Vietnam who takes care of him when he visits. An ex-boat person. Very grateful."

"Beholden," said Cody.

"Yeah."

"And cheap."

"More than she made in the rice paddy, pal," said Ray. "Now, what about you?" Cody shrugged. Ray kept at him. "I look at a guy like you, I say to myself, 'Who is this guy? Where'd he come from? What's he all about?'"

"You ever been to a motivational speaker?" asked Cody.

Ray said, "Only once."

"Zen?"

"I read a little," said Ray. "You?"

"What for?"

"Why'd you ask?"

"Just puttin' two 'n' two together."

"You ask a lot of questions, but you don't answer any."

"That's the way we are up here," said Cody. "We ain't Rome, but we got our ways."

Now Ray was pissed. "I got the feeling you're jerking me around," he said. "Why be a schmuck?"

Uh-oh, thought Buddy.

"Don't let it spoil your trip," said Cody.

"You guys ready to roll?" Ray asked Summer Joe and Buddy.

"Lock 'n' load, my man," said Joe.

Buddy looked like he wanted to stay. "I don't know," he mumbled.

Ray said, "Whatever. Joe?"

The two men started to leave, but Mel came in before they were three steps from the bar. When Cody spotted her, he got up and went to the john. His exit was obvious. It got to Mel—the unmitigated rudeness of it—it hurt her feelings—but she tried hard not to show it.

"Where have you been?" she said to Ray.

"What?" he asked, annoyed at the question.

"How long's a phone call take?" Mel shuddered when she heard herself, like some kind of shrew or something. "I was wonderin' what happened to you."

"Hey, babe," said Ray, "I didn't know I had to sign out. Tell me something: what's with that guy?"

"What guy?" asked Mel, not fooling anybody.

"The one who just turned his back on you," he said.

"Don't worry about it," said Mel. "You ready to go?"

Ray persisted. "How long have you known him?"

"Off and on," she said.

Summer Joe leaned over and whispered into Ray's ear, "First thing the cops learn about the rez: never get in the middle of a domestic dispute."

"Save your strength," advised Mel. "The guy don't bite."

"One weird mother," muttered Ray.

"Save it, I said," snapped Mel. Then, instantly realizing she overreacted, she said, "Listen, the guy's an artist. You know what they're like. He's sensitive."

"The problem with the goddamned artists," groused Ray, "is they forget other people are sensitive, too."

"He hurt your feelings?"

"I wouldn't go that far."

"Don't waste your energy," Mel went on. "You're gonna need

it. What're you here for, anyway, bear? Or some backwater stuff artist?" But Ray was unwilling to let it go.

"What is it with you two?"

"Which two?"

"You two."

"What is what?" asked Mel.

"You're not an item or anything like that?"

"Meaning?" asked Mel.

"Meaning is this getting to be some kind of problem?"

Mel grabbed a cheek of her ass in her hand. She never saw Cody walk back into the room. "See this ass, pal?" she said to Ray. "It's mine 'n' nobody else's. I run my own guide operation and nothin' gets in the way of that. The only problem we got is how we're gonna haul half a ton of grizzly back to your plane."

"That's the kind of talk I like," said Ray.

"It ain't talk," said Mel.

"I'm here for the action," Ray went on, "but I don't want any hassle with it. Bottom line is: I come to the woods to find a little peace and quiet. If you can't find peace and quiet in the boonies, where the hell are you going to find it? Am I right?"

"No, you're not," said Cody as he made his way back up to the bar.

"Back off, Cody," ordered Mel. "Let's get movin', Ray."

"I got something to tell your dude might save his life," Cody said.

"He don't wanna hear it, and neither do I," she said.

"Go ahead," said Ray. "What do you have to say?"

"Smart man," said Cody. "Peace 'n' quiet. I'm with you there. Silence in the woods is somethin' you hear very loudly. It's the loudest sound there, but, see, you really don't hear it too much, maybe two, maybe three times during the day. Dawn. Dusk. An hour before light. An hour before dark. You hear it then. It's when the beasts of the day and the beasts of the night take each other's place. If you're still, you can sense them passing through a kind of cease-fire zone as they exchange positions in the forest. So, y'see, it's nearly, but not absolutely, silent. There's still movement. Time goes by. The third silence is death. You can't deny it. I've seen predators stalk their prey. They don't necessarily carry death itself, but they carry the real possibility of it—death on the way, death to come—so they carry it in silence. That's why a man can sense an animal watching him. You can actually feel the silence. Animals leave the area or stay still as my mounts. A victim—taken prey—is death-in-fact, and that silence is deeper than any. All of a sudden, there's an absence of life in the forest. You can't not pay attention to it, it's so much there. This kind of silence—the third—isn't one of peace but anxiety, like a dark room when you're scared of what might be in it. Peace—the kind you're talking about—is only when the woods are filled with the noise that most people love and accept as quiet."

The barroom was silent until Ray said, "Thanks for the tip."

"Come on, Ray, how 'bout some sleep?" said Mel, taking him by the arm. Ray nodded and let her move him to the door when Buddy suddenly jumped off his bar stool and stopped them.

"Hold on a second," he said, "I ain't had a chance to pitch the man my story yet."

"What story?" asked Ray, really not wanting to hear.

"My blockbuster," said Buddy.

"Buddy," said Mel, "it's late."

"Five minutes," he yelped. "Ray. My man. Five minutes. Please. The profits from this picture will enable me to activate a lifelong dream."

"What's that?" asked Ray.

"I want to open up a German-Chinese restaurant," said Buddy.

"Good night, Buddy," said Ray, and turned back to the door.

"An hour later you're hungry for power," shouted Buddy, and cracked himself up. That stopped Ray. He couldn't help himself. It cracked him up, too.

"Okay, pitch me," he said. "You deserve five minutes for that one."

"Yeah. Fine. Great. Terrific," grumbled Mel.

"Five minutes," said Ray.

"Thanks, Mr. Marks," said Buddy. "You're a credit to your race."

Buddy grabbed an empty chair from behind a table and brought it over for Ray to sit on.

"Get comfortable," he said. "This is better than a bar stool." Buddy fussed over Ray as he settled him in the chair, then he cleared his throat, ran his hands through his hair, wiped his forehead with his wrist, and got started. "Here it comes. The pitch. It's a war story. About the little guys—privates, corporals . . . You don't hear about them, but they're the ones. We're off the coast of Korea. Inchon landing. I was just a kid in the Marines. Eighteen. Green. A couple of months out of PI."

"Parris Island," Summer Joe said to Ray, as if he needed the information.

"I got it," said Ray.

"Up until then it was just like a bunch of kids runnin' around playin' cowboys and Indians. Sorry, Joe, no offense meant."

"None taken," said Joe. Buddy continued.

"We'd seen newsreels and trainin' films of guys hittin' beaches. Men, y'know. Real Marines. Us, we was only kids, but come the war we found ourselves waitin' belowdecks in the hold of a troopship. We could hear the planes and battleships poundin' the beaches. Boom. Boom. I gotta guess everybody was nervous, but you didn't show it. It was still fine. I was with my pals, my buddies. They had pimples. They was makin' jokes. A lotta grab-ass. Then, this loud clanger clangs for us to come topside 'n' climb down the nets into the landin' craft below."

"LSTs," offered Summer Joe.

"Landing Ship, Tank," said Ray, smugly.

"You are the man," said Joe, and showed his appreciation by flashing Ray a thumbs-up.

Buddy continued. "When you went over the side and climbed down the nets, you had to time it just right. See, the water was real choppy, so the landing craft was banging against the troop-ship. You had to catch it when it was close to the mother ship's hull, or else the two hulls smashed together and, bam, you were roadkill. Anyway, this clanger sounds. We put out our smokes, shoulder our packs, put on our helmets. The drill was that you turned around and handed your rifle to the guy behind you who then attached it to your pack while you attached the rifle of the guy in front of you to his pack. Then, see, then, this amazing thing happened: I looked around and I don't see my buddies any-more. Their faces were hidden by their helmets. I saw Marines. Warriors. Us. Christ. It was real. A few more minutes and we could be dead. I remember thinkin' how lucky I was not to be one of the first guys off the landing craft. I don't know where they got the guts to do that. Every enemy gun was zeroed in on that ramp, and they all began firing the instant it started down. Men dead before they took a step. Guys get hit they curse God. They scream for their mothers. They shit themselves. Death ain't dignified. Somehow we got through it. Some of us. It was a time when right was right and wrong was wrong, and we had a job to do; a time, gentlemen, when honor was still in fashion."

Buddy clicked his heels together and placed his hand over his heart. Everybody in the Pingo Palace stood and did the same, even Ray, when he saw the others. Then, Buddy lifted both hands to his mouth and mimed a bugle, his thumb the mouthpiece, and "blew taps"—long and mournful and beautiful in its honesty, its pain, and its love. For a few seconds nobody in the place said a word. It was Ray who broke the silence.

"Nice story."

"Fifty-fifty. You 'n' me," said Buddy.

"Well," Ray hedged, "the story's a little long right now. Maybe it's thirty-five percent there. It needs shaping before—"

Buddy interrupted. "You're gonna produce it, right? What the hell, you can do whatever you want."

"Wise up, Buddy," said Cody. "He's not gonna do a thing."

"Hey, Ray," Buddy said, objecting, "tell him what you're gonna do."

"At the moment, the gentleman and I agree," said Ray.

"But I told you the story!" Buddy protested.

"Right," said Ray. "It was nice. But it's not a movie."

"Course it's not," said Buddy. "You haven't made it yet."

"Buddy, I told you," said Cody. "The man's not gonna—"

"Let him tell me!" yelled Buddy.

Ray sighed impatiently. "That's the trouble with dealing with people who aren't in the business. You've got to spell everything out for them."

"You think I'm stupid?" asked Buddy.

"Listen," said Ray, "it was a good story, but there are lots of good stories, lots of good war stories . . ."

Buddy got hostile. "I asked you a question."

"What?" said Ray coldly.

"You think I'm stupid?"

"Hell, no," said Ray, thinking he had to defuse the situation. "I don't think you're stupid, but let me ask you a question. Do you know what a high-concept is?"

"Yes," answered Buddy. "What?"

"It's what you need to make a picture," continued Ray. "A high-concept story."

"Meanin'?" Buddy wanted to know.

"I'll give you an example: a guy falls in love with a mermaid

who grows legs so she can come onto dry land and look for him."
Ray thought he had done a pretty good job with that one.

"Then what happens?" asked Summer Joe.

"He jumps into the water with her at the end, and they live
happily ever after," Ray finished up with a flourish.

"All right!" whooped Summer Joe.

Buddy pushed in between Ray and Summer Joe and got right
into Ray's face. "Who wants to hear a story about a fuckin' fish?
You Hollywood punks don't know dick about life. I'm talkin'
about real guys dyin', pal!"

"All right," said Ray, his patience at an end. "You want to
know the truth? Nobody gives a shit about Korea. Who the fuck
cares?"

"We died there," protested Buddy.

"What can you do, friend?" said Ray. "We've all got to die
somewhere."

Buddy became enraged, so furious he charged Ray, but Ray,
cool and disdainful, simply sidestepped and cruelly jammed Buddy with a mean dig to the ribs. Buddy gasped for air and dropped
on his ass like a sack of wet flour. Ray turned his back on him
without even looking to see where he had fallen.

"I've got to get some sleep," said Ray, and indicated for Mel
to go with him.

"Help him up," said Cody. But Ray ignored him. "I said,
'Help him up.'"

Ray looked at Mel. "You ready?" She made to follow him, but
Cody reached out and took her arm.

"Mel . . ." he started to say, but Mel pulled violently away—
"Get the fuck off me, asshole!"—and tried to follow Ray.

Cody took a skinning knife from his belt and jumped in between Ray and the door. The blade almost touched the skin at the
top of Ray's shirt, but not quite. There was power in Cody's voice.
Ray didn't move. "If you get that bear tomorrow, you don't want to
ruin your trophy. You're gonna want to know how to skin that bear

out right. This is how you do it." Cody kept the skinning knife in his left hand but used the fingers of his right as if they were the blade itself. He never actually touched Ray, but he drew the "blade" over Ray's body as he demonstrated. "Make a cut exactly three inches behind the center of the lower lip, then slice straight through the throat, the breast, all the way down to the tail. Watch you don't cut too deep into the organs, or you'll taint the meat. I'm certain you don't want to do that. Cut the legs from the inside of the feet to where you join the center cut at the groin. Gently turn the scrotum inside out and pop out the testicles. After that, it's just a matter of carefully peeling off the skin without tearing anything. You know what a bear looks like when you got it all skinned out?"

"No," said Ray.

Cody said to Mel, "You do, don't you?"

"Like a man," she said quietly.

"I don't have to put up with this shit," said Ray. "You coming?"

"In a minute," she said as he left. She turned on Cody. "My God, you can't stand to touch anything unless it's dead." Mel turned and rushed out after Ray.

Cody crossed to the bar stool, picked up the bearskin, and walked back to Buddy, who was struggling, both drunk and in pain, to get to his feet. Buddy shivered like an old dog. Cody wrapped him in the bearskin, guided him out the door, and helped him find his way home.

Summer Joe stayed put.

"How'd you get yourself invited to the party?" Sue wanted to know.

"A pure heart and a clear mind," replied Joe. "Hey, Sue, you know how to make a martini?"

"What're we celebrating?" asked Sue.

"Providence," said Joe.

"Does that mean you got the money for the drink?"

Summer Joe took a brand-new one-hundred-dollar bill from his pocket and slapped it on the bar.

"Make that drink a double," he said.

"Whoa," said Sue as she saw the money. "All I did was show him my tits, Summer Joe. What'd you do?"

"This, my dear Mel, is a two-thousand-dollar bottle of scotch," said Ray as he poured out two silver shot glasses of the stuff. They were sitting in the cockpit of his plane, where he'd suggested they go for something to take the edge off.

"I never spent that much money on a truck," said Mel, "let alone a drink."

"This is more than a drink," he said.

"I'll bite," Mel said.

"This is a dream made where smoke from the tip of a cigarette goes, an idea born as liquid magic, an elixir fashioned to smooth out the furrows in a fraught world."

"You're tryin' to be charming, aren't you?" said Mel.

"Yes. Yes, I am. I admit it."

"Well, you're pretty good at it," she said.

"You make it easy," he said, and lifted his glass in a toast. "Here's to you."

"Here's to me, too," Mel said, and took a sip. "The next sip's for you, and the next one's for your bear. Refill! Wow, that stuff goes down pretty."

"Let me sweeten it a little for you," said Ray and took a small vial of powder from under the seat.

"And that is?" asked Mel.

"A soupçon of Hollywood magic," he said, and tapped some into her silver glass. "Just a tad."

"To take the edge off," she said.

"Exactly. It helps the blood pressure."

"What's a young dude-alicious like you doin' with high blood pressure?" asked Mel. "Refill." Ray filled her shot glass a third time.

"It's a problem I have every time I sit next to a pretty lady."

"Oh, my God," shrieked Mel, delighted. "The guy just fed me a line. My first line from a Hollywood producer. That was a line, wasn't it?"

"Cross my heart," Ray said, and smiled.

"I thought so," giggled Mel. "I knew it, and I loved it anyway. Refill! Men like to think women get taken in by what they say. They don't. Ladies like style as well as the next guy. But don't ask me to join the mile-high club. That's too corny."

"Wouldn't dream of it," he said.

"You thought of somethin' better," she said. "Two-thousand-year-old scotch. Thank ya, Jesus!"

"Two-thousand-dollar," Ray corrected.

"Whatever," said Mel. "Hey, I hope there's not as many of you as I'm seein'. One's enough."

"One it is," he said. "Are you getting tired?"

"A little dizzy. Refill!"

"I don't think so," said Ray.

"You're just afraid I'm going to blow lunch in your cockpit, aren't you, Roy?"

"Ray."

"Uh-uh," she slurred. "I won't. Tell you what, though, you mind if I curl up under your arm for a couple of minutes?"

"Tired?" he asked.

"Two minutes is all," she mumbled, cuddled, and dropped off.

Mel was bigger than most of the women Ray knew, skinny things with fake tits, but what a range of movement they had!— un-fucking-believable. All those stretch classes at the gym. He didn't care if they were faking it. He was a performance junkie, and they were actresses, right? They got paid to fake it. Un-fucking-believable. Ray could lift one up under either arm, and sometimes he did. But Mel was more of a challenge. It took some pushing and shoving and twisting to get her limp body out of the narrow confines of his cockpit, and when he put her over his shoulder to carry her to her truck, there was no doubt about it, he knew she was there. Ray made a mental note to himself to work on his cardio a little more because, by the time he got Mel into the shotgun side, he was breathing hard. He managed to get the door shut before she fell out on him a second time.

Ray drove Mel's truck up to her front door, and with a fervent wish that Cody, that cocksucker, wouldn't see them, he managed to get Mel back over his shoulder and stagger up the steps. He had some trouble getting the door open, finally did, lugged Mel inside and dumped her on her bed. She sprawled but without so much as a twitch. Whew. He stretched out his back and thanked God he could still walk. That was when Ray realized Mel was supposed to sleep in her tent outside. No way did he want to lift her up and out again. Fuck it. He untied her boots and pulled them off, undid her belt, and worked her out of her jeans.

He was surprised to see that her panties were as pretty as they were. Ray figured her for waffle-weave thermals, basic white, but these, Lord, they looked like butterfly wings around her hips. Black trim. The crotch diaphanous gold. Interesting. More than interesting. He'd seen them before, and he knew just where, an exclusive lingerie shoppe in Beverly Hills on Rodeo Drive named La Perla. Laaaaa Perla. Ahhhh. The mere thought of it made him hard. Pricey but worth it. The panties were ninety-seven dollars. Ray knew because he bought them by the dozen for all the women in his life. Different colors, of course, in case they worked out at the same gym. This Mel Madden was a lady with secrets. *I wonder what's in her drawer,* he thought to himself as he walked over to her dresser and opened one. Under a layer of thermals and generic cotton underpants was a soft, sheer bra and thong set, periwinkle blue, and a flesh-colored camisole trimmed with white lace. He recognized each of them. The camisole alone was three-fifty. Ray looked down at Mel and smiled. You think you know somebody. He took off his boots, his trousers, then his shirt, and got into bed beside her.

Cody was on his second mug of coffee when he heard the first shot. It was barely light, and he had hardly slept. He tried hard to put words to what kept him tossing all night, what this stuff was that had him seething. It was like trying to catch smoke in his hand. He could see it. He could smell it. He could reach for it, but when he grabbed at it, it was no longer there. He was white water, class VI, boiling furiously down through narrow channels in the mountain. The hydraulics of chaos—wham, thump, scrape-the-rocks chaos. He was the mountain, too, and the narrow channels and all the rest of this shit storm with no safety valve, no place to shuck free. Cody heard a second shot, a third, a fourth, all heavy-caliber reports from a rifle somebody was firing at will.

Buddy rushed into Cody's shop and yelled, "Come on. Hur-ry up!"

"What's up?" said Cody.

"Mel. She's gone berserk. Get your ass down there!"

"Where?" asked Cody.

"The airstrip," yelled Buddy, already back out the door. "Somebody's gonna get killed!"

"I'll take the Bronco," Cody shouted.

They reached the airstrip in time to see Mel blow out one side of the windshield of Ray's plane. Most of Toehold was watching from the sidelines. Before Cody could reach her, she blew out the other half. Methodically, icily, with smooth Olympian aim, she had been taking Ray's plane apart, wheel by wheel, door handle by door handle, strut by strut. She ignored Cody as he ran over and yelled for her to cut it out, goddamnit! Breathe, squeeze, bam, let it surprise you, jack another round; breathe, squeeze, bam, jack another round . . .

"Mel, stop it!" yelled Cody, and tried to grab the rifle.

"Get your hands off me, you son-of-a-bitch," she yelled back.

"Don't start in on me, Mel, goddamnit!"

"That rat bastard left without me. The Indian took him."

"You know that for a fact?" asked Cody.

"Don't you fuckin' reason with me. I know what I know. Treacherous, muthafuckin' bastard!"

Cody tried to put his arm around her and gently wrest the rifle away, but Mel violently pulled away from him. "I've had enough of men puttin' their goddamn hands on me. Why didn't you do somethin', Cody? Why didn't you stop me?"

"I tried to," said Cody.

"What? You call that tryin'? What kind of tryin'? With that baseball game crap, that shit about my kid? Or when you gutted Ray Marks? What were you tryin' then?"

"I said don't start in on me, Mel."

"Oh, yeah? Who else am I gonna start in on? I got nobody else! I'm gonna track that lyin' scum down in Hollywood and put a bullet in his head. I'm gonna follow him to the studio, humiliate him in front of his big-shot friends, make that slime beg to live, and then I'm gonna shoot him anyway."

"Where's that gonna get you?" Cody wanted to know.

"Nowhere, which is exactly where I am," she answered. "Oh,

Cody, why'd this have to happen?" she asked plaintively, then, as
if she just remembered how angry she was, "Goddamnshitmuth-
afuckinshitfuckChristdamndamnshit . . ." She kicked a stone out
of the way. "Shit fuck damn it! What am I gonna do, Cody? I
could've gotten that bear good as anybody. What am I supposed
to do now? My plans. Everything."

"Lemme make you a cup of coffee," he said.

"Where do you suppose the fuel tank is?" she asked.

Cody pointed to a spot on the fuselage midway between the
wings and the tail. "Right about there," he said.

"That's what I was thinkin'," she said, and smiled. It was a
small, hurt smile, but still . . . Mel shouldered the rifle, aimed,
squeezed, and fired one more time. The 220-grain load tore into
the fuel tank, and Ray's airplane erupted into smithereens. A
lockbox filled with two hundred brand-new twenty-dollar bills
blew its hinges and flew through the roof of the cockpit. Two
hundred stiff twenties floated down toward the gawking townies.
Everybody cheered and leapt into the smoky air to snag as many
bills as they could with both hands before the money landed in
the mud.

"The just deserts of filthy lucre," said Cody. He and Mel
broke out laughing.

"You were sayin' somethin' about coffee?" she asked.

"It was gonna be warm in Hawaii," said Mel over coffee. It was
delicious. Cody had just received a new batch, a mixture the dealer
labeled Woodstock. The taste was intense and rich with a finish
like the first sip of a cup of hot chocolate. "I researched the whole
thing, sent away for maps, wrote the chamber of commerce—the

works. I really studied it—where the best volcano is that you can climb the rim and watch the sun come up like it was comin' out of its cone—I was gonna show her all this stuff. Theresa Louise Patricia Elizabeth Madden, and her mother, Mel. What a joke, huh? Except I had it all planned out. There's this one special forest, y'see, where they got nothin' but orchids. She might've got one orchid for her prom from some guy—maybe—but I was gonna give her a whole forest full. This same forest's got leaves big as truck tires, except they're soft. And there's even a place got magic mushrooms growin' right there on the ground to eat as you please, only that probably wasn't one of my better ideas seein' as how she's only sixteen. Hawaii, Maui, Oahu, Hilo, Lanai—they sound so nice, don't they? The water's so warm you could even take your clothes off like the natives do all the time. And you don't have to worry about gettin' jumped either. They understand things like that there. Imagine two ladies takin' off their clothes in the Bering Strait. If they didn't freeze to death the guys would be on their bones like a pod of killer whales.

"I gotta watch out for her. She's the same age I was when I had her. Her father—my so-called boyfriend—no, that's not right, he really was my boyfriend—I loved him. He was a jockey from Montana, said he raced quarter horses, not that you actually ride quarter horses, he told me, more like you just hang on. I was a kid. I believed anything. But I'm sure it was true. Anyway, what he was doing hangin' around a high school in Tucson I never knew except maybe it wasn't racing season. I knew he was a jockey, though, 'cause he was a little guy—not a wimp at all but little like barbed wire's little as opposed to rope—and he had real strong hands. He held me and I couldn't get away, not that I wanted to, I didn't. He told me all about huntin' gold in the Amazon and racing Arabians in the desert, and he did the best card tricks I ever saw. He was a lot older, too, like about thirty, thirty-five, but he was real nice to me all the time is the truth, so what difference did that make? I might've just been a little girl when he made love to me, but I liked it a lot, and he never made me do nothin' I didn't want to do until I was ready. That was somethin' my own mother and everybody else didn't understand—how I could have liked it. What was I supposed to do? Hate it? He was always gentle.

"One day, he came to me and told me the police or somebody was after him, so he was gonna have to go back to Montana and lay low for a while, but if I wanted to come with him, he'd be waitin' for me on the corner when I got out of school. Well, he wasn't on the corner, and I never saw him again, except I was pregnant. It'll probably happen to her, too—you know, Theresa Louise. What makes me think I can stop it? Anyways, I actually did see the baby for a little while—me 'n' her 'n' my old lady. I wanted to be her Mom, take care of her, but she wouldn't let me. Oh, Christ, yeah, sure, I could empty the diaper bucket, wash bottles, go to the store, but I couldn't decide what color dress to put on her or play her the music I wanted or even what to feed her, so that was more like bein' a maid, if you think about it. I'll tell you something: the day you realize your own mother hates you, I mean really hates you, not just pissed all the time but true, deep, and burning, the day that finally sinks in is a day to reckon with. I think the old lady took my baby so she could make me over, except not me, the baby, if you know what I mean. She told the court I was promiscuous. Not me. I was lookin' for love because I liked it so much. Then, I stopped lookin'. Then I just fucked around. Then, I ran away from home. What a mess!" Mel took a sip of her coffee. "What'd you put in here?" she asked appreciatively.

"Cinnamon," said Cody.

"Great," said Mel.

"Sometimes I sneak in a little chocolate. Want some?"

"I'm fine with this," she said, then reconsidered. "Okay, maybe a little, you sweet-talkin' daddy you." She was glad Buddy wasn't there, and she hoped he'd stay away. The two of them having coffee in the morning. She liked that. It helped to settle her.

"Thataway," said Cody. "Don't let yourself get so down." He took a golden box of Godiva chocolates from its hiding place on the shelf behind cans of paint and glue.

"When you say chocolate, you ain't just battin' your gums," she said.

"The miracle of mail order," said Cody, and plunked a truffle into each of their cups.

"Let me guess," Mel said. "Your momma used to put those little tiny marshmallows into your hot chocolate when you were a baby boy." She laughed at the thought. Cody reached back onto the shelf and took out a bag of miniature marshmallows. "I don't believe it," she gasped. "Obviously, there's a lot about you I don't know."

"One, two, three, or four?" he asked.

She held up four fingers. "In for a nickel, in for a dime," she said, and toasted him. "Here's to pounds and pimples." They clicked mugs.

Neither said a word for a while as they drank and savored Cody's concoction. How did that song go? "You say it best when you say nothin' at all"? Well, Cody should have paid more attention to the lyrics, but instead he said, "What do you say we forgive and forget? I can if you can, Toots." The instant his words were out, something clicked for Mel. She didn't know for sure what it was. She was pretty sure, but not completely sure. The fullness of the moment had snapped in two, and she had to figure this out. So she stopped sipping and said nothing. Cody, unaware of the set of her jaw, went on. "Maybe we don't always agree on what's best, but I was pulling for you, anyway. Bottom line: have what you want." He toasted her and took another sip.

It wasn't his words exactly. It was more like where those words were coming from that smacked Mel like a two-by-four clean between the eyes. "I don't believe you," she said.

"What do you mean you don't believe me?"

"I mean I don't believe you," she said. "That's what I mean.

Let me spell it out for you. *I don't fucking believe y-o-u,* you." She jabbed her finger into his chest.

"Don't," he said, stung, turned his back on her, retreated to his workbench.

"You're lyin' to the both of us." Mel was astonished as it all became clear, at least, came clear to her. "I've always trusted you, Cody, but goddamn if I do right now. Actually, right now I think you're chock-full of shit."

He busied himself organizing the tools that were out, shifting them around, doing it again. "Good," he said. "I got work to do."

Mel hounded him. "You set me up. It's so clear."

"Set you up? Are you kidding?" said Cody. "You set yourself up. I was the one who tried to stop you, remember? I spotted that guy for a bad actor the minute he walked in here."

"So why were you rooting for me to pull it off?" she badgered.

"Because it's what you wanted, goddamnit! Why else would—"

She cut him off. "Buster, you made sure you sandbagged me."

"Know what? This is lunacy. You're fuckin' delusional. And I got beaucoup work to do," he said, and began organizing a tray of glue bottles, brushes, and paint pots, anything to shut Mel out.

"Is that what you told your wife?" she asked.

"I want you outta here." Cody picked up the tray and started for the storeroom.

"The hell I will," she yelled, and kicked the tray out of his hands. Water, glass, paint—everywhere.

"Are you out of your mind?" Cody was incensed. "Look at the mess you made!" Mel was unstoppable.

"You think this is a mess? Watch. I'll show you a mess," she said, and started to tear the place apart. She pulled skins off the shelves, overturned containers, toppled mounts . . .

"Don't touch those!" he hollered, grabbed her, and bodily threw her across the room. She stopped herself by grabbing the counter, spotted the Black & Decker coffeepot, and before Cody could stop her, she heaved it against the wall. The carafe burst, and coffee dribbled down the pine wood as if it were bleeding.

"Not so neat and tidy in here anymore, is it?" said Mel.

Cody grabbed her and pushed her toward the door. "You get the hell out of here," he said.

Instead of leaving, however, she slammed shut the bolt and turned on him defiantly. "No way, Jack," she said. He tried to push her aside and undo the bolt, but Mel dug in and wouldn't be moved. "We're gonna have it out right now," she said, and Cody knew she meant it.

"Okay," he said, squaring off with her. "Let's do it!" Then Cody really opened up. "I'm good and goddamn tired of you comin' in here bitchin' and moanin' all the time, askin' for advice and never takin' it, making a mess out of your life and expectin' me to wipe up after you. I'm tired of it, you hear me? You're a loser!" On that one, Mel hauled off and hit him, but Cody deflected the blow with his arm. She stayed right on him.

"Tell me somethin' I don't know," she yelled, and backed him up. "Let's see if you can fight. Let's see if you can bleed," she hollered.

"Mel, get off me!" yelled Cody as he slapped her punches away. She did not back up.

"Saint Cody," she said. "Mr. Perfect. Mr. Sensitivity. Mr. Forgiveness. St. Nothin'." Cody retreated behind his workbench and kept it between the two of them.

"You don't want forgiveness?" he said. "Fine. You'll get nothin' the next time you need me."

Mel gave it right back. "Who the hell are high-'n'-mighty you to sit up on your throne and forgive anybody? You? Forgive me? For what? You want to hear the truth? I'd rather have somebody fuck me and fly away than fuck me and make out like it never happened, especially if the son-of-a-bitch was good at it."

That did it. That was the one. Cody exploded and slammed Mel so hard she staggered sideways.

"That's not exactly what I had in mind," Mel said as she wiped away a trickle of blood from her mouth with the back of her hand. "But now we're gettin' somewhere, and that's what matters."

Cody was instantly sorry. He wanted to cut off his hand, but he knew he'd smack her again if Mel stayed on him. He had reached his breaking point. She had pushed him and pushed him and finally he'd lost it. "Mel . . ." He meant to say "I'm sorry" but Mel quashed it.

"A little blood never hurt anybody," she said. "The weird thing about this joint is there's never any blood and guts anywhere. Other stuff artists, you walk into their shops, you know somethin' was once alive, somethin' once bled, somethin' one time felt somethin'."

"I feel." Cody hated the way he sounded.

"Feel *me*, goddamnit, me, feel me," said Mel. "All these years, I thought you were wonderful. I thought your wife must've been crazy for not hangin' on. But what was she supposed to hang on to? You weren't there. You went into the boonies, and she went out on tour. Who deserted who? You were already gone, you asshole."

"Stop it, Mel, stop it." No way. She would not be shut down.

"Maybe I am a loser. Maybe Buddy's a loser, too. What's that make you?"

"Goddamnit, shut up!"

"Cody's place—the end of the world and the end of the line. Face it, buster. You need us."

"Like I need fucking brain cancer," Cody said.

"Don't kid yourself, pal. We make you feel alive." Mel finished speaking and unbolted the door. "How's my lipstick?" she asked, turning back.

"Who cares about your goddamn lipstick?" yelled Cody.

"My date," Mel said.

"What're you talking about?"

"He's big 'n' hairy 'n' his breath smells," she said.

"You're not," he said incredulously.

"Watch me," she said, and walked out the door. Cody followed her.

"You dumb shit," he yelled.

Mel pointed over his right shoulder. "Look at that," she said, and when Cody looked, she clocked him with a hard right. "She may be dumb," said Mel, "but she's got quick hands."

No place was too far away, no mountain too high, no glacier too cold. She would hunt them down to the ends of the Earth if that's what it took. Ray Marks, the sleaze, with his Hollywood magic dust, and his partner in crime, Summer Joe, that third-world son-of-a-bitch. Joe had cut in on her dance. He thought he was so nimble, that crap artist, but when she got through with him he'd be lucky to be able to lie down without holding on. Mel would track them down, and once she did, they'd be in shit so deep the good Lord couldn't dig them out with a backhoe. They had the better part of a day on her, and Ray had taken her map. So what? It didn't matter. Mel had memorized the terrain long before, and she didn't intend to stop until she caught up with them, the scum.

Midafternoon found Mel in her canoe on the river paddling with the steady pull of a galley slave. In her mind this big, fat, sweaty barbarian with hair growing out of his ears was beating rhythm on an oversize pigskin drum. With every beat she pulled, and with every pull, she closed the distance between her and "them." The enemy. Her quarry. Them. They were no longer human. As far as she was concerned, they were traveling in a free-fire zone and didn't know enough to get down. They didn't have to. She did. But Mel didn't want this to be any long-range deal. She wanted it up close and personal. Summer Joe first. He was a nuisance, a prelim before she got to the featured attraction himself—Ray Marks. Summer Joe would cave easy. She was pretty sure of that. But big Ray, big bad Ray, he might be a challenge. He had never had to trade his hind parts for a pack of cigarettes, though she really didn't know that Joe had ever done such a thing, either. But he had been in prison, and you did hear rumors, and she wished him only the worst. Mel was a Fury on a black ops mission, a Fiend who drank the blood of her enemies from a skull, a one-woman Holy War. Out of her way! No mercy, hombre, no mercy.

It was nearly sunset when Mel took the small raft through a chute of frothing white water. Soon it would be too dark to mess with any more major hydraulics. Time to put in. Mel had just about done all the river she needed, anyhow. The rest of the way would be on foot. She raised the paddle above her head as a sign of victory. "Yes! Woman!" she cried in triumph, and made for shore. Once there, she unloaded, and overturned the raft to dry. She shouldered her pack, picked up her rifle, and walked inland toward the great, red, setting sun—a small, solitary figure making her way across an endless expanse of land. The darkness, when it came, came on quickly. It shouldn't have come as a surprise, but it always did. Mel remembered something she once read that Muhammad Ali had said, a boast: "I'm so fast I can turn off the bedroom switch and be in bed before the light goes out!" She laughed to herself. He was a beauty, that Ali. She wished she could have watched him fight live, at ringside. That would have been something to see. She remembered how exhausted and relieved he was after Joe Frazier couldn't get off his stool for the fifteenth round: "That was as close to death as I've ever come," Muhammad said. That Ali. People thought he was crazy and maybe he was, but the point was he defied them all and never gave up, just like she was doing.

Mel stopped where she was for the night and built a small fire. She always carried three or four commercial starter sticks with her and refused to feel guilty because she couldn't make a fire with just two pieces of wood. Fuck it. Nobody else could, either. When the fire was doing well enough on its own, she laid a couple of strips of dried salmon belly across the flames and waited for them to sizzle. The oil oozed out of the rich, orange flesh and permeated the air. She boiled up some tea in a camping cup she also carried, laced it with lots of sugar from a Ziploc bag, leaned back against her pack, and watched the belly strips cook. The salmon was so fat and oily that it didn't take very long. The aurora borealis shimmered and shifted above her as she gnawed the strips of fish.

The lights gave a greenish tinge to the air around her. She thought it must be what soldiers see through night vision goggles. Tomorrow night would be a full moon. She wondered at how simple it all seemed! Somewhere out there a wolf began to howl. Mel threw back her head and howled back.

When she finished eating she took three round stones that she had plucked from the river and tied them together with lengths of rawhide. After that, she spread her sleeping bag out on a caribou hide. *My little visitor is late this month,* she thought.

Probably the strain I've been under. It certainly couldn't be because of anything else. Probably a good thing, right? What made Cody such a goddamn expert, anyway? And with that as her final thought of the day, Mel fell asleep.

"Pussy," said Summer Joe.

"What about it?" asked Ray.

"Let's talk about it," said Joe.

Summer Joe put another log on the fire as Ray shook out his sleeping bag.

"All right," said Ray. "Talk about it."

"I hear it's pretty easy down there in Hollywood."

"I guess it is," said Ray.

"You don't have much trouble, I bet," said Joe.

"Let me tell you something my father once told me, a very important thing," said Ray. "He said never talk about what you do with a woman. Nobody's going to believe you, anyway, and if you don't talk about it, they're going to think you get even more than you do."

"So you don't have much trouble," said Joe.

"Why be modest? We're family, right? I guess I don't."

Summer Joe wanted to know if it was true that Donald Sutherland and Julie Christie really did it in this movie. Joe hadn't seen it, and he couldn't remember its name. Ray told him that you hear all kinds of rumors, but that, yes, things on the set could get pretty raw. Summer Joe was on a roll. He told Ray that he'd heard Errol Flynn used to put cocaine on the tip of his war club to keep it hard. Was that true? he wanted to know. Ray said, "Could be."

"I also heard," offered Joe, "that he liked to take it up the chocolate speedway."

"What?" said Ray.

"The old tunnel of love," explained Summer Joe. "The guy swang both ways. You didn't know that?"

"I guess I don't have my ear to the ground as much as you do," said Ray.

"Oh, yeah," said Joe. "It can get pretty raw down there. It can get pretty raw up here, too, y'know. Ever hear of a hum job?"

"I don't think I have, no," said Ray, feeling he was about to find out.

"It's when a lady takes your balls in her mouth and hums," explained Joe. "I once had one in Juneau hum 'The Star-Spangled Banner.' She was a super patriot. You oughta try it sometime."

"Any other tips for me, Joe?"

"Just a question," said Joe.

"You promise to get me that bear tomorrow?"

"I do," said Joe, "I solemnly do."

"One more question," agreed Ray.

"All those starlets," Summer Joe asked, "they go down on you, right? I mean hum job or not."

"That's been my experience, yes," said Ray.

"Do they swallow?"

"I make them swallow," said Ray in a tone of voice that was chilling, even to Summer Joe who, nonetheless, wanted to know, "How?"

"Trade secret," said Ray.

"Seriously," said Joe.

"How serious can it be, my friend?" asked Ray. "We're not talking quantum physics here."

"Still," said Joe, persisting, "it's a subject I care deeply about."

"That bear's as good as mine, right?" asked Ray.

"Every hair," answered Summer Joe.

"All right," said Ray, warming up to the subject. "I'll let you in on it. Get them really hot."

"I got that part," said Joe.

"Put your tongue in their belly buttons as you slowly peel off their panties. Go down on them first thing. Bitches love it, and you've got them right away. They trust you. They're into it. Then get them to go down on you. They think it's all part of the gestalt."

Summer Joe didn't get that gestalt business, but it sure sounded fun.

"You know, foreplay," explained Ray. "You do something; they do something. Back and forth. Equal rights. Get her thinking you're almost ready to move on to the next step, and just when she does, you roll the cunt over, pin her shoulders to the bed, and slam it home. Don't worry. She'll swallow."

"Wow," said Summer Joe, uncharacteristically lost for words. "You Hollywood guys really play hardball."

"It's a rough town. Lots of scripts to read. Not much time for the amenities," said Ray. "Why don't we pack it in?"

"Sure," said Joe, but as he lay there waiting for sleep he thought, *This mother is really a prick. What the hell, though, it's just business. A bear for him, cash money for me. Business. Fuck it. I don't have to sleep with the guy.* A few feet away from him, Ray had already started to snore. *Any bitch can stand that must be deaf,* thought Joe.

The next day Mel found the wrapper to a Snickers bar and figured the two men must've taken a break here. *You greedy bastard,* she thought. *You even helped yourself to my stash.* There was still a bite left, too, so she hated him all over again for wasting the one luxury in her dismal life, and then she hated herself for indulging in all that self-pitiful muck. Just because her life had turned into a mud bath was no reason for wallowing in it, right? Right? Or was it? *Uh-uh. Don't go there, girl. Keep your eye on the prize.* Think of Ray's hide nailed to the barn door. That kept her going. She was close. She could smell blood. She was . . . da da da dum . . . the *Avenger!* Pumped, Mel kept her eyes on the ground looking for sign. When she came to an old campfire, its ashes still wet from the water poured on them, Mel knew, when this night finally fell, that vengeance would be hers.

The moon appeared, and with it the northern lights. Coral and golden, they pulsed in and out depending on when the cloud cover hid the moon. She thought of a poem she learned in school—likely the only thing she did learn—where the moon was a ghostly galleon—something like that—sailing across a turbulent sea. Mel watched the moon dipping in and out of the clouds and marveled at what a wondrous picture the poet had come up with. He was anonymous, but wait a minute, if "he" was anonymous, why couldn't he be a "she"? Why automatically jump to conclusions? *They got us brainwashed from birth,* she thought to herself. *Now, it's payback. Vengeance is mine, sayeth the Mel.*

Way out there in the distance she could see a pinpoint of light flickering on the ground, as if a star had fallen to Earth. The coral from the aurora had now taken on a deeper hue, which made staring across the terrain like looking through an infrared lens. Mel homed in on that flickering pinpoint of light, moving only when the clouds covered the moon. Two men sat around a campfire, with no idea they were being hunted, no idea that she was out there, and Mel intended to keep it that way. They would know the minute she wanted them to know and not a second before. She crept closer. From fifty yards she could see them clearly. Summer Joe laughed. It sounded phony like the way you do when a joke's not really funny. *Laugh now,* she thought, and hunkered down in the darkness to wait for them to sleep.

Three a.m. Time to move out. Mel had seen the two men crawl into their sleeping bags, and there had been no other movement from them for hours. Take your time, girl. Don't blow it. She crept closer. Which one was making such a racket? Jesus, it was awful! Mel chose to see it as a blessing in case she stepped on a twig or kicked a rock by accident, but damn, it was loud. The fire threw a small circle of light. Mel stopped, stretched prone, watched, and waited in the darkness just beyond it. So Ray was the bull-roarer in the outfit! Oh, wow, was it obnoxious! Honk, snort, wheeze, rattle, gulp, buzz, blam, honk. . . . All that noise made the inside of her head feel like a hard break on a rack of billiard balls. She'd love to stuff a sock in his mouth, but Mel had plans for Ray and she preferred to savor them. The man was in for a rude awakening. Oh, yeah.

Under cover of a particularly loud bleat that sounded more like an elephant than anything else, Mel crept forward. Ray slept on the far side of the fire. Summer Joe was the closest, just the way she hoped he would be. She crawled closer until she could touch him, then closed her hand over his mouth. Joe woke up, immediately saw the knife at his throat, and froze.

"Hi," said Mel. He started to struggle, but Mel whispered,

"Be smart for a change. You move or make a single sound before I tell you, I'll carve a smile in your throat like a pumpkin." Joe froze. "Now," she whispered. "this hunt's history as far as you're concerned. Start walkin'." Joe mumbled something. "What'd you say?" she asked and warned him, "Whisper."

"I need my boots," said Summer Joe.

"Crawl on your belly like a reptile, sport. Crawl very, very far away. If I see you out here again I'm gonna make General Custer seem like a friend of the family."

"Those boots cost good money," he protested.

"So does a funeral. Move it out."

He reached for his rifle. She pulled him back.

"How 'bout my rifle?"

"Jack out the rounds," she said.

"Everybody's playin' hardball these days," Joe grumbled and did what he was told.

"Crawl, muthafucker," she said, and he did.

Ray woke as it broke daylight. "Come on, Joe," he said. "Time to saddle up." He looked over to where Summer Joe should have been. *Uh-oh. Her!*

Mel said sweetly, "Ain't it a shock to the system to go to bed with one person and wake up with somebody else?"

"What do you want?" Ray asked.

"A deal's a deal, Ray. If I were with the mob, you'd be sleepin' with the fishes. *Capisce?*"

"Where's Summer Joe?" Ray wanted to know.

"Gone," said Mel, as she took her hat from her head and held it over her heart.

"You didn't . . ." gasped Ray.

"I did," said Mel.

"Killed him?"

Mel used her finger to make a cut across her throat from ear to ear. "History is full of injustice," she said. "Get over it."

"I don't want anything to do with you," he said, clearly shaken.

"I'm what you've got," said Mel.

"Forget it." Ray went for his rifle, but Mel whipped out the bolo she had made with the round rocks and rawhide, and caught him around the ankles. Ray went down, and Mel was on him. She straddled him, pinning his shoulders with her knees.

"It's very important," she went on evenly, "that you see our relationship from the proper perspective, Ray. We got a deal. I'm gonna come through, and you're comin' with me, or I'm gonna commence to break every bone in your thoroughly despicable body."

Credit where credit is due. Mel had to give it to him: the man could walk. Ray's body might've been store-bought, but it was in good condition. Much of the tundra was a hard, punishing terrain to cross, especially the vast fields of hummocks, which, if you took them personally, were devised by the Creator, along with pingos and frost boils, as punishment for your sins. Hummocks were the size of human heads, thousands of them, on cylindrical bases each a foot high, surrounded by damp crevices caused by Summer melt that eroded and enlarged them. What made them (again, if you are so inclined) the product of a Divine Malevolence was that they moved and shifted when you stepped on them, making it damn near impossible to keep your balance. In a field of hummocks there was no such thing as solid ground. You could step in between them, but that's like being a football player in training camp who has to hop and run through tires. By now, Mel was used to them and could move through them with relative ease, but when she first came into the country she found herself praying for a steep mountain to climb because there, at least, she'd be on solid rock. Ray was determined, and he didn't complain. Mel guessed making movies was tougher than she thought. The man had stamina.

Every so often they would stop and glass the surrounding countryside looking for bear. Once they spotted a nice-sized specimen with a chocolate hide on a hillside a mile away. That would have taken a stalk, and even though the wind was right and the big bear didn't seem to be in much of a hurry, they'd be lucky to find him still there by the time they were in position for a shot. Mel was pretty certain it was a boar because of its size. Ray wanted to go for it, but she said no. It would have been well worth the stalk had it been the sun bear, but it wasn't.

"Why not?" he asked in exasperation. "It's big enough."

"You're not the kind of guy who wants 'big enough,' Ray," said Mel. "You want the biggest. That one's just a cocker spaniel compared to the one I've got in mind."

"You're looking for a bonus," said Ray.

"Yes, sir, I am," said Mel.

Later the same afternoon they had to cross a seriously boiling river. The current was enough to knock them off their feet were it not for an old spruce tree that had fallen across the river. Mel half expected to see Ray sit on his butt, straddle the log, and scoot across, but he took it on two feet with barely a wobble. *Nice one*, she thought grudgingly.

They rested on the other side of the river. It was too noisy to talk so they simply sat there as the roar of the water wiped all thought from their minds. After a while Mel became aware of movement other than the water not twenty yards downstream from where she sat. She saw it through a spray and her first re-action was to shake herself out of what she thought must have been a dream. But it was not a dream. It was one of those mo-ments in the wilderness that seem so wondrous they couldn't possibly be true, that catapult you into a one-one-thousandth of a second glimpse of a world not yours alone, which goes on whether you are in it or not, a dimension to which the word *behold* applies.

A silver-tipped sow was trying to cross the river with two young cubs. The little ones were frightened and hung back on the shore, but one at a time, she nudged them into the water and guided them across. First she took one, then returned for the other. When all three of them were safely on the far shore, the sow shook herself like a big wet dog and led her cubs into an alder thicket where the three were soon hidden from view. Mel was so taken with what she had witnessed that she had forgot-ten to nudge Ray. When finally she turned to him, she knew he had not seen what she had, and she was genuinely sorry for that.

"C'mere," she said. Mel was hunkered down checking out some bear tracks on a sandbar further downriver. Ray joined her and squatted down for a better look. "See how clear they are?" she pointed out. "He was standin' here havin' a drink when he caught our wind. Look here," she said, following the tracks. "This is where he wheeled around. This is where he ran. See how the wet dirt's tossed up? Put your hand in there." Ray placed his hand in one of the tracks. The track was more than twice its size.

"Big," he said.

"Not as big as the sun bear, buster," said Mel. "I'm talkin' starting team here, son, not sixth-round draft choice."

"I gotta see this beast," said Ray.

"Keep the faith," said Mel. "Let's go."

They moved off and continued to follow the shoreline, unaware that the scrub willow alongside the tracks had begun to rustle with something of great size moving through it. Two enormous, golden-haired forelegs emerged from the scrub, followed by the rest of him. He padded over to the set of tracks, sniffed them, snorted, popped his jaws, huffed. His nose was as big as a football. He lifted his head and tested the air downriver, then stepped into the first bear's paw print and dwarfed it.

Later on that afternoon, when it was nearly time to stop for dinner, Mel and Ray spotted a big, fat, snow-white arctic hare hopping upright on its hind legs. The tips of its ears were black. Other than that it was spotless.

"What's that rabbit on?" asked Ray.

"It's not a rabbit. It's a hare," said Mel.

"Looks like a rabbit to me," said Ray.

"Rabbits are born blind and naked," she explained. "Pretty near the most helpless things you ever saw. These guys got fur, good eyes, and can run almost as soon's they're born. The other point is rabbits don't hop on two legs like that."

"Weirdest thing," said Ray.

It was hopping along a good fifty yards away when Mel snapped off a shot and put one right smack through the rodent's head. Ray's jaw dropped.

"Remind me not to get you mad," he exclaimed.

"You already did," said Mel.

"Remind me not to do it again," said Ray.

Mel had the hare skinned and cooking before ten more minutes had passed. They had both worked up such huge appetites that every shred that could be eaten was. Mel gnawed the last piece of meat off the last bone and tossed it in the fire.

"So much for Thumper," she said.

"Tasty," said Ray.

"Liar," said Mel.

"Just trying to be friendly, Sunshine."

"Don't," she said. "You've been too damn friendly already."

"I have?" he asked, surprised.

"Be coy with me, buster, and you'll wind up like that rabbit," said Mel.

"Hare," he corrected.

"Smart fuck."

"What are you talking about?" He seemed genuinely at a loss. "Of what am I accused?"

"Of fucking without a license." Mel threw the words at him.

"Honey, I have this gut feeling that we're not on the same page," said Ray.

"Don't call me 'honey'!" she snapped.

"Fair enough," he said.

"You slipped me some damn date rape drug, carried me back to my bed unconscious, and did me in my sleep."

"I did not," protested Ray.

Mel put on the pressure. "You didn't give me some drug?"

"I did."

"Carried me back to my bed?"

"Yes."

"And—"

"No," Ray interrupted. "That I did not do."

"Then who the hell took off my jeans?"

"I wanted you to be comfortable!"

"You were just bein' considerate," Mel said sarcastically.

"Believe it or not," said Ray, "I have my moments."

"Why'd you gimme that drug?"

"To knock you out."

"Uh-huh. Why?"

"So I could go out with Summer Joe. Sleazy, but I admit it."

"Why'd you carry me back to my bed?"

"I thought it was the decent thing to do."

"And you expect me to believe—"

Again, Ray interrupted. "Check for evidence." That stopped her. "Well, did you?"

Mel went through the steps: "My jeans were off. I was in bed. I was unconscious . . ."

"But nobody took advantage."

"I'm supposed to roll over and believe you, just like that?"

"You've got satellite TV up here. Check out *Forensic Files*. You need proof, and in order to have proof, you need evidence. Got any? I really don't see how you could. There was nothing carnal between us."

"I'm not even good enough to diddle in my sleep? Is that what you're sayin'?"

"I'm saying I respect you too much as a woman."

"You are so full of shit."

"Maybe. Probably. But not right this minute."

"What about my stash of Snickers bars?"

"Guilty. I took your Snickers but not your knickers."

Mel didn't think it was anywhere near funny.

Mel lay awake on the other side of the smoldering campfire. Except for the occasional honk and snort, Ray didn't do too much snoring. *Thank God,* thought Mel. *Maybe I can actually get some sleep.*

In truth, Mel preferred to sleep outside rather than in, saw no need for a tent and never carried one. Why, she reasoned, when a person was in the midst of so much natural luxury, would she want to be encased inside a polyethylene bag? She wouldn't be any safer inside where she couldn't see, would she? Mel wanted to be out there. If something was going to get her, well, come on, then, let's have at it right here in the open. She wasn't about to whale around blindly in a tent.

Before Mel fell asleep she thought about Theresa Louise, as she always did. *How many sixteen-year-old girls have a mother who's hunting a bear so they could have a nice place to live?* The oddest thing: Mel felt more confident hunting a bear than she did about being a mother. She practically never had one herself, so what did she know? Esther Nanachuk told her there wasn't but three things a mother had to do: keep 'em dry, keep 'em full, and love 'em like there wasn't nothin' more important in this wide world. The first two were the hard parts. The third one was as automatic as air, said Esther. Maybe for Esther, Mel thought at the time, but there's a helluva lot of women with kids who don't feel that way. The bars were full of them. What was that country song? "You picked a fine time to leave me, Lucille. With four hungry children and a crop in the field." Suppose she was like Lucille, one of them? Mel was pretty sure most of them didn't start off with a plan to be evil. She was pretty sure they probably couldn't help it, not that this was an excuse, but still, there it was. What made Mel think she was qualified? Well, nothing. That was the point. She wasn't even so sure she could pick Theresa Louise out in a crowd. Even a goddamn seal could pick out her pup in a crowd, and every damn seal looked like every other damn seal, and there were thousands of them, hundreds anyway. The high hundreds.

So how was she supposed to take home a sixteen-year-old girl whose hormones were probably going kablooey and whom Mel hadn't seen in fifteen years and ten months? Mel might be able to feed her and keep her dry (though she figured—hoped—that wouldn't be a problem), give her a roof and a bed, but could she make this kid feel like she was home when Mel didn't know what that felt like herself? Then what would happen if she did somehow love this kid but the kid didn't love her back? That would certainly suck big-time.

She didn't want to think about this anymore. She wanted to go to sleep, but, shit, she couldn't. *Let me think about the good stuff,* Mel said to herself. Let's see. First tooth was out. First step was out. First birthday. First day of school . . . This could get depressing. Anxiety racked her system like a bout of yellow fever.

Mel had finally fallen asleep, but she was asleep only a short while when something woke her. It wasn't agonizing about Theresa Louise. It was something else, but she was foggy and couldn't quite get at what. Remember those old-fashioned radios when you turned them on but nothing happened until the tubes warmed up? She saw one once in a science museum. Well, that's what Mel felt like. She had been turned on, but her tubes hadn't yet warmed up. Something brushed against her sleeping bag. Mel groaned and turned away in annoyance, but it happened again. There was heavy breathing. She opened her eyes. Something nuzzled the back of her head. Was that shifty son-of-a-bitch at her again? She almost bought his bullshit. Goddamn him!

"Listen to me, you son-of-a-bitch," she growled as she turned to face him. But, oh, my God good Jesus, it was the bear, the sun bear, the golden one! Ray was still asleep on the other side of the campfire. The bear was inches from her face. Its breath was hideous. Its mouth was open and it seemed to be smiling. Mel wondered if this was the moment of her death. She froze. She ached to roll over into a fetal position, protect her organs, cover her head, but she was too terrified to move, and anyway, a sudden move like that might provoke an attack. Stay still. Freeze. Except every fiber in her body said run.

The bear nuzzled her face, licked it. She thought she would puke but hoped she wouldn't. Too sudden a move. Its tongue felt like the sandpaper you'd use to strip a floor, and, oh God, it stank. She prayed. *Don't kill me, please, don't kill me.* The bear popped its jaws. His saliva fell on her face. He popped his jaws again, but backed off with a huff. Mel stared after him, willing herself to be still, to do what her body screamed not to do, knowing movement was almost certain to bring pain, and, maybe, death. The great bear left her to circle Ray, then went to the edge of the campsite, turned, stared at her, snorted, and ambled back into the darkness. Mel looked over at Ray. He was still asleep.

"Hey," said Mel as she shook him by the shoulder. "Ray, wake up."

"Wha'?" he mumbled, still groggy with sleep.

"You had a bad dream," she said.

"What're you talking about?" he asked, confused.

"Check it out," said Mel. She unzipped his sleeping bag. "Come on. Get out. I want to show you something."

Ray squirmed out of his bag. "It's still dark," he protested.

"Get your flashlight," she said. He did. "Take a look, sport." Mel pointed to the paw tracks.

"My God!" exclaimed Ray when he saw them.

"Big as dinner plates," said Mel. "You could be a turd by now. Excuse me: a bigger turd."

"When?" For once, Ray was a little bit rattled.

"In the recent past," she said. "Like about ninety seconds ago."

"You saw him?" he asked.

"I even smelled him," she said, nodding her head.

"What'd he do?"

"Sniffed us both," she said, and wiped her cheek. "Got some of his spit on my face."

"Jesus!" exclaimed Ray. "How come you're so calm?"

"I'd've had a different answer for you about ninety seconds ago."

"You think he'll come back?"

"He knows where we are. He knows he can. He's onto us. What he's gonna do I don't know. A friend of mine told me that if you're huntin' grizzly the bear knows it," said Mel.

"Come on," scoffed Ray.

"We're huntin' him, right?"

"Right."

"And who found who?"

"You're sure he's the one?"

Mel nodded. "A golden hide, thick and fat for Winter. Put your hand in his track." Ray did as she told him. "Yours don't look any bigger than a baby's. That was him, all right." A loud huff and a sharp, quick puff and intake of breath came from the brush beyond the campsite. "He's still out there," said Mel.

"Now what?" asked Ray. He grabbed his rifle and jacked one in the chamber.

"For Christ's sake, don't shoot unless he comes for you! We don't know for sure where he is, and the last thing we want is a wounded grizzly."

Mel and Ray spent the rest of the night sitting at the camp-site with their backs against each other and their safeties off. She stoked the fire to keep it as large as possible, though Mel knew a blazing campfire wasn't always a deterrent. They could hear the bear moving in the brush, actually saw a sapling, silhouetted in the moonlight, bend and snap back up. No doubt the animal was agitated. Every so often they'd hear him whuff and snort and pop his huge jaws.

"What's he doing back there?" whispered Ray a little too loudly.

"Probably trying to figure out what we're doin' out here," said Mel.

The movement and the noise from the brush stopped about an hour before daylight, and an hour later Mel thought it might be safe enough to take a look. The big tracks led directly from the campsite into the brush. The claws alone must have been three inches. On a black bear track, you didn't see the claws, but on grizzly, you did. Mel cautioned Ray to stay about ten feet behind her and went ahead into the brush. She saw at once what the bear had done. The sapling had been bitten in two, and the ground had been torn up in a twenty-foot circle where the great bear had shuffled and jumped and angled sideways in anger. The only thing she could figure had kept the bear from attacking was that she and Ray hadn't moved and hadn't crowded him. The grizzly knew they were something he didn't like, sensed something that could be a threat, but he didn't know what. Even a half ton of bear can have his doubts.

"This is where we separate the men from the boys," Mel said

to Ray, "but not necessarily the men from the bears. Ready to track him?"

"I'll even go first," offered Ray.

"Wouldn't be ethical," she answered. "Keep just behind me. When it's time to shoot, you'll be out front. Ready?"

"Let's do it."

It had been easy to follow the tracks where they led into the brush because they were large and clear, but once inside the thick scrub there was too much tangle to see them anymore. Mel could see where the bear had moved out, however, because the vegetation was bent and trampled, and twigs were snapped off from the gross poundage of a big animal moving by. Mel and Ray combined made up less than a third of the sun bear's weight, yet this enormous animal could move without a sound.

What also amazed her was how any animal that big could remain hidden from view when it was practically on top of you. She remembered reading about a grizzly attack in one of the national parks a few years back. A young woman, a college student, was the victim. A three-year-old grizzly of some four hundred pounds came into the young woman's campsite one evening while she was eating dinner, grabbed her, and dragged her into the brush. Rescuers could hear the woman as she begged for help. The cry came from close by, but they never heard the bear at all, and they could not locate where he and his victim were. At one point, the victim cried out, "My God, oh, my God, he's eating me!" That was the last sound anyone heard. When it was daylight, what remained of her was found not twenty-five yards from where she had been snatched. The bear had covered her with a mound of dirt, twigs, and stones, which meant that he planned on coming back to finish his meal. A professional hunter set a trap for him, and tracks showed that the bear had indeed come back, but the trap was never sprung and the girl's remains were left untouched.

His Latin name was *Ursus horribilis*, horrible bear, and for good reason. Yes, it is true that a sow suckles her cubs and defends them to her death against attack, but it is also true that, since the grizzly has no predator except man, the creature she is usually protecting them from is a boar bent on killing and cannibalizing her young. Sometimes you might spot a full-grown grizzly sliding on its huge butt down a snow chute, and sometimes you will see it ambling for miles across open country, seemingly out for nothing more than a carefree walk, but this is not a cartoon bear out of Disney's *Jungle Book*. It is not playful like an otter, communal as a chimp, nor has it the sleek beauty of a cheetah. You see a grizzly, you see power, a creature that owns the mountain and knows it. It walks arrogantly with those massive shoulders rolling forward, and it sports a hair trigger capable of launching an attack with astonishing quickness. It is a brute unlike any other beast on Earth, but it is not a dumb brute. It is one of the most clever. How else did it know to avoid the trap set for it next to the young woman's remains? What it cannot see it hears, and what it cannot hear it smells. The bear's sense of smell was so keen that old-time hunters used to say a bear could tell the color of your Uncle Jake's boxer shorts by scent alone. And more than one guide tells the story of a client so cowed by the sight of his first grizzly that he laid down his rifle and quit the hunt. Nothing prepares you for the sight of a grizzly up close on his own turf. One old-timer swore he told his clients to pack an extra set of drawers. "Better to be safe . . ." he said.

This was pure grizzly country—exposed rock, thousand-foot precipices, no trees at all. The only other creature up this high was the mountain goat that clung matter-of-factly to ledges so narrow two skinny goats could not stand side by side. Mel had been in this country before, once when a storm had raged. Lightning bombarded the heights. Thunder rolled across the ridges. Rain pelted her unmercifully, but when the storm stopped, there were those goats in exactly the same place. The only effect the storm seemed to have on them was that their white coats looked whiter, like they'd been dry-cleaned.

They had been climbing for a couple of hours—Mel and Ray—but she was more impressed with his endurance than he with her gut instinct. Mel knew the golden bear had come this way. Goddamnit, don't ask her how she knew, she just did! But Ray wanted proof.

"The proof will be his hide," said Mel impatiently. She did not want to be questioned. She did not want to have to speak. Mel felt the bear out there and needed to allow herself to navigate by automatic pilot to keep on track. Her internal radar picked up minute shifts of light and wind and temperature, gradients, boulders, ledges—anywhere a bear might be or might have been. What did any of it mean? The computation was endless. Random bits of information fed into the feral part of this obsessed woman. Sometimes she would circle around some ridiculous distance to turn back and cover terrain that, to Ray's mind, they could have crossed straightaway. The key, of course, was always to stay downwind. To do that meant keeping the breeze in your face. If you were upwind, that is, if the wind were behind you, it would carry your scent to the bear, and chances were you'd never see him. Once he caught your wind, he'd be three mountains away before you could say "shoot."

Mel was right, and Mel was wrong. Mel felt the bear, and the bear was there. She had been on the money when she and Ray followed the route the bear took when he left his cover near their campsite. But he had traveled only a short distance before he circled back and took cover in a stand of alder a scant few yards from where he tore up the Earth. He lay down and slept while they slept, and watched as they broke camp and followed his lead out of the thicket. Mel's instincts were firing on all eight cylinders. They told her to climb, that the golden bear's keep was the ramparts and parapets of the mountaintop. She was right about everything except this: the bear was behind her, always in cover, his nose as keen as the eyes of a hawk, transfixed by their steps.

A bear's sense of curiosity is legendary, so maybe that's all it was. Maybe he sensed their threat, and his instincts prodded him to keep track of them without exposing himself. Or maybe he was hungry. A bear doesn't go after food because he's hungry. His hunger is triggered when he senses food, whether ripe berries or vulnerable prey, and then he goes after it with all the might, cunning, and desire at his disposal. Whatever his reason, he was there, and nothing told him to be anywhere else.

Ursus horribilis.

Lewis and Clark first heard tales of the devil bear from Indian tribes as their expedition made its way up the Missouri River. Their journals recorded many accounts of its fierceness as well as its iron determination in the face of devastating musket fire. The great bear never backed down. It was revered because of its many great strengths and reviled because of the death and damage it could wreak. Hunting parties were always in multiples of men because a single hunter was too vulnerable. He could be (and often was) ambushed without ever having known he was being stalked. The single way of stopping a grizzly's charge was to kill it, and that could take as many musket balls as there were men in the party.

The *vaqueros* in the early days of California played a perverse game with the bear. They were great horsemen, these vaqueros, but as savage as the animals they loved to kill. A group of them would surround a grizzly on horseback, and one by one they would rope the bear until it was caught and pulled in every direction. To hear a trapped grizzly bawl in pain was, from all reports, a horrifying sound. The roped bear would rear and charge only to be pulled off its feet. The vaqueros taunted it for its efforts, and the fury of the bear became awful to behold. One of the friars who witnessed such a sight wrote in a letter home that the infuriated bear bit through one of the ropes, charged a vaquero, and dragged him from the saddle. The other riders fired shot after shot into the angry bear as it mauled the man it caught. It pinned his chest with one giant paw, tore his scalp off with the other, and ripped his face and throat with its teeth, all of its deadly gifts going at once. The musket balls seemed to have no effect whatsoever until the bear finally fell dead upon the body of its victim. When they cut the bear open and skinned it out, there were thirty balls in its carcass, and what remained of the vaquero did not look human at all.

Ursus horribilis.

They were at ten thousand feet when they stopped in the lee of a large boulder to refuel with cheese, crackers, raisins, and Snickers. Breezy crosscurrents streamed around at random, making it impossible to keep the wind in their faces. Mel figured it a good time to take a break. To be honest, she also felt that the bear was suddenly somewhere else.

"We lost him, didn't we?" asked Ray.

"What makes you say that?" she wanted to know.

"You stopped," he said.

"Listen up, Ray. Just because you lose the trail don't necessarily mean it's the end of the trail," she said.

"I'll bet you go to cowboy poetry slams. Am I right?" he said.

"Aren't you always?"

"So we did lose him."

"Don't go south on me, son. If you got the will, I got the skill," she said. An old boyfriend who had been an Army Ranger taught her that one.

"What now?" asked Ray.

"There's a reason why they call this hunting, you know," she said.

"Mel, all I'm asking is what now. A civil question. I'm not trying to pull your chain."

If I were that bear, she thought, *where would I be?* Mel looked around carefully and tried to assess all the opportunities this place offered. She continued to keep her thoughts to herself. *Not much water, if any. Not much food. Ground squirrels maybe. Just an hors d'oeuvre. No chance for a goat. Can't get above them. I could den up here for the Winter, but that's still a ways away. Still . . .*

"What're you thinking?" Ray wanted to know.

The breeze shifted again, and this time, when it did, Mel's head swung sharply with it. Her heart began to pound. "You smell that?" she asked.

"What?" asked Ray, pulling the hood of his parka up over his head. He had cooled off since they sat down, and now the chilly wind was getting to him.

"Take your hood down." He could see how serious she was and paid attention. "That!" she said sharply. "You smell that?"

He sniffed the air, sniffed again. "I don't smell anything," he said.

"Bear," she said.

"Where?"

"I can't tell. I just caught it for a second. Once you've smelled it you never forget it. All the carrion it eats makes it stink something fierce."

"You think he's here?" asked Ray.

"Here somewhere," she answered. "Jesus, there it is again. You didn't smell that?"

"No," he said in frustration. "I don't smell a goddamn thing."

"Be still," she said.

Suddenly, two bears—a large one and a small one—broke from cover uphill about a hundred yards away and took off running down the mountain. Their appearance was so without warning they seemed to materialize from thin air.

"There he is!" yelled Ray as he brought his rifle to his shoulder for a quick, offhand shot.

"Don't shoot!" Mel hollered, but Ray was beyond hearing her and cranked one off. The bullet went low and spit up dirt between the larger bear's legs. "Don't shoot, goddamnit!" she hollered again. "It's a sow and her cub, for Christ's sake! Don't shoot!" Ray reluctantly lowered his rifle. "You don't shoot a female with a cub," said Mel.

"You think you caught their scent?" he asked.

"Maybe," she said. "I don't know. If I say 'don't shoot,' damn it, then don't shoot!"

"She tore ass out of there, didn't she. Man, she was traveling," said Ray.

"Lemme give you a tip, sport, in case you spot your bear uphill again. Shoot high, or you'll shoot under him, like you did this time."

Ray did not like this woman telling him how to shoot, not one bit, but he knew she was right, which of course only made it worse.

"Don't worry, Ray. These things happen to men sometimes," said Mel, coyly. "You'll make up for it next time I'm sure."

Did she say what he thought she said, or what? He started

to answer her back, but she threw up her hand and hissed, "Shh," and pointed toward a scraggly clump of scrub and a small boulder some fifty yards away. "*We* didn't spook those two bears," she said as she stayed focused on the spot. She snicked off her safety and cautiously moved forward. Ray jacked a round and followed. After a few yards, Mel motioned him in front of her, and when they were ten yards away, she tapped him on the shoulder to stop. Again, Mel motioned Ray forward only to stop him maybe ten, twelve feet away. "*Mano a mano,*" she said softly.

What Ray hoped was that he wouldn't start shaking on the outside because, all of a sudden, the switch on his internal wind tunnel flipped, and he was shaking on the inside like a light plane in a bad storm. He had to get it under control. Sudden fear gripped him by the short hairs. It was more intense than anything Ray had ever felt before. He had to fight it off. He had to wrench himself back from the edge, to breathe, to focus, to use the fear, to stay alert but loose. How did you do that? Alert. Loose. *Concentrate, Ray. Focus on what must be done. Breathe. You do not want to die, so breathe, damn it!* His heart thundered against his ribs. The bear had to have heard it, had to be listening—right now, had to have his muscles bunched—right now, ready to rush from the bush—right now. This image whipped into Ray's mind: he stood on a gallows with the noose around his neck waiting for the trap to drop from under him. *Make your move, bear! Jesus Christ Almighty, make your move!*

"Goddamn!" yelled Mel as she suddenly broke the silence and slapped the bush with the butt of her rifle. The wind in Ray's face carried with it an awful smell that damn near triggered his gag reflex.

"Where the fuck did he go?" she asked, more to herself and maybe God than to Ray. "And how the fuck did he go there?" She walked to the other side of the bush. "Ray," she called, "come here." He joined her and both of them stared at a pile of fresh scat the size of a Thanksgiving turkey. "Still steaming," Mel pointed out. "Smells like he sold his ass to the devil, don't it? How the hell does a thousand pounds of pure bear disappear practically right before your eyes?" she wondered aloud.

"Don't I pay you to know the answer to that?" Ray asked.

"Shut up, Ray," she said. "I'm trying to concentrate. This is spooky." Mel was talking to herself again. "Got to be some kind of magic act. I'm the bear. Where am I?" Then, as if the magician suddenly revealed his trick, she saw him—two hundred yards away and loping downhill in the same direction the sow and her cub had taken. "Ray!" she hollered, but he had seen the bear just about the same time as she did. His rifle was already at his shoulder. It was hard to tell the color of the bear's hide because he had the sun behind him, but he was big, and he had led them there. "Crossing shot. Hold low and lead him a little," instructed Mel. Ray fired. Dirt spat up into the bear's face, and then he was gone again. Disappeared. Out of there. Racehorse fast. Down the mountain gone. Gone. Gone.

"Let's go get him," said Mel, and crossed at a clip to where they last spotted the bear as he sprinted down the mountain. "Here's his front paw," she said, pointing out a partial track. "Here's where your bullet hit. You almost had yourself a big one. Come on, let's stay on him."

Ray asked, "Think it's the same one?"

"We'll find out," said Mel as she "cut for sign." Ray was right there with her, the two of them joined at the hip, predators after prey that had already turned back on them once, and might well turn again. Mel's best guess was that the sow and cub would keep the big male busy, but that was all it was, just a guess, and it wasn't any more educated than she was.

They hunted hard all the rest of the day. Mel was meticulous. She scouted every speck of terrain she could with a jeweler's eye. Ray glassed the opposite slopes, trying to will that bear into his field of vision. He stared so long he felt like his eyeballs would pop. Their hunt took them down the mountain, and by the time they reached its bottom slopes, the light of day was on the way out. They had seen no sign whatsoever of any bear at all. A couple of squirrels chastised them from the topmost branches of a nearby spruce. A raven soared above, croaking raucously. Mel took it personally. She didn't like to be laughed at. On top of everything, Ray was in a real bad mood. He'd raised a blister on his left foot, so each step was a limp and a grimace.

"Got any ideas?" he growled. None that she felt like telling, so she kept them to herself. "Bear got your tongue?" he asked. Did this guy think he was clever or funny or what? "Say something," he said.

"I was thinking you were having too good a time hearing yourself talk, and I didn't want to interrupt," she said.

"I don't think I have ever wanted to inflict pain on a human being as much as I'd like to inflict it on you," said Ray.

"I'll take that as a compliment," said Mel.

"Did you ever want to strangle somebody so badly your palms ached?" asked Ray. "Hang them out to dry and watch them dangle slowly, slowly in the wind? Yearn with all your heart to deliver them up to Vlad the Impaler?"

"Vlad who?" asked Mel.

They reached a thicket of alder and willow. They could hear running water on the other side, but busting through this jungle was going to be a bitch. Mel led the way in; it quickly closed around them. Between the tangle and the lack of light, they could barely see three feet ahead of them. *A perfect place to be ambushed by a bear*, thought Mel, but she stifled it. Instead, she concentrated on moving forward with great caution, her rifle poised nearly to her shoulder. If she had to, she could fire in an instant, which was probably one subatomic particle more than all the time she'd actually have. But with each step forward she became more certain that, had the bear been there, he would have attacked already. That took some of the edge off. Maybe easing off the edge wasn't such a good idea, but Mel had a gut feeling that she and Ray were the only two good-sized mammals currently in this tangle.

Still, the going was rough and slow. Sharp twigs and stickers poked and snagged them from every angle. Finally, they had to crouch so low it was easier to crawl forward on their bellies. This was the type of thicket that seemed as if it would never end. It was tedious and boring and taxed the patience of even the most resolute. A thicket like this made her wonder why she didn't move to Hawaii and live on the beach. Mel pushed a branch aside as she crawled by, then allowed it to snap backward. Ray yelped with pain as it caught him in the face.

"Damn it," he said. "Watch it!"

"Sorry," she said. She wasn't really, but the undergrowth was so vicious and demanding that the act of inflicting pain on Ray (something she would ordinarily have enjoyed) didn't make Mel crack so much as a smile. A few minutes more and they emerged from the thicket to find themselves on the edge of a cutbank that overlooked a gravel bar that ran alongside a river not too wide and only knee deep but flowing swiftly. Downstream just a bit, on the opposite side, was an overhang. Mel felt that she'd been here before, felt strongly that this was where she first laid eyes on the golden bear.

The sun had long since peaked and had nearly completed its descent. Shadows had grown longer. The air had taken on an icy feel. Ray shivered.

"What now?" he asked.

"We wait," said Mel.

"It's going to be dark soon," said Ray, a bit uneasily.

"Do you need your blankie?" asked Mel.

"I've got another suggestion," said Ray.

"You're kidding," she exclaimed incredulously.

"Uh-uh," he answered.

"Let me get this straight. You hate me."

"Right."

"You want to kill me."

"Right."

"But you still want to have sex with me."

"You find that unusual?" he said, all charm and with his best smile.

"Sweet dreams," said Mel.

It seemed to Mel that she had no sooner fallen asleep than she was jolted awake by the awful sounds of bears fighting. Ray was still asleep, his rifle clutched to his chest. How could he sleep through such a murderous racket? She kicked his foot.

"Get up!"

"Huh?"

"Shh!"

She motioned with her head, and he crawled after her as she crept to the edge of the thicket where it met the cutbank. It turned out to be a ringside seat for a war that two grizzlies were waging on the bank of the river only a few yards opposite. They faced off upright on their hind legs and struck each other slashing blows with their forepaws, any one of which would have eviscerated a human being. They raged at each other. Spittle flew from their mouths. Their jaws popped like steel traps. They didn't roar so much as they howled. Like all the devils of Hell. Unearthly sounds tore out of them. Mel pointed to the thicket behind the fighting bears. A much smaller bear was nearly hidden by the tangle.

"Cub," said Mel, pointing.

At that moment, the smaller of the two fighting bears feinted, grabbed a forepaw of the other between her teeth (it had to be a sow), and shook her head from side to side as she tried to rip it off. She took everything the larger bear gave her, but none of it forced her to let go. Now the big one wanted out and tried to pull away. He pulled away so hard he left half his paw in her mouth. She spit it out and lunged for him again, snapping at his flanks with no mercy as she drove him further and further away from her cub before she finally allowed him to retreat. The cub, less than a year old, came out of the thicket and loped toward its mother. The old sow cuffed her baby on the head, but whether affectionately or to teach him a lesson Mel couldn't tell. The two of them, sow and cub, started back to the thicket when something stopped them in their tracks. The female stood on her hind legs again and tested the air. Whatever was there made her instantly drop to all fours, swat her little one on the rump, and nudge it upriver. They passed so close to Ray and Mel, Mel could have touched them with a pool cue.

"Why'd they . . . ?" Ray started to ask.

"Shh," cautioned Mel.

"What . . . ?" he persisted.

"I mean it," she whispered harshly, and stared so intently at the thicket opposite that it seemed as if lasers would leap from her eyes. The two of them lay there without making a sound, barely breathing, wound so tightly they might spring at a touch. It was utterly silent. Nothing moved but the water. They listened so hard their ears hurt. There was no wind, and yet an expanse of thicket across the river moved, slowly, in waves, as if something mighty were passing through it. An alder sapling swayed above the brush, then came a sharp crack, and the sapling went down. Ray looked to Mel for a sign. She nodded her head. Still in prone position, he shouldered his rifle, put the scope on the brush, and tracked the movement. Whatever moved through that thicket was drawing closer and closer to the edge. Another few seconds, it would clear the brush and be visible. Another second. It was that close, so close. Beads of sweat ran into Ray's open eye, but he quickly blinked them away.

Mel whispered, "Take a deep breath. Hold it. Hold it . . ."

Ray's finger tightened on the trigger. *Squeeze it, Ray,* he told himself. *Squeeze, don't jerk.* He had moved to a zone in time and space where nothing existed except the deadly connection between the hunter and his prey.

Mel whispered, "Hold it . . . Hold . . . it . . ."

Another instant more. Ray would have his shot. Another . . .

But in that instant, the one next to last, Cody's voice rang out, "Hey, fellow nimrods, whatcha doin'?"

"What the fuck?" said Ray.

"Oh, shit," said Mel.

Whatever animal was in the thicket stopped short and left by a back door. Gone.

"You guys need any help?" hollered Cody, still out of sight.

"Where is the son-of-a-bitch?" Ray cried out.

"The son-of-a-bitch is right here," said Cody.

Mel and Ray crawled forward a couple of inches and looked down. There was Cody relaxing against the riverbank just a few feet below them.

"Hi," he said ingenuously. "Seen anything?"

"You blew my shot," shouted Ray.

"Did I?" asked Cody.

Ray and Mel jumped down beside him, both furious.

"What the fuck are you doing here?" asked Mel.

"You two have a nice night?" asked Cody.

"You are so low," said Mel.

"Why's that?" asked Cody, all innocence.

"He had the shot. He was comin'," said Mel.

"Must've been a squirrel," offered Cody.

"That big?" Mel fired back.

"Hey," said Cody, "this is Alaska."

"You're an asshole, you know that?" said Ray.

"I do, yeah," said Cody. "She told me."

"What the hell are you doing out here, Cody?" Mel demanded again.

"Well," said Cody, "we need to talk."

"On my fucking time?" asked Ray.

"Couldn't it wait?" asked Mel.

"Not in my opinion," said Cody.

"Great," snarled Ray. "One asshole and one dumb . . ." Cody clobbered him before Ray finished the sentence and dropped him on his butt. He looked up at Cody in shock, cleared his head, jumped to his feet, and assumed a karate stance. With a weird smile he said, "I always wondered if this would work." And then he advanced on Cody.

"Check this jerk out," Cody remarked snidely to Mel. "Take your best shot, Ray, baby," he challenged, and stuck out his chin.

"You don't want to see this," Ray cautioned Mel.

"Sure I do," she said brightly.

"Bet on me," said Ray.

"I would," replied Mel, "but who'd bet on him?"

Ray decided he'd had enough of these two. He cracked his knuckles, stretched his neck, and launched a flurry of punches and kicks that Cody avoided with surprising speed and agility.

"Float like a butterfly, sting like a bee," he taunted Ray.

"You go, Cody," cheered Mel.

Cody responded with a fair imitation of the Ali Shuffle. "Check it out, Ray. I'm fast, and I'm pretty." Ray stalked Cody, trying to close the distance, cut off escape. Cody stepped aside and feinted with his left.

"Attaway, Cody!" hollered Mel. "Jab him! Jab him! Come in behind your jab, baby!"

Cody hooked off his jab and tagged Ray with a smart left.

"I like what I see, Cody," yelled Mel. "You got him worried! You got him scared!"

"Will you shut the fuck up?" snapped Ray.

"Make me!" taunted Mel.

"When I'm finished here," said Ray, and landed two quick shots to Cody's ribs.

"That was good, Ray," said Cody. "Make it a fair fight."

"Is that all you got, Marks?" said Mel. "You punch like a pussy."

Ray feinted with his right and connected with an uppercut designed to blast Cody's head into space. "Not that time, mutha-fucka," gloated Ray.

"That's one for you," said Cody, staggering some and trying to clear his head.

"Watch out for number two, schmuck," Ray said, and launched himself through the air feet first, aiming for Cody's chest. Cody jumped aside, snatched Ray before he landed, and slammed him to the ground.

"What number are we on now, Ray?" asked Cody. Ray didn't answer. He also didn't move.

"Jesus, Cody, you think you killed him?" asked Mel.

"Come on, Ray, goddamnit, get up," said Cody. "I know you got more in you than that. We were just getting started."

"Maybe he is dead," said Mel. A rasping sound escaped Ray's throat. "Think that's a death rattle, Cody?"

"Jesus Christ," yelled Ray as he pushed himself to his knees. "I could be dying down here, and you two morons are having a conversation about it."

"I can see how that might prove aggravating," said Mel.

"Here," said Cody as he offered his hand to help Ray up.

"Watch him, Cody. The man's a snake," she warned, just as Ray tightened his grip on Cody's wrist and yanked him off balance. His left hand came up off the ground clutching a rock and slammed it into the side of Cody's head. Cody lurched to one side and fought to keep his balance. A sidekick caught him full in the chest and sent him flying into the river, where he hit his head once more and sank facedown.

"Cody! Oh, my God!" screamed Mel.

Cody's body bobbed to the surface where the strong current began to carry him downriver.

"Cody!" she screamed again, only this time Mel jumped into the river and battled her way through the water until she reached him. She slipped and fell, losing her rifle, and the current swirled Cody away, but she managed to grab his belt and fought to get him back to the gravel bar. Ray stepped in and tried to help her haul him out of the water.

"Get your hands off him!" she cried.

"He threw the first punch," protested Ray.

"That's what they all say on death row, you creep," she shot back. Cody was still unconscious. Mel cradled his head in her lap. "Come on, Cody, wake up," she said. "Don't be dead."

"He's not dead," said Ray.

"You're an expert," she said sarcastically as she put her mouth to Cody's and breathed air into his lungs. A couple of breaths more and Cody came to.

"You need to do that one more time," he said weakly.

"You're okay?" she said, still worried.

"I think my ribs are broken. Why are there two of you?" he asked.

"Because I want to make your life twice as miserable," she answered. "Come on, Cody, stand up. I got a bet on you."

"Wait a minute. Am I hallucinating, or did you actually almost sound affectionate just then?" he said as she helped him to his feet.

"It's a weakness," she said with a begrudging smile. "I admit it."

"I am not paying good money to listen to this shit," said Ray. They had forgotten he was there.

Cody, still seeing blurred and double, glanced at the thicket across the river. He shook his head to clear it, but what he saw wouldn't go away. Something was happening there. He couldn't believe it but there it was: the golden bear, grand and enormous, vivid as a dream.

"My God," he said to Mel. "You weren't lyin'."

"Not a bit," said Ray who, very slowly, so as not to create any unnecessary movement, lifted his rifle to his shoulder and put the scope on the bear. Ray breathed, held his breath, put pressure on the trigger, his crosshairs steady on the great bear's heart. Pressure on the trigger, a split second more . . . and . . .

Suddenly, Mel had had it. This thought rammed home as surely as a round jacked into the chamber: that mighty beast deserved a more noble death than at the hands of this crap artist. The instant this became clear was the instant Mel grabbed Ray's rifle, threw off the shot, and tossed it in the river.

Where it sank.

"What the fuck did you do?" Ray was wild. "Are you crazy? You're a fucking lunatic!"

The great bear looked over their way, a little above their heads as if they didn't matter at all, turned majestically, and vaporized back into the brush. Ray screamed and lunged for Mel, but when she pulled out her big .44, he hit the brakes like Wile E. Coyote.

"First the shoulders," she said as she assumed the position, "then the heart."

"You wouldn't really shoot a man," Ray taunted.

"Nope," said Mel, "but I'd sure shoot you."

"You are some work of art," Ray shot back.

"Nice to be appreciated," said Mel.

"What the fuck did you do that for?"

"The short list or the long list?" she said.

"Shit," was all Ray could manage as he splashed into the river after his rifle.

"How we doing, sport?" Mel said to Cody as she helped him to sit on the trunk of an upturned tree.

"I should have known. The guy's from Hollywood. They fight dirty there," said Cody.

"There's still a little matter," said Mel, "of my fee. Where am I supposed to get it?"

"Hear me out, Mel. I think I got that covered."

"I'm not gonna borrow it from you. I told you that," she said.

"Did I say borrow?"

"How else . . . ?"

"Did you hear the word *borrow* cross my lips?"

"Okay," she settled down. "What?"

"You're gonna love this," said Cody, and started to tell her, when she jumped up so abruptly he lost his balance again and nearly fell backward off the log. "What the fuck, Mel!" he exclaimed, then caught himself as he watched dumbstruck at Mel sprinting across the gravel bar hollering and waving her arms to get Ray's attention. He had found his rifle and now brandished it above his head as he whooped and stomped through the water in some kind of victory dance. Now Cody saw what Mel had seen and Ray still hadn't: a grizzly cub angling through the shallows toward Ray. Its small size and curiosity made it this season's. Its size was not the problem. Both Cody and Mel knew that. Its mother was the problem. Both Cody and Mel knew that, too. So where the hell was she?

That question no sooner entered their minds than the answer bawled like she swallowed a beehive and exploded from the brush. Ray saw her now and froze. Gravel spit from between her paws, but she stopped just short of the water as her cub came barreling back to her. The big she-grizzly still threatened to advance on Ray. Ray snapped an offhand shot at the bear but his rifle didn't fire. The bear chomped her jaws. Spittle flew. She swung her head from side to side as she closed the distance with Ray. His rifle was useless.

"Toss it," yelled Mel as she angled for a shot with the .44 Mag. "Try to distract her."

Ray, desperate enough to try anything, swung the rifle around his head like a club. When the grizzly looked up at it, Ray slung the rifle to one side and slightly behind her. It twirled like a baseball bat. She turned and pounced where it splashed back into the river, and in another instant came up with the black walnut stock in her mouth. Her teeth and claws gouged out scars in its exquisite finish. Ray winced.

"Just back away, Ray," cautioned Mel. "Slowly, amigo. Cut your losses before they cut you." The bear was too busy mauling Ray's rifle to pay him any mind. Ray did what he was told. Slowly. Mel covered him as he crossed the gravel bar toward Cody's position on the upended trunk.

"Got room for a brother?" Ray asked, and indicated the spot beside Cody on the log.

Cody nodded. "Too bad about your rifle. You did good, though. Didn't panic. Mess your drawers?"

"No," said Ray.

"I'll know if you don't tell me," said Cody.

"I said no, goddamnit."

"Just checking."

The small cub disappeared back into the brush. Once more hidden in thick cover, it bawled for its mother. She dropped Ray's rifle where it was, twirled, and followed her cub into the brush. Mel holstered her pistol and began to cross the gravel bar to where the two men sat watching her approach.

"Like I said, a fucking work of art," muttered Ray.

"I assume you meant that as a compliment," said Cody.

"Actually, I did," and Ray had.

Cody applauded as she walked back to their log. She smiled at him and then her smile turned to terror as the furious she-bear broke from cover behind the two men. The sow had circled around and come in for a second attack. She sidestepped the two men on the log, rushed Mel, and knocked her down. Mel scuttled backward as the bear came at her again.

"Mel, cover your head!" yelled Cody, and grabbed his rifle, but when he brought the stock to his shoulder, the pain from his cracked ribs cut through him like the swipe of an enraged grizzly's claw and drove him to his knees. The sudden drop distracted the she-bear's attention for as long as it took her to grab the rifle in her mouth and shake it back and forth as if trying to break its neck. The stock snapped like a chicken bone. She flung it away and turned back to Mel, who had curled into a tight ball, legs tucked, hands over her head to protect it from bites.

It occurred to Mel that the bear's breath was everything Cody had said it was—vile and damp, the stench of dead meat. She lay there and clenched herself tightly as the bear nuzzled her in an attempt to turn her over. If she squeezed herself and kept squeezing harder this would all go away. This would all be fine. She had to believe that or give up and give in, and that was not Mel Madden. Its nose was rough. Those teeth. She thought she felt them graze her forearm but she wasn't sure. It didn't hurt. So far nothing hurt. Mel wasn't sure that she heard Cody yelling but maybe she did. The bear's snuffling as it continued to nuzzle shut out other sounds. Then everything stopped for a few seconds or however long it took before pain unlike any other Mel had ever borne ripped through her right thigh as the bear's teeth tore the meat and minced the bone. Even as the bear's jaws ground through her thigh, Mel found it impossible to grasp that such pain could ever exist anywhere, anywhere at all, yet here it was, and there would never be an end to it until she was dead.

Running side by side with the pain, like scalding water through the same hot pipe, was the most primal fear of all: the utter dreadfulness of being hunted and eaten, terror of the most fearful kind, what the movies want you to feel, only the attack doesn't stop after the next frame. It doesn't stop at all. Mel felt herself lifted off the ground by strength beyond imagining. She beat on the bear's snout with her fists, but it was like cinder block. Pain did not abate. Pain obliterated everything except the struggle to get rid of it. She flopped in the bear's mouth like a salmon, her head dragging on the gravel bar as the bear carried her toward the brush. This thought broke through: *Cody.* Where was he? But the thought was gone as soon as she thought it. Pain was all there was.

Mel did not know that Cody had taken his broken rifle by the barrel and was smashing it over the bear's head, finally forcing her to stop and swipe in his direction. Then Cody bought two seconds off the raging sow by poking it in the eyes with the tip of the gun barrel, but the bear wheeled away with Mel still in its mouth and outdistanced him. He heard Mel screaming his name. He'd never heard a sound like that come out of anyone, but it had to be Mel. Mel screaming his name. Yet he was helpless to do anything except watch the beast finish its kill. There was a moment beyond which Mel would be dead, and Cody watched it coming in dread.

There was no more time, and then, suddenly, there was all the time as the small cub ambled out from behind cover and tagged along behind its mother. When it bawled for her attention, she dropped Mel's body and turned to care for her baby. The cub sauntered off, and its mother followed. The humans were forgotten. The bears waded into deep brush and disappeared. It became as if they never were. Except for damage left behind.

Cody raced for Mel as quickly as he could. He knew she was alive when he heard her screaming for him.

He reached her. "Cody, Cody," she screamed. "She took my leg, Cody. She got my leg." Cody used his lock-back to slice open the torn and bloody right leg of her jeans.

"It's a mess, but it's still there, baby," he said. "Lemme get at this." He intended to begin dressing her wound, but she clung to his neck and sobbed his name over and over and over.

Ray looked on awkwardly. Mel's wound was horrible, her jeans chewed into her flesh. He forced himself to look at it. He sensed he owed Mel that much.

"Am I gonna lose it, Cody?"

"She took a chunk, Mel, but she left you plenty," he answered, and began plucking strands of denim from her wound. "Got a T-shirt?" he asked Ray.

"On me," said Ray.

"Take it off and tear it into fourths," said Cody. "Get a fire built, and boil some water."

"Boil it in what?" asked Ray.

"Small saucepan. My pack. Also some fire-starter cubes," said Cody without looking up from Mel's wound.

"I can start a fire," said Ray.

"No need for a pissing contest," said Cody, tore off his own T-shirt, and blocked Ray out of his conscious mind. Mel was starting to shake and chatter. "Hold on, Mel, I got something for you," said Cody. "Ray," he called. "Gimme the pack."

"I can find it," said Ray, misinterpreting Cody.

"Gimme the goddamn pack!" Cody bellowed. Ray jumped to. Cody reached deep into the pack and pulled out a plastic box, something like a pencil box. He took a morphine syringe out of this box, pulled Mel's jeans down to expose her buttock, and injected her. A spasm of pain took Mel.

"Cody, Cody, Cody, Cody," she screamed, and hung on to him.

"It's going to be all right, Mel. I gotcha here," he said, and held her as the morphine took effect, and Mel sagged with relief. He held her a while longer as her breathing evened, and she fell asleep. Then he laid her down gently, and finished cleaning and bandaging her wounds. He amazed Ray with how gentle and meticulous he could be. The only time Cody left Mel's side was to get some split pea soup started. Cody offered him some, but Ray had no appetite at all.

"That was death, Cody," Mel said between spoonfuls. "Wasn't nothin' kind about it."

He told her a little while later, "We'll spend the night here, get some rest. In the morning, I'll leave you food and water, hike out, and send the rescue chopper back for you."

"No," she insisted. "No! You leave me here waiting for that chopper, and I swear to God I'll crawl out on my knees, so help me Jesus Christ!"

"Fine. We'll take you back fireman's carry. It'll be a lot harder on you, though," warned Cody. "You don't want to bang that leg around."

"I could probably hop a little if I hung on to you," she said.

"Don't worry about it," said Cody. "Ray'll spell me." The man had offered, and the offer was genuine. But Mel wouldn't hear of that. She didn't want anybody near her that wasn't Cody. They traveled three days for one. Each of them was in so much pain that every step was an act of will, but they made it back to Toehold the way Mel wanted.

A couple of nights later, Mel lay in her hospital bed in the clinic with her right leg in a sling. Cody sat on the bed beside her. She rested her cheek gently against the bandages that bound Cody's ribs. Alaska being Alaska, Cody asked the doctor could he stay in Mel's room, and got yes for an answer. Cody promised the young doc that he would sleep in the chair.

"That leg should not be jostled," the doctor warned.

"Nothing's gonna get jostled, Doc, I promise," assured Cody.

It was late at night but neither Mel nor Cody felt sleepy, yet. The *Toehold Weekly Gazette* lay on the floor open to the headline: "Mel Mauled!" Mel laughed when Cody brought it to her and said, "Xerox some copies and include it with the brochure. That oughta bring in some business." The only illumination in the room came from a thick candle on the bedside table. They talked and talked. It was a wonder to each of them that there was so much to say.

"For better or for worse, I'll tell you something," said Mel. "I really didn't want to kill that big griz. He don't need me to help kill him off."

"He'll die off soon enough without anybody's help," said Cody.

"Yeah," said Mel. "We're forcin' him to the ends of the Earth, that's why. If he weren't so damn big 'n' strong, maybe he'd stand a chance. But the stubborn bastard needs to go his own way."

"He thinks he don't need a damn soul in the world to help him out, but he does whether he knows it or not," mused Cody.

"He'll keep runnin' 'til there's no place left to run, won't he?"

"Yep," said Cody.

"And then he'll die."

"Yep."

"And then what?"

"He'll be dead," said Cody.

"That's it, then?" He didn't answer her. "Will you please put your arm around me, Cody?"

They passed the night that way.

The village of Toehold went back to normal. Ray had gone positively berserk when he saw his plane in little pieces strewn around the airstrip, but no one in Toehold, absolutely no one, professed to know a thing about it. When Ray would ask, one citizen would say to another, "I didn't see anything, did you?"

"See what?" came back the answer.

The next day Ray hopped a bush plane to Fairbanks, where Air Alaska then carried him back to L.A. That was the last anyone heard about Ray Marks. Everybody had even forgotten to ask him the name of his movie, so when it finally came out, whenever that was, nobody would be able to see it. Anyway, it was a drive of over two hundred miles to the nearest movie theater, so the prevailing sentiment was, *Forget it, we'll get it off the dish.* Buddy did ask Cody, just before the medevac took off, whether or not Ray had said anything about his story, but Cody just glared at him, and Buddy walked away grumbling, "All right, all right."

It wasn't too much longer after Ray's departure that Winter finally stepped up and slammed one home. Snow fell for three days without stop. Gusts of wind tossed the flakes about like white gypsy moths caught in the high beams. The wide wings of a huge, gray bird settled over all the Arctic. The river froze thick and hard. It would stay that way for many months. Thirty below? Forty? Only to be expected. Ten below was considered balmy. Once Winter let him know that it wasn't going anywhere, Cody no longer had an excuse to be outside, so this was the season he caught up on a backlog of work. This time of year his focus was near complete. Most of his time was taken up by a diorama he had promised to a private natural history museum in oil-rich Qatar. The sheik who owned it had commissioned Cody before, but nothing this extensive or dramatic: five wolves, the lead one white, bounding across open tundra. To look at it was to gasp, to fear they were coming for you. Buddy was there when he finished.

"It's perfect," he said. "Beautiful. What means more than *beautiful*? Gimme a word. That's what it is. Exactly. That's what it is!" Mel stomped the snow from her feet at the front door and came inside.

"Do you think the plane will be able to make it in today, Cody?" She seemed nervous.

"Take a look," said Buddy, pointing to the wolves.

"Wow, Cody," was all she could say.

"He'll have his skis on," said Cody. "Don't worry. Dwayne's flown in lots worse."

"Oh, yeah, Mel, by the way, here's this letter for you," said Buddy. "It got stuck inside my *Field and Stream* last time the mail came in."

"That was a week ago, Buddy," she said, obviously annoyed.

"'Thank you, Buddy,'" he said sarcastically. "'What a pal you are for delivering my letter!'"

"Hand it over," said Mel.

"I didn't know you were still in the business," he exclaimed, and double-checked the address on the envelope. Mel slit it open with a knife from Cody's workbench and read the letter.

"Cody! Cody, check this out! It's from a guy in Chicago. 'I am interested in a high-quality Spring fly-fishing trip for grayling and arctic char.'" She waved a check in the air. "Here's his deposit."

"Can I see?" said Buddy. Mel handed him the letter.

"'Golden Bear Guides,'" Buddy read. "'Cody and Mel at your service.' Is this for real?"

"What you do not know, my man, is that you're lookin' at a family operation here. We even got stationery," said Mel proudly.

"I get it," said Buddy. "Cody, you're gonna lead 'em to water, and Mel's gonna lead 'em to drink."

"Very funny," said Mel.

"Think it's too cerebral?" asked Buddy.

Mel picked up an ax handle. "I think you're tap-dancin' on quicksand," she threatened.

"Ease up, for Christ's sake," said Buddy. "You're heading for a change of life."

"You're heading for a change of consciousness," Mel retorted.

"I meant that sincerely," Buddy explained. "Really."

"I believe he did," said Cody, coming to Buddy's defense. The sound of a small plane passing overhead snagged everybody's attention.

"That must be it, Cody. Sounds like Dwayne's Cessna, doesn't it?" said Mel.

Sweet-ass Sue stuck her formidable head through the front door and hollered, "Mail call, guys. Who's with me? Let's see some blood on that door!"

"On my way," said Mel, except she didn't move.

"Don't you think your brain needs to send a message to your feet?" asked Sweet-ass Sue.

"Let's go," said Cody. Mel suddenly seemed very nervous. She fidgeted. She didn't know what to do with herself. "Mel?" said Cody. "Come on. Shake it out."

"I'm there," she offered, and followed him out the door. Cody and Mel jumped into one truck, Buddy and Sweet-ass into another. Both trucks spat gravel as they tore out and careened toward the airstrip. The speed limit, like those in every other bush community, was, to put it loosely, "flexible," determined solely by how fast you could push whatever rig you were driving. At this moment, Toehold resembled the dirt track of a demolition derby. Seemed like everybody in town was speeding toward the airstrip. Dwayne, skis attached to his Cessna, circled the icy strip looking for the best approach. By the time Mel and Cody got there, Dwayne was bringing her in. Every vehicle in town, including snowmobiles, was parked on both sides of the strip with their headlights on high, making Toehold at that very moment the best-lit dirt airstrip in Alaska. As Dwayne landed the plane smoothly and taxied to a stop, every single citizen in Toehold broke out in applause. Everybody continued to applaud and circled around the Cessna as Dwayne opened his door and got out.

"Hey, Mel," he said. Mel and Cody were right there. "Got your Snickers in the front seat," he told her, and walked around to the other door. Mel followed him closely and stood right behind him as he opened it and stepped aside. Sure enough there was a fresh case of Snickers, only it sat in the lap of someone muffled up to the eyeballs from the cold. The eyes were wide and green with an expression both expectant and cautious. Wide, green eyes which Mel recognized as her own.

"Theresa Louise?" she asked.

"Yes, ma'am," answered the girl with the case of Snickers in her lap. She spoke with a soft, Loretta Lynn–like lilt.

"Darlin', baby?"

"Yes, ma'am?"

"I'm your mother," said Mel.

Acknowledgments

My life has been blessed with friends and family. This book is for them.

George E. Barrett, there from the beginning.

Brooke Adams and Tony Shalhoub, good friends and true, loving counsel, unconditional support.

Mark Ammons helped bring these characters into the third dimension. Ellen Stern and Peter Stern gave me constant encouragement and critical reads. Mark Reiter, my agent, advised me to write a novel, and Peter Kaminsky, my old hunting buddy, advised me to call Mark. And every writer should have an editor with the grace and savvy of Lexi Beach.

Finally, always, there are my children: Sevi Donnelly and Madden Rose. Thanks, guys.

About the Author

Stephen H. Foreman received his BA from Morgan State, an MFA from the Yale School of Drama, and taught writing and literature at various universities before moving to California to work as a screenwriter and director. Having trekked across the Alaskan wilderness, bushwhacked through tropical rain forests, and hunted for gold mines in Arizona, he now makes his home in the Catskill Mountains, with his wife, Jamie Donnelly, and two children.